UGLY

KELLY VINCENT

KV Books LLC

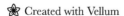

To everyone who struggles to figure out who they really are in the face of constant judgment and criticism—I see you

Chapter 1

The school hall was as packed as ever, but one boy was weaving through kids, heading right toward me. He shouted, "Give me five, bro!" and slapped another boy's raised hand.

I needed to stay out of his way, so I leaned against my locker and waited for him to pass.

Then he careened toward me. "Put five right here!" he said, hand in the air and grinning like a maniac.

I tentatively raised my arm, and then his face fell.

"Oh. I thought you were a guy."

Someone else barked a laugh behind him.

The high-fiver dropped his arm, and I realized I was still holding mine half up like an idiot, so I let it fall, just as the laughing guy said, "She might as well be a guy. She's a big lesbo."

I blushed fiercely, and they both cracked up and moved on like it was nothing. I stood there stupidly, wanting to sink into the floor. I looked around and heard a couple of snickers.

I grasped my books to my chest and headed toward class.

Why did everybody have to say all that stuff? I was aware that I didn't dress all girly—it just felt wrong, and I couldn't have done it if I'd tried. What was wrong with wanting to be comfortable? So what if I liked jeans and unisex t-shirts. So-freakin'-what?

I lifted my head to navigate around a corner, squeezing past a group of girls who didn't mind at all doing their makeup and wearing cute clothes. I made sure not to look too closely, lest I get some kind of snark.

God, I hated this shit.

And I didn't think I was a lesbian, anyway. But everyone acted like I was. How could everyone else know something about me that I didn't know myself?

Chapter 2

Later, in math, Mr. Martinez was going on about algebraic expressions, an x here, a y there. He was writing on the whiteboard in blue. I was trying to pay attention because I was actually interested. I'd hated geometry freshman year and was glad to get back to algebra. I had my notebook out and was copying the latest expression down when I saw Carlos's hand shoot over and grab my white eraser.

I looked at him. His fingers closed around the eraser, and his eyes twinkled.

He was cute. He had light brown eyes and wavy dark brown hair that sometimes got a little long, but it wasn't now.

I reached for the eraser, invisible in his big hand, and he pulled away, a mischievous look on his face. He was goofing around with me, something that most people didn't do.

Wait—was he flirting with me?

I couldn't believe it.

I didn't know much about this stuff, but I did know you

weren't supposed to seem desperate, so I turned back toward Mr. Martinez and started taking notes.

Carlos set the eraser down on top of his notebook. I reached for it, and he grabbed my wrist firmly, still grinning. "I don't think so, Nic," he mouthed.

Okay, flirting, definitely. He'd touched me on purpose. The heat in my wrist where he was holding it felt new and exciting.

Kyle was on the other side of him, watching this, clearly amused.

Carlos was strong. I could see the muscles flexing in his forearm.

Is it weird that I thought that was kind of cool? I'd never thought about how boys were stronger than girls before, except in the they-can-beat-you-up way, but it was right there. General male strength. And I liked it.

He still had my wrist. What should I do? Tug it back? But then he might let go.

My heart sped up, because no boy had touched me in an inoffensive way since elementary school. I stopped reaching for the eraser, and he let me go with a sidelong glance, so I got back to taking notes. Not that I could concentrate.

Lately I'd been thinking if I could get a boyfriend, things might be better. Maybe people would treat me less like a freak—and more like a normal person. Carlos would be perfect because he was so normal. I loved the idea that a regular guy was flirting with me, even if I'd never thought of him that way before.

If he liked me, I wouldn't turn him away.

Although I eyed the eraser several times through the rest of class, when Mr. Martinez let us go, Carlos snagged it and tossed it in his backpack. He and Kyle grinned at me, and I followed them out, getting squeezed out by another couple of girls in the class, who gave me one of those all-too-familiar looks. The down-the-nose look, followed by the dismissive head turn away. I told myself I was numb to it.

I was pretty much used to it. I was sort of a last-picked-for-the-team kind of girl here at Emerson High School. I didn't know who they thought they were, though. Everyone knew it took forever for trends to make it to Oklahoma. We were forty-five minutes from Tulsa, and it wasn't like that was culturally cutting edge, either. All the things kids here thought were so cool were probably totally passé in places like New York or L.A. by now.

Whatever. Just three more years here, and I was gone. I couldn't wait, and wondered how I was going to weather it.

Chapter 3

All afternoon, I obsessed over the whole Carlos thing. Could he really like me?

Admittedly, it could have simply been that I was there, and he was bored. But I didn't think so. I had a good feeling about this.

About time.

I missed having my eraser in chemistry because I decided to sketch out the periodic table while the teacher rambled on about something or other, and I messed it up counting out the transition metals. Plus, I'd need it over the weekend. Once I was on the bus, I put my headphones on and cranked up some Killers.

My asshole brother Caleb flicked me on the head when he passed me, heading for the back. He was such a douche now.

Still, the only thing in my head was Carlos, and how he maybe liked me.

My best friend Sam—short for Samantha, but she'd die if I called her that—was always getting on my case about not being brave enough socially, so I tried to think of what

I could do that would be proactive and maybe even bold. We had a plan, called Operation Social Interaction for Nic —or OSIN for short—to wrangle some friends for me. She'd be proud if I did something on my own. I just had to figure out what.

It would be hard to talk to Carlos the next day with Kyle there, so it wasn't like I would be able to ask him out or anything. The idea that I'd just go up to a boy and be like, "Hey, wanna go out some time?" was sheer insanity anyway. It would be much better if he would ask me.

We rolled over a speed bump heading out of the parking lot, and a light bulb went on in my head. I knew where Carlos lived, after all. We'd ridden the same bus since elementary school, even though he'd stopped at the beginning of this year.

I'd be avoiding the bus soon, too, because I was getting a car when I turned sixteen next month. Thank God. It would be nothing fancy. We'd already agreed on a budget of $5000.

This idea—this was an awesome idea. I could walk over there and ask for my eraser. Maybe he'd invite me in, and things would go from there. Good things.

After forty-five minutes of bus torture, because I was the second-to-last-stop on the route, I finally was able to get off into the late summer heat. My forehead beaded with sweat before I even made it to the yard.

Caleb—just ten months younger than me and a brand-new freshman—went in the front door ahead of me. I stopped to get the mail from the dented mailbox and headed up the walk to the front entrance. We had a nice covered stone porch that Mom had put a white bench and several plants on.

Of course, Caleb had shut and locked the door so I

had to use my key. He was such a dick now. To me, to Izzy, our little sister, to Mom and Dad, to everybody.

I grabbed a pack of off-brand berry fruit snacks and headed up to my room.

My room was completely ridiculous. The walls were pale peach. The double bed had an antique metal frame painted white and sat centered on the wall so it seemed to take up the whole room, especially because it was tall. There were white hooks in the ceiling that drapery used to hang from because Mom had thought I needed a canopy bed.

Me, a canopy bed.

Just no.

At least she had Izzy to be her little princess of a daughter.

Not that I had a problem with Izzy. She was my favorite family member. But her princess-ness was impossible to deny.

Fortunately, my room also had a little built-in desk and shelves in an alcove. I'd been able to make it my own by claiming it for my Testors paint bottles and the little metal fantasy character figurines Sam and I painted.

I climbed onto the gray and peach bedspread because I needed to think a bit. Make a plan.

Okay, so I'd walk over there. I'd knock on the door. Carlos probably wouldn't answer—maybe his mom would. I'd just ask her if he was home, and she'd get him. No big deal. Normal people did this kind of thing all the time, I was sure.

Sam would be so impressed. I'd have engaged the en … not the enemy. No. I'd have initiated a potentially risky social encounter on my own.

The AC kicked on with a groan and whoosh. The air was freezing because my skin was already wet from sweat

—from the heat and what I was thinking about doing. But I *could* do it.

I headed out. No need to leave a note since I'd be back before either of my parents got home, unless things went really, really well. I didn't want to jinx myself by assuming the best-case scenario.

I shut the door and crossed the street. Most of the houses on this long street were two-story, in various colors. Normal, boring house colors. I'd always thought it would be interesting to paint our house bright blue, but it wasn't allowed. Not that my parents would do something so unusual, anyway.

It was a long walk down to get to a cross street. I started thinking maybe I should have left a note. What if things did go really, really well?

I replayed the scene from math class in my head. The looks Carlos had given me. He had to have been flirting. Why else would he have done all that? I mean, we'd known each other for a long time, since third grade, when he'd moved here from somewhere. Tennessee, I thought. I'd always thought he was cute. Because he was. He was a little awkward, but kind of tall, so he was still hot. He played baseball, too.

I was about halfway down toward the side street and I was drenched in sweat. I might not have thought the whole thing out all that well. My face was bound to be pink from the heat, and I'd be halfway to a sunburn.

It would have been so much better if I already had a car.

I passed the house that gave out celery sticks with peanut butter on Halloween. It was a friendly Black lady, but celery? Seriously.

I trekked further, sweated more.

There was the biggest sycamore in the neighborhood,

in front of a white house with gray stonework. Finally, I reached the corner and turned, walked past the two corner lots, and turned again down Carlos's street.

Was this really a good idea? Would I look a little desperate? That was probably bad. But I had no experience with boys. I'd never been invited to those middle school spin-the-bottle parties I knew went on. I'd never sat around with a bunch of girls talking about boys and doing each other's hair or painting each other's nails. And it wasn't like I'd ever wanted to do those things, either.

I wiped the sweat off my forehead. Was it getting hotter or was it all nerves? I tugged my short sleeves back down where they'd ridden up my arms. Too fat. Which was too bad, but I didn't know what to do about it. I didn't think I had a worse diet than anyone else.

It was okay. If Carlos was interested, it would be good. I liked him.

Okay, there it was. It was a one-story on a block of mostly two-stories. But the front yard had loads of bright and warm-colored flowers—red, orange, yellow—and I guess some would say it was well-manicured. There was a set of stones that led to the mailbox, so I followed them to the door.

I stood on a small covered porch, surrounded by walls painted a dull gray that seemed in contrast to my intense emotions.

This was it, the moment of truth. I took a deep breath and knocked. Sam would be so proud of me when I told her.

After a short delay, during which I did not even ponder running, an older boy opened the door. Oh, shit—I hadn't thought of this. His eyes widened into that judgy look I was all too familiar with from school. Lip slightly curled.

Oh, God. My stomach plummeted.

"What?" he asked.

Okay, at this point I faltered. I hadn't been expecting someone else from school. "Um."

His deadpan expression didn't change.

I swallowed as a droplet of sweat trailed down my forehead. "Does Carlos live here?"

"Hold on," he grunted.

He left the door open and disappeared behind it. After a moment, Carlos appeared. He was looking off to the side when he stepped into the doorway. His brother was saying something from inside the house, though I couldn't make it out.

So for a millisecond, I got to admire his profile and be glad I'd come. He had a nice nose and full lips. I imagined what it would be like to kiss him and run my fingers through his soft-looking hair. What would that feel like?

I had never kissed anyone yet. Which was pretty embarrassing at fifteen, but maybe that was all about to change.

He turned toward me and his eyes widened in alarm, and then got wider.

Oh, God. This was worse than his brother. He was *horrified* to see me. I needed to crawl into a hole and die.

It was like I'd stubbed my toe, except it was my heart. The heat flared in my cheeks as a humiliating blush exploded onto my face.

He still stared, his hand on the door—knuckles white—and I swear the door moved like he was thinking of closing it. In my face.

I stared at him. He stared at me. Say something. Anything. "Can I have my eraser?"

"Yeah." He pushed the door almost shut and disappeared again. I stood there, dizzy with shame. His brother opened the door again, looked at me, shook his head in obvious disgust, and breezed off.

This was a fucking nightmare. I felt like puking.

Soon Carlos came back holding the stupid white eraser between two fingers like it was a stinking dead thing.

I stuck my palm out, and he dropped it in my hand, not touching me.

My tear ducts and cheeks were burning, and I knew it was a matter of time before I started crying, so I muttered, "Thanks," and turned around. The door clicked shut.

I stepped back along the stones to the street. God, I was a fucking idiot. How could I have actually thought he liked me? I really, truly should have known better. Probably if I'd been remotely normal, I would have.

But I knew what it was. The problem was that I was an ugly freak. Everybody knew it, and I did, too, though sometimes I forgot. Apparently. I still had this traitorous well of hope deep inside me.

I clenched the eraser in my hand, wishing it could erase what had just happened.

I was not going to tell Sam about this. She'd probably pity me.

Chapter 4

Saturday was a new day. Time to forget Carlos and the eraser and my idiocy. It was 7:55 a.m. and Sam and I were waiting to board the school bus that would take us, Ms. Tolliver, and eleven other art club members to a couple of Tulsa art galleries.

Maybe I should tell Sam about Carlos. I didn't want her to feel sorry for me, but what if she somehow found out at school? Carlos could tell people.

The idea made me sick. And Sam might be mad if she found out from someone else.

Ms. Tolliver and her wild hair were off to the side of the bus, where she was talking to a man, probably the bus driver. The yellow bus's engine was already running. It was one of the smaller buses since there weren't that many of us.

Sam yawned, which made me yawn, and both of us laughed.

Ms. Tolliver clapped her hands. "Alright, everyone, let's go." She followed the driver onto the bus and we all started filing on.

Sam and I chose the back seats, each of us taking one, but we both sat near the aisle so we could talk easily.

Once everyone was seated, Ms. Tolliver stood at the front of the bus. "I just want give you some info about the two museums we're going to visit, in case you haven't read up on them. The first is Philbrook, which has both a gallery and a lovely large garden with paths for roaming. It has a fairly diverse collection, with a lot of American and Native American art, and also some Asian and African pieces that are fascinating. It also has a decent amount of European art, including a work by the Renaissance painter Cosimo, and one by the French painter Bouguereau.

"The second is Gilcrease Museum, and it's probably best known for its Western collection, especially the art of Frederic Remington."

"Oh, boy, Western art," Sam said.

That made me laugh. "Yeah, like we don't get enough of cowboys every day."

Ms. Tolliver was still going. "... many of his bronze sculptures and oil paintings. They are incredible. There are also a lot of Native American at pieces that are exciting to see. Another important thing to see is the new exhibit on the Tulsa Race Massacre, even though there isn't a lot of art in that collection."

She took a breath and continued, telling us about the schedule. We were supposed to eat lunch at Philbrook, either in the restaurant or ideally in the garden. She finished by saying, "Make sure to manage your time wisely at both places."

She turned to the bus driver and nodded at him before sitting down in the front seat behind him.

"Speaking of not caring about cowboys, maybe you should put a cowboy in your dragon drawing," Sam said.

"Ha."

"Have you started it yet?"

"I did the complete preliminary sketch already, but that's it." She'd seen the various sketches I'd done in my sketchbook.

"Cool. I'm so excited to see it."

The bus started moving, heading toward the exit of the empty parking lot.

The drawing was going to be so cool. In the foreground was the back of a dragon in flight. It was facing what was in the middle ground, which was the top of a mountain. Then, and this was the really cool part, another dragon was just emerging from behind the mountain to face off with the one in the foreground. I was doing it all in pencil. I wished I was better at colored pencil, but I wasn't, so regular pencil it was.

I loved dragons. At least, the western version of them. Chinese dragons didn't do much for me, but the kind you see on the front of classic fantasy novels—yeah, I was all over that. Probably because they were so inherently powerful, and I was not. I also loved that they came in bold colors.

The foreground dragon was in the bottom right while the other dragon was mostly on the upper left. And the mountain was a mess—it had snow-covered shrubbery but the fight the dragons were having had caused some collateral damage, and some of the shrubbery was burning. It would be hard to balance the fire with the snow, which would obviously be melting.

"I'm a little worried I won't be able to draw fire," I admitted.

The driver pulled out onto the main road, and we were off.

Sam laughed. "Just practice first. That's what your sketchbook is for."

"Yeah." Sam was a better artist than I was. While we were both in art club, she took band instead of art for her elective.

"It's like me with guitar." She laughed. "I just need to practice more."

"Whatever, you're amazing at all your instruments."

Sam shrugged.

But she really was amazing. She played the oboe for band, but had played some other instruments in middle school—I could never keep up with what—and she learned keyboard last year. I was jealous of that one, because I really felt like I could learn to play that. And it might open up the social world for me. Music did that. But my parents wouldn't just get me one without a reason. And although my birthday was coming up, I wouldn't be getting anything except the car they'd promised. Which I wasn't complaining about. Maybe I could put it on my Christmas list.

"Okay, so, OSIN," Sam said. "We need to talk about this."

"Right." Operation Social Interaction for Nic. This reminded me painfully of Carlos and my stupid trip to his house, which made me feel sick again. Should I tell her?

"We need a plan."

"Okay." I had no ideas. My only attempt had been a crash and burn situation. I didn't want to tell her, but a good friend would confide.

"We should start by looking at opportunities we already have. There's Key Club and of course art club. You should try to talk to people today."

"Yeah." Problem was, I didn't really want to talk to people today, to be honest. None of these people were as interesting as Sam was.

"People can be fascinating when you get to know them a little," she said.

Like she could read my mind. This is why we were friends. "Are they?" I still wasn't convinced.

She laughed. "Well, not all of them. But the ones worth meeting. And people are worth knowing, you know."

We fell forward as the driver stopped at a red light.

I really needed to change my attitude. I was genuinely shy, but the years of friendlessness and bullying had made me distrust people in general. Sam and I knew each other in sixth grade, but we weren't really friends until seventh grade.

"Okay," I said. "You're right. I mean, it's probably not common that you find someone who agrees with you on everything. But I still can't be friends with someone who thinks *The Bachelorette* is quality TV."

"Ha. Fair enough."

She was talking me into trying, but the old fear of rejection returned as I thought of Carlos. "What if people really just don't want to be friends with me, though? I mean, everybody thinks I'm ugly. I'd be a liability to them."

"Come on, you're not ugly." Sam rolled her eyes.

The bus got going again.

"I don't know. People say that. You know they do."

Sam frowned but didn't say anything.

"I don't really understand why, though. I mean, blue eyes are considered a plus, but not on me. My nose and mouth aren't overly large. And pale skin and freckles are cute on some people. Why not me?" I had fine teeth after having had braces, and I didn't even have an acne problem. I always had one zit that migrated around. Now it was on my left cheek. My brown hair was straight and halfway down my back. Boring, but I wasn't sure why it made me ugly. Though, obviously, being fat was a big factor.

"I don't know. It's stupid. I think they just pick up on your shyness. Sometimes they misinterpret it, too. Like they think you're stuck-up or something. I don't think everyone really thinks you're ugly. They're just being mean. Some people just go in for the kill."

"Maybe it's the baggy shirts. My mom always says I'd look better in close-fitting shirts. They're just not comfortable." Actually, she said I'd look less fat in closer-fitting clothes.

"I know. My mom says the same thing." Sam usually wore unisex t-shirts, herself. But not as loose as me.

"Izzy wants me to wear makeup."

"I can't see that ever happening," Sam said with a laugh. "You wearing makeup before me? As if."

"I know. I'm sure if I just slapped some makeup on my face and tried to dress cute, they wouldn't pick on me so much. I just can't." It was hard to explain, but it felt deeply wrong.

It wasn't like I hadn't tried. I mean, there were pictures of little me with lipstick and eye shadow all over my face, but that interest was one I'd outgrown pretty young, like five or something. I'd started hating the way it felt—both in the physical sense and in the social sense. Everybody could see it and knew you were playing the game, and I couldn't stand that.

"I know. It's stupid."

We were waiting at a light about to turn left onto the highway that would take us into Tulsa.

I scooted forward and put my knees up against the seat back in front of me. "It is." I thought again about Carlos, and considered bringing it up.

Sam yawned and stretched out lengthwise on her seat, feet on the aisle floor. "I think I'm going to sleep."

"Cool." More time for me to think about trying to be more socially adept. And work up the nerve to talk about Carlos.

Chapter 5

Sam and I were waiting for our orders at the restaurant at Philbrook, standing at the counter at the side.

"So what was your favorite thing?" she asked.

"I liked *The Little Shepherdess* because it wasn't ornate and overdone like most of the Renaissance work. I mean, there's only so many religious figures you can look at."

"True. For some reason, I liked the one with the sheep. It seemed peaceful."

The girl at the restaurant called my name and I took my bag. Sam's came right afterward, so we headed out to the garden.

We walked out into a large sculpture garden, but decided to skip it for the moment. There was a picnic area further on. We walked down these broad steps flanked by green lawns toward a large fountain at the bottom. Paths bordered by low hedges criss-crossed the lawns and garden areas. The whole way down, I tried to think of a way to bring up Carlos.

"Let's sit over there," Sam said, pointing to a spot close to the creek we'd just crossed.

It was a sunny day, still warm but not uncomfortably so, and the surroundings were nice and peaceful, even though there were other people around.

I pulled my sandwich out of the bag and started unwrapping the plastic wrap.

I decided to tell her. "So, Sam. There was something that happened Friday."

"Oh, hey," Sam said, which made me look up.

Lily, the president of the club, stood in front of us. "Hey, guys. Are you having a nice time?"

"Yeah," Sam said.

I nodded stupidly, struck dumb for no reason. I just hadn't been expecting a social interaction.

"Good. Just wanted to make sure. Also, don't forget we're doing the fundraiser next month." She looked at me and my half-unwrapped sandwich and smiled before leaving, heading towards some of the other kids from our group.

"That was sort of passive-aggressive," I whispered.

"Oh, I don't think so. I mean, we do need to raise money for stuff like this."

"She acted like she cared just so she could remind us about the fundraising."

Sam laughed. "It's normal to say something nice before asking someone to do something."

"True, I guess." I finished unwrapping my tuna salad sandwich with sprouts and realized I was pretty hungry. So much for telling her about Carlos right now. I took my first bite as Sam opened her wrap.

I looked over and saw a calico cat sauntering our way. "Look," I said, pointing.

"Oh, cool. That's Perilla, I think," Sam said. The garden had three friendly resident cats that helped with pest control and entertained visitors.

Sam waggled her fingers. "Come here, kitty." She whistled a little. The cat slowly approached, smelled Sam's fingers, and turned away.

I laughed. "She doesn't like you."

"I'm so hurt."

Perilla wandered off toward other people.

"She didn't even bother to sniff your fingers," Sam teased.

"Cats kind of weird me out. Maybe she could tell."

"Usually those are the very people they gravitate toward."

We finished up our lunches and lay back in the grass.

Eventually, I checked my phone. We had twenty-five minutes. "We'd better get going if we want to look through the gift shop."

"Let's go the back way," Sam said.

We headed the other way and crossed a nearby bridge before heading up some steps to a small house and fountain. Once we'd dumped our sandwich wrappers in the trash cans and found the store, we only had fifteen minutes. That was enough time for some browsing.

As soon as we got inside, one of the other club members, a stocky girl whose name I didn't know, said hi to Sam. "Are you going to Nate's tonight?" she asked.

I was instantly worried. Was this girl friends with Sam? She already had enough other friends, with all the band kids.

"No, I don't think I can," Sam answered.

The girl looked at me before saying, "Cool," and heading out of the shop.

"Why didn't you say anything, Nic?" Sam asked.

"She was just talking to you."

"No, she wasn't." She sounded kind of annoyed. "You've got to try harder."

I felt like a dumbass. I'd just assumed. That's how it had always been. When I was younger, I frequently mistakenly believed I was being addressed, only to get told off for responding. It stayed with me.

We split up and I looked at the art books and some of the art supplies they had.

"Look, they have a Philbrook garden cats t-shirt," Sam said from the other side of the store. She didn't sound annoyed anymore, thank God.

I moved over to the rack she was looking at. It was a heather gray shirt with three cat faces on it.

"I think I'm going to get it. It's kind of cool."

I laughed.

"Come on, it's a fun idea. I like cats. And I want to remember this trip. It's nice to spend time with my best friend without parents or brothers around." She smiled at me.

That warmed my heart. "Me too."

What would I do without Sam? I was a social disaster. But I had to have faith in OSIN. It had to make a difference, with Sam on the case.

Chapter 6

Monday morning I slept past my alarm, so I was running late. Caleb was in the shower and I had to wait for him, but I really needed a shower. So I was sitting with my stack of clothes on my bed when my phone dinged.

A message from Sam. —*there's something I need to tell u*—

—*ok. what?*—

This didn't sound good. My stomach made this noise and I couldn't tell if it was hunger or sudden nerves.

—*not over text*—

—*call me then*—

The shower turned off. Caleb should be done any minute. But I still had time for a quick call.

—*can't. have to talk to one of my teachers. see you at lunch*—

She wouldn't have her phone in class and I never saw her in the mornings because of where our classes were. I would have to wait until lunch.

My stomach twisted again and I suddenly wondered if she was going to friend-break up with me. Everything had been fine Saturday, but I'd experienced things like this before.

But no, that couldn't be it. Maybe she'd started dating somebody and wouldn't be able to do lunch with me anymore.

What if it was something bigger than us? About her family? Oh God, what if she was moving?

I heard the bathroom door squeak open and raced across the hall to shower, all the bad thoughts swirling in my head.

Chapter 7

There was only one more class before I would meet Sam for lunch. I'd been stressing all morning over what she was going to tell me.

Of course, I also had to face Carlos before that. In minutes. I was sweating again.

I rifled through my locker trying to find my English notebook, which was buried under my backpack and some other random papers. I always managed to turn everything into such a mess so fast—it was just the third week of school. Then this group of juniors walked past, and one of them held his fist up to his mouth and cough-said, "lesbian."

I turned back into my trash pit of a locker, and my face burned.

More kids were coming and going and as they disappeared into the crowd, one of the other two laughed and said, "She's so fugly."

Assholes. I spied the corner of the blue spiral sticking out from under my chemistry book and yanked it out, already pissed off. Who did these people think they were, and why did they go out of their way to attack me?

I looked back down and headed to English with my notebook, pen, and a beat-up copy of *The Scarlet Letter*.

When I stepped into the room, the first thing I saw was Carlos and Kyle sitting against the yellow-painted cinderblock wall opposite the door.

There go the feelings again. Why couldn't I just not care? Why did I always have to start sweating or end up with shaking hands? How did other kids pull it off?

I slunk to the seat right by the door and slid into it.

But, just my luck, Carlos looked over right as he was laughing at something Kyle said.

His smile fell away, and he averted his eyes. I studied the top of my desk—a sort of mystery color somewhere between beige and pink with little black bits of something mixed in.

When I glanced up, Kyle was looking at me. His laugh, a sort of bark, drew the attention of several of those around him and made Carlos roll his eyes.

Carlos must have told him.

I was such an idiot. I still couldn't believe I'd thought— I truly had—that it was possible Carlos liked me. Remembering his face on Friday—as well as how it looked now— was making my cheeks flame again.

I hated how easily I blushed. It announced to the world that I cared what it thought.

I hunched over my opened notebook and wrote the date at the top before flipping through the novel. I was about a quarter of the way through it and hated it. I was a reader, but preferred stuff written since the mid-1990s or so. I'd forced myself to read some 1970s sci-fi out of respect for the genre, but they weren't my favorites.

But with *The Scarlet Letter*, I found it infuriating how the main character was treated. I know it was true to the times, but it was not okay. Why do we want to read about slut-shaming, Puritan-style? Then we have to have all these idiot boys in class saying things like, "She should have said no," and so on. Applying that period's idiotic moral code to today was more than irritating.

The teacher started the class by clearing her throat to get everyone to shut up. I spent the whole period focused on my half of the classroom so as to not inadvertently catch Carlos's or Kyle's eye. Eye contact was dangerous. It triggered interactions.

What a nightmare. And it would be even worse because we had assigned seats in math, which meant I was going to be right next to Carlos—today, and the rest of the year.

God, why had I gone to his house?

Finally, the teacher stopped talking and let us go. I shot out of there so Kyle couldn't say anything to me. I guessed Carlos wouldn't. He didn't strike me as the go-out-of-his-way type.

I headed to my locker to drop off my crap and raced to the cafeteria to snag a burrito before the line got too long. I pulled open one of the rust-colored double doors and was hit with the din you'd expect from the throng of kids already in there. This place would get even busier. I could feel my heart from speeding up due to anxiety.

I got in line and listened to kids talk about the week-end. They'd had a lot more fun than I had, for sure. Wild parties, apparently. My Tulsa trip was cool, which was fine. Still, I was tense and feeling inferior, listening to everything other people got up to.

I edged forward, eventually getting to the trays. I didn't need one, but the food was almost within reach. We inched ahead even more, and finally I was able to grab a couple of the small burritos and some salsa packets. I headed over to the register, eventually getting through that line and out the door, into the September heat. For once, it was a relief—just to be away from so many people.

My pulse approached normal as I went back into the main building and into the stairwell where Sam and I often ate lunch.

She wasn't there yet, so I sat cross-legged on the scratchy brown carpet against the wall facing the stairs. What in the world was she going to tell me?

I unwrapped my first burrito and squeezed some salsa on before taking a giant bite. I was positively starving. I had my sketchbook with me in case Sam was late.

Some kids came down the stairs and stared at me sitting there against the wall, but fortunately they didn't say anything. Thank God. They went through the door. Still no Sam.

Sam was cool. She didn't wear makeup either, which really was weird here, where all the girls slathered on goop millimeters thick. Somehow she still came across as a little cute, even though her long, dark blonde hair contrasted with her super-pale skin. She didn't meet the official American standard of beauty, but she was definitely not ugly like me.

I knew I wasn't supposed to think things like that about myself, but I really felt like a bit of self-awareness can take a person far in life. Or at least keep me from doing stupid shit—like thinking any boy could truly like me.

The door opened, and Sam came in bearing a paper-wrapped burger. She had on yellow board shorts and a Killers t-shirt, and her face was strained.

"What's wrong?" I asked.

She flopped down next to me, sitting close but not quite touching my shoulder. We weren't very touchy-feely.

"My God, the worst thing!" she announced.

I stared at her, imagining all the horrible things. Her dad died. She has cancer. She was moving.

"We're moving!"

Gut punch. My only friend. "You're moving? Where?"

"Scotland!" Her eyes were wide. She must still be in shock.

What? Oh my God. "Holy shit. When?"

She shook her head and looked down. "Three weeks."

Then we stared at each other, and my mind raced, trying to figure out all the ramifications. There were so many. I wouldn't have anyone to paint my figurines with. We'd never manage to find a D&D group. I'd never get to drive her around in the car I was getting after my birthday next month.

I wouldn't have any friends at all.

But worst of all, I wouldn't have my best friend. I mean, we'd been friends for so long and had so much in common. We weren't friends because we thought we'd be good for each other on the popularity scale—we were real friends. She was the most important person in my life.

Sam frowned and looked at the burger she was still holding. "My mom sprang it on me during breakfast."

I studied the second burrito in my hand. It looked like a normal, dried-up cafeteria burrito—pasty refried beans tucked into a flour tortilla that was curled up on the edges where it had gone crunchy. This would forever be the meal I'd remember when I thought of losing my best friend.

I looked over at her and saw she was upset. She never cried, so I knew that wouldn't happen, which was good because I wouldn't know what to do.

"Are you okay?" I asked.

"Yeah," she said, unconvincingly.

"This really sucks."

She nodded, staring into the distance. "You know what else?"

"What?"

"We're going to have to step up OSIN."

"Yeah. Only three weeks left." I was relieved that she was still thinking that way. Maybe I still had a chance to make even one new friend before Sam left. "What's the plan?"

"You will have to be braver, for one. But I'll see who I can get to come by at lunch so you can get to know some of the band kids and other people I know."

The thing was, Sam was once as unpopular as I was. In seventh grade she still hadn't been allowed to shave her legs, but there was no way to avoid wearing shorts here, so she got made fun of a lot. She always cited facts about how only a small proportion of women in the world shaved, and so on. I'd admired her for it because I'd been too chicken to hold out and had started that year.

Kids had called us the manly girls. On the first day of eighth grade she came in with jean shorts and smooth legs. Her mom had finally relented. That had been the beginning of her rise on the popularity scale. She wasn't at the top now, by any means, but she was somewhere in the middle.

"The band kids seem kind of snobby," I said.

"They're not snobby, just insular."

"Because that's totally different."

She snorted. "Okay, true. They are kind of snobby."

They weren't snobby like the popular rich kids. They were band geeks, after all. But it always seemed like most of them looked down on other uncool people. I guess, in their world, wearing those dumb hats carried a bit of prestige. I wouldn't want to walk around with a plume sticking up from my head, personally.

"And really," Sam said, "You should try harder with Zach and Evan on Wednesday. They're nice."

Yeah. At least, Zach was. I wasn't so sure about Evan, who was in band with Sam. He didn't seem to like me. But what was new? No matter what I did, that's how it was.

Ugh. Why did I always have to think like that? Other people didn't constantly beat themselves up.

It was different with Zach, on the other hand—I'd definitely caught him staring at me in the rearview mirror a bunch of times when he was driving us to Key Club. I didn't think he'd had a disgusted look on his face, either. I knew what those looked like.

Despite what people said, I couldn't be a lesbian if I liked Zach this much. Could I? And, I mean, I was probably being stupid again, but maybe he could actually like me back?

Chapter 8

Tuesday at lunch, I opened the door to the main building and headed toward Sam's and my stairwell. The carpet in the halls was brown, and the lockers were painted gray. It all looked so industrial. At least the classrooms had some color. I passed the last bank of lockers and turned down the hall before heading into the stairwell.

I'd beat Sam again. So I sat down, the carpet scratching the skin on my calf. Sam was supposed to be bringing some friends today, and my pulse was already speeding up in nervous anticipation.

She was true to her promise and showed up with a boy and girl in tow. Unfortunately, I didn't feel very hopeful. I'd spent most of the past twenty-four hours feeling shitty, between Sam moving and the Carlos thing.

"Nic, this is Ryan and Lizzy."

"Hey." My face heated as I said it. So stupid to already be nervous. Nothing had happened.

Ryan lifted his head in greeting, and Lizzy did a finger-waggle wave. Ryan looked preppy in tan shorts and a pale plaid shirt. Lizzy had on jean shorts and a layered top.

Sam and I sat in our normal spot against the wall, and the other two plopped down on the adjacent wall, a place which was a little darker because it was under the stairs.

I was about to say, "Are you guys in band?" but then they started making out.

O-kay. This was awkward. I averted my eyes. I shouldn't watch that. Sam smiled and shrugged.

"So, I had this idea," Sam said between bites of cheeseburger.

"Yeah?"

She finished chewing and then said, "So, you know how my parents are making me get rid of stuff?"

I nodded. I'd been over at her house yesterday, and they'd already started going through their belongings. They were getting professional packers, but there was still a lot to do before they arrived.

"Do you want my keyboard?"

"For real?" Sam had this awesome eighty-eight-key digital piano. She had a stand for it and everything. Even a little stool. And it could change everything for me. Music brought people together. If I could get good—good enough that I believed it—maybe I could meet new people. Make friends.

"Yeah. I hardly use it anymore."

She'd moved on to guitar a while back, plus she still played her oboe for band. As exciting as it felt, I'd always had my doubts about myself and music. I was a terrible singer, for instance. "Do you think I could learn to play it?"

"Totally. You're smart enough. And you're good at math. I think it's all related. It's not that hard to get the basics and then it's just a matter of patience. And practice. I'll give you a bunch of books, too. And the library will have the basic how-to books, so you should be good."

I grinned and nodded, cogwheels turning and stirring

up hope, then grimaced at the sounds of smacking lips coming from a few feet away.

Sam took another bite of her burger, and I unwrapped the first of my three taquitos. It looked like the happy couple weren't going to eat anything except each other's faces.

"My brother will totally be jealous," I said.

"He'll mock you and say you're selling out to EDM."

Caleb had a guitar and thought he would be famous some day. It seemed unlikely, given his skill level.

"Yeah, especially since there's all those pre-recorded tracks." I laughed, feeling better than I had since the Carlos thing. All three of us liked real music, not the electronic crap that everybody preferred now.

Still thinking about it all, I started on the first taquito.

This keyboard could be just the thing I needed socially. I could learn it and maybe find other kids who played. At least I'd have something to talk to them about. That was half my problem—I didn't know how to make small talk, which I knew was what primed a group for real conversation. I mean, you couldn't simply walk up to someone and start talking about the giant plastic island in the Pacific.

I kept imagining fabulous scenarios while we finished eating in silence punctuated by the annoying slurping and rustling fabric sounds coming from under the stairs. Then I remembered again why the keyboard opportunity had come up. Sam was moving. My mind raced. What was I going to do when she was gone? I'd be eating in the stairwell alone, or going to the library. And my weekends would be so desolate.

"So are you going to be able to join the band at the school there in the middle of the semester?" I asked as I crumpled the wrapper and dropped it next to me.

Sam's eyes went wide and she wadded up her own

paper and swallowed. "You won't believe this! They don't even have marching band. I looked it up."

"They don't?"

"No, because you know they don't have school sports the way we do. Kids who play sports do it for fun outside of school. They don't have them in college—I mean, university—either. So no marching band."

"Huh." It was sinking in that she would be gone soon. I wouldn't have anyone, if today's make-out session was any indicator of the potential success of OSIN.

Unless the keyboard worked out. Then I'd have something in common with more people.

"I mean, they do have jazz bands and stuff like that, they're just not associated with the schools, really."

"So will you join one of those?" I pulled the hem of my t-shirt down where it had ridden up in the back.

"Probably. Why not, you know?"

I nodded. Man, things were going to suck here.

"You know what else?" she asked.

"What?"

"The way they do school is different anyway. You basically pick these subjects and study them in depth. You can choose how many to do, though you have to do a certain number of them to qualify for university, of course, plus do well enough on each final test—which is also your whole grade, if you can believe that." She punctuated her explanation with her hands.

"Huh." That sounded so different.

"You know, there's always OAMS for you, if you want a change yourself." The Oklahoma Academy for Mathematics and Science was a boarding school in Oklahoma City. It was free once you got accepted because it was considered public.

"If I could get in."

"Come on, you could." She bumped my shoulder. She had more faith in me than I did.

I wasn't sure. Plus, they didn't have a great art program, and I wanted to go to a good art school. I'd need to keep developing.

"Do you think you'll go to college over there?" I asked.

"I don't know. Maybe, if my parents stay. That could be kind of cool."

I nodded.

This got her started on universities in Scotland. I didn't have anything to say. The excitement from the keyboard had faded a little. It wasn't that I didn't care about what she was going to go through, but I didn't want her to leave. It would suck so hard.

Chapter 9

I raced up the stairs to the art building after school, already covered in sweat from the heat. Ms. Tolliver stood in front of an easel next to her desk. She was wearing her messy, formerly-white apron that was covered in clay and paint. She had this wild hair that looked permed but I guessed was natural. She was cool.

"Nic! Hi. Can I help you with something?"

I made a beeline for the ceramics shelf, passing all the gray tables and the shelves of painting supplies. "Just picking up my hand."

"Oh, I love that piece. So creative, and you did a really good job on the shape. It's so mundane yet fascinating, and your choice of glaze—I adore it!"

"Thanks." I'd glazed it a deep, glossy midnight blue. It was kind of awesome. "I like how it turned out, too."

"What's your next piece going to be?"

Okay, I did like her a lot, but she could seriously talk. She seemed to genuinely like me, too, which was rare. Most of my teachers didn't. So I had to stop for a second, even though I needed to hurry if I was going to catch the bus.

"I'm not sure."

"Listen, Nic, I know I mentioned the art contest in class, but I think you should really put some thought into it. You can enter as many categories as you want."

I nodded. The contest wasn't until the spring. "So I should choose my class projects carefully, to cover as many of them as possible, right?" I thought I had a chance. I was a better artist than most of the kids in my class. I thought I should be nervous about putting my work out there for the world to see. But I wasn't.

"Yes, exactly."

I needed to leave, so I started edging toward the stairs.

"I know you want to go to art school, don't you?"

"Yeah." I was halfway to the door.

"It's good to have both breadth and depth in your port-folio. So if you make this year the one you produce work in a variety of media, you can work on the depth in your junior and senior years."

Now I was in the doorway but I stopped. "Okay. That makes sense. I, uh, have to go catch my bus."

"Oh, go ahead, honey! I didn't mean to keep you. Off you go." She smiled and teasingly waved me off.

I rushed down the stairs and through the outer door into the gravel lot. I raced back toward the oval and turned the corner on the bottom of the U. I couldn't move very fast because I never ran—the way I looked was just too humiliating—plus I needed to keep the blue hand safe.

Then the first bus pulled away. Mine was the fourth in line. It would be hard to make it if I didn't hurry, so I started speed walking.

Then the second bus went, and I started jogging. A

bead of sweat rolled into my eye, and then I was behind the fifth bus when the third one pulled away.

Shit, shit, shit. I broke into a run to try to catch mine, but it left just as I passed its brake lights, leaving me in the wake of a few taunting faces from the back windows of the bus and some tasty bus exhaust. Jeremy from up the street who'd spit on me once threw his head back in laughter, and one girl whose name I didn't know twirled her finger around her ear in the universal sign for "you're crazy."

I stopped running, blushing with embarrassment at what an idiot I looked like chasing a bus. Of course I'd missed it.

I flopped onto a green metal bench in front of the building, which was long and made of tan brick with a tacky greenish overhang protruding from the top. Though at the moment it blocked the sun, so that was nice.

As my breathing slowed, I realized it wasn't the end of the world. I'd just call Mom.

"Hi, honey, is everything okay?"

"I missed the bus."

"Oh, Nic. I don't have time to come get you. I've got to be at work in twenty minutes."

Shit. She had an early shift. She worked at the City Flame Grill, one of those sit-down chains. Her having a job was a new thing, and I wasn't used to her schedule yet. I didn't say anything.

"You'll have to call Dad, but you know he won't be able to come until after work." That meant at least six. Which left me with over three hours to kill. I probably could walk home, but I really didn't know how long it would take me.

"Crap."

"I'm really sorry, honey. Why'd you miss the bus?"

"I went to pick up my giant blue hand."

"Oh, great. I'm excited to see it in person." My mom liked my art so I always showed her pictures of the in-progress projects. "What are you going to do until Dad can come?"

"I don't know." I pictured the bus ride into town. "There's a coffee shop downtown."

"You have some cash?" Her voice sounded strained, like it did whenever she mentioned money.

"Yeah, a few bucks."

Something was going on with my parents, with our pantry full of a lot more off-brand labels than we were used to. I guess that was why she'd started the restaurant job.

"I've got to go, Nic. I'll see you tonight. I'll probably be home by seven thirty or so, assuming we're as dead as normal for Tuesdays."

"Right. See you tonight."

"I love you, honey."

"'Kay." I hung up and called Dad.

He could come at 6:30, so I headed downtown. It wasn't far, just a few blocks along streets that lacked curbs, which was different from my neighborhood. We may not have had sidewalks, but we had curbs, at least. I lived in the north side of town, which was generally the upper middle-class part.

I wiped away sweat and turned onto Main Street. It was only a few shops down.

When I pushed the door open, the cold air immediately cooled my damp skin. It felt sort of glorious, such a relief.

There were tables lining the wall on the left all the way to the back of the narrow shop. Thank God the last table was empty. The other tables were swarming with kids from school, all of whom I didn't know.

Then I heard a laugh I'd have known anywhere and turned to the one table that was in the front window, to my right.

Zach. I stared for a moment at his face as his eyes crinkled with laughter. He drove Sam and me—and his friend Evan—to Key Club, this service club, every month. And he was the one I'd actually had a proper crush on since last year. He was blond and also tall, even if he was a little on the chubby side. Not that that took away from his cuteness. And I swear, he always looked at me in the rearview mirror when we were in the car. I'd been hoping he liked me back. Seeing him got my hope machine going again.

He was with some other junior guys so there was no way I'd approach his table. Before I could get to the counter, he saw me and smiled again and waved. My heart beat a little faster. It was his smile and the way his blue eyes sparkled that I really loved.

I wouldn't say he looked ecstatic to see me or anything, but he wasn't embarrassed to acknowledge me, which was a big step in my social world. He could like me. At least he could be a friend, maybe something more.

I returned the wave and was unable to prevent a stupid grin from stretching my mouth way too much, so I stared at the menu instead of him. I wanted an iced vanilla latte, but it was too expensive.

"What can I get you, man?" the barista asked.

Great. He thought I was a guy. I looked away and felt my cheeks heat slightly.

I swallowed and then ordered an iced passion tea and had it sweetened to make it palatable. Whenever I saw health nuts drinking tea without sugar, I was just like, No.

I set the ceramic hand down on the table and settled in. I pulled out my math homework, which made me think of Carlos and Kyle. Why did Kyle have to be such a jerk about it? Why was it so horrible that I sort of indirectly expressed interest in Carlos? Maybe I'd really only wanted my eraser back.

No, I mean, I got it. Being liked by me was an insult to a boy. That had been clear since a particular incident in middle school.

Anyways.

I worked on my homework. I actually liked math. It was very logical, and there were usually multiple ways of getting to the right solution, which reminded me of art, even though the final product in art was always unique. It was the impact that the art had that was either right or wrong—it moved someone or it didn't.

I worked for a while. Where I was sitting, I couldn't see Zach. Though to be fair, I could hear him, on and off. Which was distracting. I strained to hear what he was saying, and I couldn't quite make anything intelligible out. I had to keep forcing myself to get back to my homework.

While I evaluated a polynomial expression, I heard a door squeak open behind me, and a guy snorted and said, "Hey, can you lend me a hand?"

I looked up and saw Logan, the son of two of my parents' friends. I seriously couldn't stand the guy. I couldn't stand his dad, either.

So of course I'd run into Logan in a coffee shop because he was a total coffee snob. He was also a short guy and had on a pale yellow polo shirt and khaki shorts. His smirk made my stomach go queasy. It took me a second of staring at him before I realized what he was talking about. The blue hand.

And while what he'd said might sound innocent or even friendly, I knew him well enough to know it wasn't. So of course—and I fucking hated this—I blushed, and he laughed and sauntered away.

God, I despised Logan. Still, that was a fairly tame interaction. Usually he said something shittier.

I put my head in my shaking hands. Eventually, my heart slowed a little.

Then I looked up to see Zach approaching with purpose. My pulse sped right back up.

He slid into the booth across from me with a smile and said, "Hey, Nic. What's up?"

"Not much." I didn't know what to say. "I missed the bus."

"Ah. Yeah, I've never seen you here."

"No." It was amazing I even got that out, I was so flustered by him.

"You missed the bus?"

"Yeah." Idiot. Say *something*. If only I could think over the racket the butterflies in my stomach had raised.

"Do you need a ride home?" He flashed me that smile. "I know where you live."

I laughed, hoping he didn't notice the nerves laced though it. "Sure."

"Ready?"

"Oh, sure." I started cramming everything into my backpack. I'd just need to send Dad a text.

"Did you make this?" he asked, stretching his hand across the palm of the giant blue hand. I liked the idea of his fingers on the sculpture of my own hand.

"Yeah." His fingers were a lot longer than mine and they filled more of the piece than my own did. His hands were probably strong.

"It's awesome."

I blushed again. I loved that he noticed it and didn't make fun of it.

He had to like me. At least a little. Right?

Please let it be true.

I zipped up my bag and we left.

Zach drove a new Honda Accord, but it was black, so it was baking when we got in.

"So hot," he muttered as he rolled down the windows and cranked up the AC.

I couldn't believe I was here with him. Alone.

We backed out and he did a U-turn. As soon as all the hottest air was sucked out of the car, he rolled the windows back up, and the air from the AC blowing on my face felt great.

I sat with the ceramic hand in my lap. He glanced over and smiled again.

"So cool. Was that inspired by the praying hands in Tulsa?"

"Jesus, no!"

He snorted, and his infectious laugh filled the car. The praying hands he'd referred to made up the giant bronze statue that adorned the entrance of Oral Roberts University in south Tulsa. We'd lived nearby when I was a lot younger. You'd never be able to imagine what they were like until you'd seen them. They were sixty feet high and, well, insane.

"Not half a pair? You could display them side by side like they're requesting alms." He chuckled.

He was teasing me, but not in a mean way. Wasn't that flirting?

Not that I was qualified to judge. Clearly.

"No chance," I said.

He was still laughing while we left downtown.

Halfway to my house I realized I wasn't that nervous anymore. It had to be a good sign that he put me at ease, didn't it?

"Key Club's tomorrow," he said.

"Yeah." Was he looking forward to it? Another chance to see me?

"Are you doing the car wash next weekend?"

"No." Girls did that mostly so they could wear skimpy clothes and get all wet and look good. Obviously that wouldn't work with me, so no.

"Me neither. Who wants to spend hours outside?"

See, we felt the same about the weather. We had even more in common than I thought. I was talking to Zach without losing my words. This made my heart pinch. "Not me. The sun's fine as long as it's on the other side of a window, as far as I'm concerned."

He chuckled.

We chatted some more until he pulled into my driveway. He put the car in park and said, "So I'll see you tomorrow at six thirty?"

The Key Club meeting. I nodded and got out. "Thanks for the ride."

"No problem. See you."

I headed to the front door, wondering if I should have stood there and waved at him or something. To let him know I was interested.

Well, there was always Wednesday. Maybe I'd get a chance then.

Chapter 10

After eating a Lean Cuisine cheese ravioli, I tossed the plastic tray into the trash and dropped the fork in the dishwasher.

Back to my drawing, which I'd been prepping since I got home. I was set up in the dining room because I was working on a poster-sized piece of thick white paper. It was almost as big as the desk in my room, so there'd be no way to do it in there. I was lucky my mom encouraged my drawing.

I'd done a super-light sketch of the whole drawing to get the scale right. It would be so awesome. It would be my best piece for the contest. And I needed to do well in the contest this year and next year if I was to have any chance of getting into a good art school.

I looked at the paper, trying to decide where to start when my dad came in from the den. He was still in his nice work pants. His curly hair was getting long.

"Nic?"

"Yeah?" I was thinking I'd start with one of the snow-covered shrubs since it was roughly centered. I could work out from there so I didn't end up squishing one of the dragons off the page if my scale was off.

He stood next to me. "When your mom gets home, we're going to have a family meeting."

"What?" I turned to look at him and saw a barely perceptible frown on his face, which was weird. Also, we had literally never had a family meeting before. This made my shoulders tense a little.

"She shouldn't be too much longer." He rubbed his beard, one of his nervousness tells.

I checked my phone and saw that it was already after seven. I was too weirded out to ask anything else. Something was going on. Were we moving? It would be hilarious if we ended up moving to Scotland, too. And awesome.

I mean, I knew that wasn't it, but it was a nice thought. Better than the thought of Sam leaving and me staying.

"More dragons?" he asked.

I looked at the paper. "Yeah, this one's a battle scene."

"I can't wait to see it." He went into the kitchen for a beer.

My dad didn't get art, but he tried with me. I mean, what could you expect from an accountant?

I focused on envisioning the final drawing in order to get Sam's move out of my mind—plus the family meeting that was making me increasingly tense.

I googled shrubbery to get a good idea of what mine should look like and started putting it to paper.

Before I got anywhere, Izzy came in and sat in the chair next to me. "Nic?"

"Yeah?" I looked at her. She had on her jeans with the crystal rhinestones that lined the pockets and hems, with a pink shirt with a unicorn on it. Most of her clothes were pink.

"What do you think the meeting is about?" she whispered. "Are you scared?"

"No, I'm not scared. It should be okay, Izzy."

"Isabella," she said.

"Isabella." She was on this kick where she hated her nickname, even though that's what we'd called her her whole life.

"Do you think we're moving?"

I shook my head. "I doubt it."

"What could it be?"

I pulled Izzy into a side hug.

"I have no idea." I didn't, but I wondered, too.

Chapter 11

Caleb and I sat at opposite corners of the pale pink couch in our den with Izzy in the middle, all of us waiting to find out what was going on. Mom paced in front of the armoire and Dad sat in the old wingback chair next to it, tapping the fingers of one hand on his leg while rubbing his beard with his other.

I glanced between each of my parents. Mom was still wearing her City Flame shirt—red and yellow—and her black pants, but fortunately had taken off her apron. She had something on the side of her shirt and I was curious to know what it was. Cheese?

Dad had his official lounge wear on: gray sweats and a t-shirt with holes and stains all over it. He picked up his beer from the table. Liquid courage, perhaps.

"What?" Caleb said in that surly way boys have patented. I'm sure he had a video game to get back to.

"Caleb," Dad said. "Lose the attitude."

Whoa. Dad disciplining? Or close to it? Never happened. I frowned. I glanced over at Caleb just as he snorted, obviously surprised, too. He tapped the arm of the couch, which had one of those arm covers that was askew and about to fall off.

There was silence until the fridge made this moaning sound we'd gotten used to, though it suddenly seemed very loud.

I was so focused on the sound that it surprised me when Mom said, "Why don't you start, Mark?"

He turned to her, also surprised. Mom was the one who ran everything. Dad kind of floated along, bringing some money home and changing a light bulb or two, since he was tall enough to reach without a step stool. Not that he was a bad guy, just kind of passive.

He cleared his throat. The three of us stared while Mom looked toward the kitchen. Izzy leaned against me.

"We are having some serious financial problems, and there are going to have to be some changes." He stopped, stared at the ceiling, and tugged at his beard.

What kind of changes would there be?

Dad started, "Izzy—"

"Isabella!" Izzy said. "That's my name."

Dad's eyes widened. "Okay, sorry. Isabella, we have to stop your dance lessons, and Caleb, we will have to stop your tennis lessons."

Caleb jerked his head back. "What? No!"

"Mom!" Izzy said at the same time. Mom frowned at her, eyes worried.

My stomach roiled from nerves. I needed to know what it was for me.

Dad continued, hand still on his beard, "There's no other way. And Nic, you won't be getting a car for your birthday."

No! Sam and I were counting on that. Or not Sam, now. A wave of sadness about her moving washed over me and I wanted to cry. No car and no friends.

"At least there's that," Caleb muttered.

Dad glared at him. "And neither will you."

"Oh," Caleb said.

I glared at him, too, just because he was such a jerk now.

We were all silent until my mom said in a thick voice, "The allowances, Mark."

Oh, no.

"Izzy, you'll get ten dollars every two weeks."

"That's not enough!"

"We don't have a choice, honey," Mom said. "I'm sorry."

"But now I can't have my craft of the month!" She teared up. She spent her allowance on one of those clubs that sent her a box of craft stuff every month. She always needed my help to complete the projects. It wasn't my thing, but we had fun anyway.

Still, as bad as I was feeling for Izzy, I was worried about what would change for me. Besides the car.

Nobody had said anything, and Izzy's tears had developed into full-on crying. She got up and ran out of the room. A few seconds later, I heard her bedroom door slam.

Mom looked in that direction and Dad said, "Nic and Caleb, you'll be getting twenty-five every two weeks now, plus fifteen a week for lunches."

"Fifteen bucks?" Caleb asked, echoing my own thoughts. "What am I supposed to do with that? That's maybe three lunches."

"You will have to start packing a lunch some days. Or use some of your allowance. Nic, you can get a job, and Caleb, you'll be able to get one soon."

Caleb grunted, again echoing the way I felt. You know things are bad when we're on the same page. Though getting a job might be okay.

"What happened?" Caleb asked.

I glanced at Mom, who was wiping tears away. Neither of them said anything at first. Caleb and I stared at her.

"Your dad's promotion fell through," Mom said. "We'd been counting on that to help us get out of credit card debt."

I didn't know what to think about that. I mean, Mom was obviously upset. But could things really be that bad?

On the way back to my room, I stopped outside Izzy's. I couldn't hear anything. Poor Izzy. Maybe I could help her pay for her craft box. I wondered what she was doing and if I should go in, even going so far as to make a fist to knock.

But I wasn't sure I wanted to give her some of my money. Maybe I'd have to see how far my new allowance went. In the end, I went on to my room.

Lunches would be rough. And Mom and Dad never mentioned art supplies, but I already had most of what I needed. I'd have to be good with my allowance in case I needed new stuff.

But now Sam and I wouldn't be making trips to the art supply store in my own car any time soon.

Oh, yeah. We wouldn't have anyway. She was leaving before my birthday.

Man, this sucked. I felt hollow. *Everything* sucked and there was absolutely nothing to look forward to.

Chapter 12

I lay on my ridiculous canopy bed and felt sorry for myself. After a while, I texted Sam.

—my family is officially poor. im not getting a car—

—what? why?—

—we just had this horrible meeting— I replied.

—whats going on? call me—

I called, and she picked up on the first ring.

"What happened?" she asked.

I went over the meeting.

"Man, that sucks."

"Yep." I still couldn't believe it. Were things really as bad as they said, or were they overreacting? I hoped they were freaking out over nothing so things could get back to normal soon.

"Well, at least you'll have a new keyboard to play with."

"Yeah," I said.

"I'm not sure what to do with all my D&D figurines. My mom says I can't bring them. I barely convinced her to let me bring my drawings. So I might sell the figurines at the game shop."

"That'd be cool. Get a little money. They're good enough to sell." Maybe I should do that with some of my own, too.

But now my ability to buy new ones was at risk, with a weak allowance and broke parents.

"I could give mine to you if you want them," Sam said, almost like she was reading my mind.

But I didn't know if I wanted hers. Most of the fun was painting them the way I wanted to. I'd feel weird repainting somebody else's. "That's okay," I said.

"So, I was wanting to talk to you about OSIN. You've got to emotionally prepare yourself for Wednesday, right?"

The Key Club meeting. "Yeah. I'll be more sociable. I'll make an effort."

"Awesome. Once you get going, it's not that hard. People are mostly nice." She spoke from experience. "But I was also thinking, you should branch out a little on your own. Aren't you friendly with Carlos and Kyle?"

Oof. A punch to the gut. God, Carlos.

"Maybe you could become real friends with them," Sam continued. "Especially Kyle—he's not a jock, after all. More anti-jock."

Kyle could be funny, but always at the expense of someone else's feelings. Like, for example, mine. Still, that was par for the course with most guys. But he and Carlos were both off the list.

Here was a perfect opportunity to tell her about what had happened with them. But I couldn't do it. Too embarrassing. I didn't know what she'd say exactly, but she'd feel sorry for me. It was one thing to tell her about my family's thing, but if she knew I'd been dumb enough to think

Carlos could like me … No, I couldn't do it. I crossed my ankles.

"I have another idea, too," Sam said. "A party."

What? "You want me to throw a party?"

"Ha! No! We should go to a party."

"I thought your mom wasn't okay with that."

"I'll work on it. But even if I can't convince her, you could go with Zach and Evan. I bet Zach would pick you up."

"Yeah." My stomach fluttered. Could I really go to one without her? But maybe she could convince her mom. I didn't think I had enough nerve to go with only Zach.

But then again, maybe I did. I'd ridden in the car with him, and I hadn't made a total fool of myself. But it wasn't like Zach and I would be the only ones at this hypothetical party. There'd be all those other people, and somebody might say something that would make me feel like shit. That would screw with my head, and I'd be a wreck the rest of the night.

"You've got to convince your mom," I said.

"I'll work on it. It's got to be this weekend or next, or I'll already be gone."

Oh, right, that. A wave of desperation washed over me, and my stomach clenched. OSIN *had* to succeed.

Chapter 13

Sam and Evan were already in the car when Zach arrived to pick me up Wednesday evening for the Key Club meeting. I gave a general greeting to the group as I climbed in behind Evan and we got going. Then I steeled myself for a night of being sociable. I'd even been doing the Wonder Woman pose—fists on hips and legs spread—in my bedroom before I went downstairs to wait. I saw this TED talk about how doing it for a few minutes was supposed to make women braver. We'd see.

Zach and Evan were chatting about a video game so Sam said, "I'm working on getting my mom to let me go to a party. There's one this Friday that Evan mentioned, so I'm shooting for that. Have you asked your mom?"

"No, but I'm sure she'll be okay with it. I know she wishes I had more friends." It wasn't like she thought I was a loser for not having friends. She was shy as a kid, too, so she got it. She just felt bad for me.

I caught movement in the rearview mirror and saw Zach glance at me again. It warmed my heart, even though his expression didn't change.

"Yeah, me too," Sam said, arching an eyebrow.

It made me laugh. "I'm going to try tonight."

"I have faith in OSIN. I'll try to find people for you to talk to tonight."

"Awesome."

Zach and Evan were still going on.

Sam and I used to play fantasy role-playing video games, but lately we were too busy with other hobbies. Art and the figurines, mostly. Would I play video games with Zach if we started going out?

Not that that was likely to happen, but it seemed not impossible.

What would that really be like, having a boyfriend? I guessed we'd eat lunch together every day. I thought I wouldn't be into PDA. But what would it be like to kiss him? I was a little weird about touching in general, ever since that thing with my dad's friend when he stayed at our house, but I thought I'd be fine with kissing. I already thought about it enough.

"Did you guys see Nic's hand?" Zach asked.

"What?" Sam looked over at my hands.

"I mean the sculpture one," he said with a laugh.

"Oh, right," Sam said. "Not the real thing yet. Just the picture. Totally cool."

Zach nodded. "It is cool. You have a picture of it on your phone, Nic?"

"Yeah," I said. He wasn't looking at me.

"You should show it to Evan."

I brought it up and handed the phone forward. Evan reached back but didn't turn around. He looked at it and sort of grunted, then muttered, "Cool."

Yeah, the guy didn't like me. He was like most people and acted like I was a total leper at risk of infecting him. I didn't know why Zach was friends with him, because he seemed like a real jerk from where I stood.

He handed the phone back, and I stuffed it back into my front pocket.

Once we got parked and inside the auditorium, we had about fifteen minutes before the meeting started.

Showtime for OSIN.

Zach and Evan went off to the other side of the room where a group of juniors were mingling, and Sam and I stood in the doorway glancing around. There were lots of kids of all grades here. Evan was talking to this skinny guy whose name I couldn't remember, but I did remember him being a dick to me at some point.

"Oh, there's Lizzy," Sam said. "Let's go talk to her."

Lizzy of the make-out couple. This made me a little nervous. Talking to someone who'd kind of dissed me already, even if it probably wasn't personal.

"And Nic?"

"Yeah?"

"I *know* you can do this. You're braver than you think."

We headed over to where a group of about four girls were standing and broke into the circle. They all glanced at us, and Lizzy acknowledged Sam with a "Hey," but she either didn't recognize me or chose to ignore me. They were all talking about *Game of Thrones*, which I didn't watch. We didn't have HBO.

I forced myself to smile, since I guessed that was what was expected. Or maybe they'd think I was deranged. I made sure it wasn't a giant smile.

Sam did have HBO, so soon she joined the conversation, and I was just kind of there feeling out of place, like always. I crossed my arms and then uncrossed them because I'd heard that made you seem closed off. Then this girl came up and put her hand on Sam's shoulder, and they talked about band for a minute before Sam took off—after giving me a you-can-do-this smile—leaving me with the group.

"He's so hot," one of the girls said to the group, talking about one of the actors. I had no idea who.

"Have you noticed how Will Kohl looks sort of like him?"

Will was a senior who played football, so everybody knew him. He was good-looking, but a total stereotypical jock. He'd made a nasty comment or two to me. I wasn't a fan.

"Oh my God, you're right!" someone said.

The conversation degenerated even further.

"Gaby's going out with him now."

"No way."

"I heard he got with Michaela last week."

Et cetera. Boring. I was desperate to pull out my phone but instead looked around the room and saw Zach still talking to the juniors.

I couldn't take this. I smiled and stepped away from the group, feeling sick to my stomach with nerves. I leaned against the wall and considered that I had nothing in common with these people.

"Hey, Nic, I didn't know you were in Key Club." I turned to see Mia, this southeast Asian girl from my art class. I always found her a little intimidating because she made everything look effortless, both with art and being cute. Still, we sat next to each other because we were the most serious students there. She was nice, and we even talked a little in class.

"Yeah," I said, not adding that I'd been coming since last year.

Though to be fair, I hadn't noticed her either, so I shouldn't judge.

"Are you going to enter the art contest next semester?"

"Definitely. You?"

She nodded. "What categories are you thinking?"

"I'm working on a big realistic pencil drawing at home, but otherwise it will depend on what else I get done by then."

"I've heard there's a grand prize of two hundred dollars."

She seemed genuine. I didn't think she was just sizing up the competition—or not too much, at least.

"Really? Ms. Tolliver didn't mention that. That's cool." It was. My dragon drawing could clinch it, I was sure. Unless Mia decided to enter something amazing, which she might. She was good, and her art was more palatable to adults. It was delicate and precise, as opposed to my looser and freer style.

"Oh, there's my friend," she said. "Talk to you later."

"Sure."

That had gone okay. I mean, she didn't introduce me to her friend so I didn't think we'd end up being real friends, but at least she was nice to me outside of art class.

Sam was over talking to a group of kids from band, so I just hung by the wall, crossing my arms because I didn't know what to do with my hands. Finally, the president of the chapter had us all sit down.

The meeting went fine. They talked about the car wash coming up and a few other things. One group did monthly visits to the local children's hospital. We also had a monthly campus clean-up, which Sam and I sometimes did. We were doing a food drive for Thanksgiving. The two of us had helped with that last year. And there was a planned visit to a nursing home for December. The club was also going to help at the winter Special Olympics. You had to do a certain number of volunteer hours to stay in the club.

I glanced over at Sam, next to me. It would be so weird with her gone. Thinking about it made my chest ache.

Finally the president ended the meeting, and everyone got up and started heading up the aisle to the door. I saw Evan and the skinny boy from earlier in front of us.

"It's not my fault—she's just always there."

The other boy glanced back at me and snickered, which made me blush again.

But then I was mad. My fists had clenched without any conscious instructions from me. Why did Evan hate me so much?

Once we were in Zach's car, he said, "Do you guys want to go to Sonic?"

Sam shrugged. "Sure. Though I don't have any money."

"That's cool, I can cover you." Zach looked at me, making my heart race stupidly, so I squeaked, "I don't have any money, either."

"No problem."

I rested my head against the window on the way there, reliving that stupid moment when that kid with Evan laughed at me. I was alone in a car full of people. After a couple of streetlights, Zach pulled into a space at Sonic.

We sat at one of the outside tables, instead of in the car. I ended up across from Evan, which was awkward as he sat with his whole body turned away.

"What do you two want?" Zach asked us after he ordered his sundae and Evan's fries.

He really was a nice guy, and I loved that. Thinking about him warmed my whole body. Soon they came out with our two cherry limeades—this time, Sam copied me, because I knew a good drink when I saw one.

"So you're coming to the party Friday?" Zach asked.

"Maybe," Sam said. "I've got to convince my mom."

Evan looked at Sam. "This is your last chance, though, right?" I guessed he'd heard in band.

Sam nodded while Zach's brow furrowed. "Why?" he asked.

"I'm moving."

"Really? Where to?"

Evan's gaze landed over my shoulder again again. It looked like he wasn't interested in their conversation.

"Scotland."

"Oh, that's cool. Where in Scotland?"

How had I never thought to ask this? Like Scotland is one single place.

"Glasgow."

"I've been to Edinburgh," Zach said. "But never there."

They continued talking about Scotland, and he told a funny story about eating haggis. Which sounded positively disgusting. I felt a tiny bit left out, but I didn't think Sam was going after him, and it saved me from having to figure out something to talk about. Evan made me so self-conscious. My shoulders automatically tensed when I was around him, as I was always on alert for him to say something.

When Zach dropped me off, he smiled at me in the rearview mirror and said, "See you."

"Stairwell lunch, tomorrow?" Sam asked me.

"Sure." But I was thinking more about Zach and all the possibilities than about any lunch.

Chapter 14

My parents and I got into my dad's white Buick Friday night. I sighed heavily after clicking my seatbelt shut.

"Stop moping," Mom said. "You get along fine with Alyssa and Kayla, Nic."

Dad pulled out of the driveway.

I sighed again, more quietly this time. Kayla and Alyssa were fine when we weren't at school. At school, they strategically ignored me, but at their houses they were nice enough. We just had literally nothing in common except being girls. And that wasn't enough.

Still, my parents and I had this argument every time they got together with their friends. They always made me come with them if I wasn't doing anything else. Caleb never had to come since none of the other boys would be there. Izzy often came, but she was spending the night at a friend's—probably already giggling about boys and makeup. But in general, unless I was at Sam's, I had to go. And Sam was with the band.

Which meant it would be even worse when Sam left,

since I'd literally never be at her place, and would therefore never be doing something else.

There was no party with Sam and Zach, since she hadn't been able to convince her mom.

So here I was. While my dragon drawing languished on the table at home, desperate for my attention.

"Nic," Mom said, "I want you to promise me you'll try this time to socialize with Alyssa and Kayla. You know you need to make a little effort if you want to have a social life. This could be the perfect opportunity."

Maybe Mom was right.

"You promise?"

"Okay, fine." I guess maybe I could try, even though they were so boring. I got out of the car and dragged my feet up the walk so noticeably that Mom called me on it.

As soon as we were inside, Gina Sheridan—Alyssa's mom—pushed a red plastic cup into Mom's hand. "Margarita! Woo!"

My guess was that Gina had already had a few. I could totally picture her going crazy on some high school spring break trip and ending up on one of those "Girls Gone Wild" videos. She and Kayla's mom were oh-so-classy. It took all my control to not roll my eyes.

My parents laughed and Dad headed into the den, where they had a folding table set up with one of those poker tops. There were stacks of colored chips spread around and a couple decks of cards. The guys all sat around the table, and a couple of them shouted greetings in our general direction.

Too many people. I was already feeling the familiar twinge of nerves, even though I knew most of them.

Gina finished hugging Mom, who headed into the dining room, where half of their long brown dining room table was covered with chips and dip, a mini Crock-Pot with Ro-tel and cheese, and wings. A couple of the women sat at the other end of the table chatting and snacking off a veggie tray. They looked up and said hi to Mom, who headed in there.

Gina was still standing there holding the door open, so I stepped in some more so she could shut it. "Kayla's back with Alyssa in her room."

In other words, Get out of here. "Okay."

When I moved into the hall, I heard my name. I turned back and saw my mom's friend Bridget standing in the foyer, a red cup in her hand, too. My heart nearly stopped because she was Logan's mom and that meant he might be here. But probably not. I hadn't seen him since the coffee shop and didn't want to. But she was smiling at me.

"How are you, sweetie? What big project are you working on now?"

She always asked that, which I liked. She was nice. "I started a drawing that will be of a couple of fighting dragons," I said. "It's pretty big." I motioned with my hands to indicate the size.

"Wow! I can't wait to see it." Bridget had this shocking red hair—especially when I saw it outside in the sun—which she wore like everyone else's: long and straight.

"Well, it's barely started."

She stepped forward to squeeze my shoulder. "You're so talented! You have such a good eye for detail. And that elf was gorgeous—that shimmery robe looked so real I wanted to touch it to feel the smooth velvet. But I've loved everything I've seen you do."

"Thanks." I smiled back at her.

Then there was a slightly awkward moment, until she held her cup up and said, "Have fun with the girls."

"See you later." She would be so pissed at Logan if she knew how he treated me. But it wasn't like I could tell her.

Or, I could, but that would make everything worse. Too much of a risk.

I knocked on Alyssa's door, and Kayla opened it. She smiled and moved to let me in. Alyssa was sitting on the floor leaning against her bed, a day bed with a frilly white and pale pink quilt, which fit her way better than mine did me. Bizarrely, it also matched her t-shirt today, which was pink and had the words "stay weird" printed upside down in white. Oh, the irony. She was as weird as I was normal.

Kayla sat back down next to her as I shut the door. She had on yellow shorts that showed off her tan legs. But she was kind of stocky, and it was obvious when she sat that way. I felt bad even noticing, but I only did because everyone knew her parents were always putting her on diets since she didn't look anorexic. I thought they were assholes. I didn't have to guess what they thought of me.

"Is Logan here?" I asked. I had to make sure.

"No," Kayla said. "Thank goodness."

"He's such a pretentious jerk," Alyssa said. She lowered her voice and continued, "'A Frappucino isn't a real drink because Starbucks invented it. Black cold brew only. Cream and sugar are for pussies. Blah blah blah.'"

Kayla and I laughed at her imitation because it sounded just like him.

"Sit down," Kayla said.

I'd been standing awkwardly barely inside the door, but I sat next to her. "What are you guys doing?"

"Looking at Pinterest." Kayla moved the laptop they had on the floor in front of them so I could see.

Fashion crap I wouldn't care about. I mean, I know they were trying to be inclusive, and I had told my mom and myself that I'd try, but God, this would be a long night. I wished my parents had let me stay home so I could draw. I'd been making good progress tonight when we'd had to leave.

They continued looking at the pictures and going on about different outfits while I sat there playing on my phone. The next thing I knew, they were standing in Alyssa's closet, tossing clothes onto the bed. Then Alyssa was mixing and matching stuff and modeling it for us. I knew it was kind of antisocial of me to just sit there, but I wasn't remotely interested. And I wasn't good at faking it.

"Nic!" Alyssa said, all animated in her current outfit of a short green skirt and fitted white t-shirt. "You should let us give you a makeover!"

"What? No!" I had to suppress a look of disgust. I couldn't think of much that I would less want to do tonight.

"You totally should!" Kayla said.

"You can wear one of my scarves to dress things up a bit!" Alyssa added.

"No." I said it as firmly as I could. The idea was horrible. Not only did I not want to do it, I actively wanted to *not* do it.

"Yes," Alyssa said, smiling.

Kayla squeezed my upper arm, which freaked me out a little. I wasn't used to people touching me, except for Izzy and Mom, plus Sam every once in a while.

She said, "It will be fun. And who knows, maybe you'll like it."

"Not likely," I muttered.

"Please?" Alyssa said, giving me a pout that was so ridiculous that it made me laugh.

"Yeah?" Kayla asked. "We can do a natural look. Nothing extravagant."

With both of them looking at me, I felt like such a spoilsport. Maybe it would be okay. They did say natural.

"You can take it off when we're done," Alyssa said. "It will be fine."

I didn't give in right away. But they kept on, and finally I surrendered to what felt like the inevitable because I just didn't have the energy to resist.

Ten minutes later they had me sitting on the floor and were both on their knees inspecting me.

"You're so lucky you don't have zits," Kayla said as she spread some white cream over the top of my cheeks.

"I do. I always have one somewhere. Now it's on my forehead."

Kayla leaned in to look. "Oh, yeah. But it's small." She started spreading this cold, tan-colored cream all over my poor face. The sensation was odd and unnatural, and also weird to have someone this close to me.

Alyssa picked up a palette of eye shadow colors, which she opened and held up. "Which one?"

God, how was I supposed to know? This was insane. "I have no idea."

"Let's do brown for a natural look," Alyssa said with finality. "I'll be back—I'm going to go get a scarf."

After she left, Kayla said, "This is really cool, Nic. This is what you need—it could change everything."

I didn't know what to say so I smiled weakly, resisting the urge to stand up and run away. I wasn't going to look good. I was going to look like an ugly fat girl with makeup.

Okay. I shouldn't think like that.

"Here, look up for a bit."

I did and she spread the cream almost all the way to my bottom eyelids, which made me nervous. I didn't want anything in my eyes. Then she got out some powder and brushed it all over, too.

"What are you doing?" I asked, relaxing my eyes.

"This sets it," Kayla said. She smiled at me. "Now I'll just do some quick blush."

She got another brown plastic disc-shaped thing with powder in it and brushed that on. "Just a little highlighter now."

Kayla took an applicator with some whitish powder and spread it on my nose and cheekbones and then patted over it with a sponge.

She grinned at me, apparently having fun. I knew it wasn't meant to be at my expense, but it still made me uncomfortable.

"Go ahead and close your eyes for a bit," Kayla said.

I did.

"Not so tight. Just try to relax."

I did my best to oblige, but nerves were congregating in my stomach. I was beginning to feel ungrounded. It was like everything they put on me was another layer that erased the real me. Eventually I'd be all gone.

She spread the eye shadow on, all over, up to my eyebrow and almost to my lashes, which made me jerk back. After a moment, I heard the door open and close.

"You'll look so good," Alyssa said, sounding almost gleeful.

At least they were having a grand old time.

None of this would change the fact that I was considered ugly, even if it might make people accept me more. I got that—part of the social contract was simply to play the game, and people hated me for not doing that.

Why couldn't I do it? Play the game, get people to leave me alone? Maybe this would be it. Maybe I could just wear makeup, and everything would be a little better. I'd have to start slow—definitely I wouldn't be spending this much time on it, or people would totally make fun of me. You can't go from zero to sixty and have people not notice.

Kayla stopped for a second so I opened my eyes. The brightness of the room surprised me.

"Not yet," she said. "One more color."

I groaned, which made both of them laugh.

"Most girls do this every day," Alyssa said.

Kayla started spreading eye shadow to the sides but then across the brow a bit, too.

I heard some more shuffling, which reverberated in my stomach, before Kayla said I could open my eyes.

Kayla moved over and Alyssa scooted in with a black tube of something.

"Liquid liner," Alyssa said. "Relax your eyelids and hold still."

As soon as she reached in, I blinked because it was too close to my eyelashes.

"You can do this," Kayla said.

I wasn't sure if she was talking to me or Alyssa, but Alyssa tried again, and I guess I held still enough for her to drag the applicator along my eyelid and off to the side a bit, on both eyes.

Kayla handed Alyssa another tube and Alyssa announced, "Mascara."

Oh, God. What if her hand slipped?

She came at me with this terrifying brush and said, "Blink a few times. It'll be fine." She brushed along the eyelashes, which felt like someone was pulling them out. So freaky.

Alyssa sat back, and they studied me.

"What?" I asked, my stomach going jittery.

"This is awesome," Kayla said. She handed Alyssa what looked like a pink colored pencil. "Push your lips out a little, Nic."

I couldn't believe I had let them do this to me. I was already regretting it, and I hadn't even seen the results. I probably didn't want to.

Alyssa finished outlining my lips and then put on some lipstick that was also some shade of pink—as an artist, I knew there were many shades of pink, but I didn't think I'd seen so many in one place. She made me do all this weird stuff with my mouth while she was putting it on.

I'd just given up.

They did my eyebrows and then wrapped the scarf around my neck in a loose knot. I was glad I didn't have to change into another shirt in front of them or something equally horrific.

At least the scarf was a nice color, a dark teal. But it was kind of fluffy. Nothing I'd ever wear in real life.

Finally, *finally*, they took me to the bathroom and let me look.

The first things on my made-up face that I saw in the mirror were my eyes. The lashes towered over them and the eye shadow made them stand out way too much. And all my freckles were gone. I had this unnaturally smooth skin. My cheeks were a horrid pink, as was my mouth. And the little black flare beside my eyes made me look like a—I don't even know. Not me. The real me was simpler and more straightforward.

Natural look, my ass.

Oh, God. I fell forward, both hands on the sink and felt my long hair cover my ears. I was dizzy. I looked up and frowned at myself as a wave of despair washed over me. How could I have thought this would be the solution?

I could see tears glistening in my eyes and barely had the presence of mind to grab some toilet paper and dab at them. They'd make everything run, and then I'd look like a sad clown. I absolutely had to get this stuff off my face.

The more I looked, the more my gut twisted, which also made me want to throw up. It felt like someone had ripped my soul out and thrown it somewhere because it definitely couldn't be behind this face. My ears were ringing and my heart was racing and I felt like everything was closing in.

I was frozen. Kayla and Alyssa came in all excited.

"Come on, let's show everyone!" Alyssa said. She grabbed my right elbow, then Kayla grabbed my left, and I was powerless to resist. I had to snap my jaw shut.

They got me down the hall so we were back in the foyer. It was like I was in a walking coma—I couldn't do anything on my own. The men at the poker table looked up. Alyssa's dad whistled—whistled!—and said, "Wow, Nic, you clean up good!" Then two more of them whistled, and it brought me out of the fugue state. I blushed and closed my mouth. But I was still frozen despite the fact that I was burning with humiliation.

Dad was looking at me in confusion. He rubbed his beard. I'm sure he didn't know what to think.

"What's going on?" Bridget said as she and the other women came into the foyer from the dining room. Kayla and Alyssa turned me to face them.

"Oh, wow," Kayla's mom, Susan, said. "You look great."

They all gushed and I cringed and collapsed into myself. When I glanced at Mom, I could feel that she was tense.

I wanted to die but nobody else seemed to notice, and they continued discussing how great I looked until they went back to their cauliflower and Ranch. Kayla and Alyssa dropped my elbows and I relaxed a tiny bit. I calmly walked back into the bathroom, where I looked in the mirror and started to freak out again. I stared at myself. I no longer felt like a person. Panic crept up my spine. I wanted to claw everything off my face. It wasn't even my face anymore.

Kayla and Alyssa came in, still all hyped up by the apparent success of their venture. "What's wrong?" Alyssa asked. "You look really good."

Kayla nodded. "You look great."

"Tell me how to get it off!" I said in high-pitched panic.

"Okay, okay," Alyssa said, wide-eyed. She glanced over at Kayla, who looked a little concerned, too. Then Alyssa said, "It's okay—it all comes off." She showed me the montage of products I needed to use, and I proceeded to remove it. My face felt so weird afterward that I even put on some of the lotion that she'd pointed to.

But when I looked one last time before leaving, I noticed I hadn't quite got all the fucking mascara off, so I had to work more on that.

When I got back to the room, they were once again sitting in front of the laptop.

"Are you okay?" Alyssa asked.

"Yeah." I felt much better now. At least it was over.

Kayla smiled. "You're all fresh-faced. Do you feel refreshed?"

"I guess." Not at all. I only felt like me again. They were so oblivious. They had no clue what they'd done to me. And they acted like they were doing me this big favor. They'd never actually cared about *me*—they didn't before and didn't now.

I glanced at the computer screen. Pictures of me. My heart nearly stopped.

"You put it on Facebook?"

They looked at me innocently. "Yeah," Alyssa said.

"You looked so good! See, look." She turned the laptop so I could see better.

I felt sick and put my hand on my just-moisturized forehead, hitting that stupid pimple, which hurt. "Please take them down."

"Oh, come on, Nic," Kayla says. "Be a good sport."

"People are going to make fun of me." I slowed my breathing and tried to exude calmness. "You know they will."

Alyssa shook her head. "No, they won't."

"They will." She obviously had no idea what my life was like.

"Okay," Kayla said with a sigh. "I'll delete them."

"Thanks." Thank God.

"But why are you so opposed to makeup?" Alyssa asked. "We were only having fun."

I shrugged. "I don't know. It's just not me."

They both looked at me in honest confusion. They couldn't understand me, and I'd never understand them. It was how it was.

The rest of the evening was a little tense. I went to Facebook on my phone to make sure the pictures hadn't made it out, and they went back to looking at Pinterest, laughing at a few Snapchat posts. Then they moved on to cat videos.

Neither Mom nor Dad said much on the drive home, but she followed me to my room and leaned on the end of the bed when I climbed onto it. "Are you okay?"

I wanted to cry, thinking about the whole debacle, with everyone a witness to it. Now they'd think I should always do that, and since I wouldn't, they'd judge me even more.

"Fine."

"I could tell you were really upset, honey."

I shrugged.

"Was it so bad?"

"I *hated* it." I spat it out.

She jerked her head back in surprise. "Nic, you just … you get so intense sometimes. It's only makeup. You don't have to wear it."

I looked over at my desk and saw some of the figurines I'd been working on recently. That's who I was. "I know."

She got up and came over to hug me, which made me want to cry. Why did I have to be so weird? Why couldn't I be okay being like other people, and go through the motions?

I honestly didn't know.

I lay on my bed and said a little universe prayer that no one had seen the pictures. Then I thought about how stupid everything was. Makeup. The whole idea that women have to modify their bodies just to be considered acceptable. Remove natural body hair. Paint their faces. Punch holes in their ears.

The whole reason lipstick and blush came into being was that when a woman is sexually aroused, her lips and cheeks get redder. The first women to wear lipstick were prostitutes, to better attract clients. And eye makeup makes eyes stand out more, right? This had to be related to the fact that mammal babies have proportionally oversized eyes. So, what—were women trying to make themselves look like sexually aroused babies?

Why? Why was this the norm? Why was *I* the freak for not doing it? Society was really fucked up.

Chapter 15

Saturday morning I was sitting at the dining room table working on shading the last few leaves on the drawing's mountain shrub. You know, minding my own business.

I heard the whooping sound of the fridge being opened, and then Caleb said, "Nice pictures, Nicole."

My hand stilled.

Oh, God. Did he mean …?

The photos *had* gotten out. My heart went crazy.

No, they couldn't have. They'd promised!

I wiped my forehead and felt actual sweat there.

Caleb was pouring a glass of something, the sound sharper than I would have expected. "But I'm not sure we can afford to buy you a bunch of makeup now." He snorted.

Either they'd reposted them, or someone had snagged them before Kayla pulled them down. My cheeks burned and I felt queasy, my go-to feeling for life.

Caleb stood in the doorway into the dining room, smirking at me and holding a glass of orange juice. He wore a pair of ratty jean cutoff shorts and an old Nike t-shirt. Even though he played tennis, he was a little chubby, too—it ran in the family. Basically, he was the male version of me.

When he was done mocking me and had downed his OJ, he went through to the den and told Mom he was going out, before heading back upstairs.

Of course he had something to do on a Saturday. As big, unpresentable, and douchey as he was, he still had a whole group of friends, many of whom were older, so he always got rides everywhere. It so wasn't fair. It was different for guys. They weren't required to entertain the rest of society with their looks. They could simply go about their business, doing stuff, and nobody cared.

But girls were punished if they didn't look perfect. I knew this was true even for those women and girls who did play the game right. For me, I just had people going out of their way to let me know I wasn't acceptable.

I tried not to think about it. Izzy was lucky that she was normal, maybe. Being normal, she wouldn't have so much trouble. She was at the mall with a friend's family right now. I guessed she'd become a full-on mall rat soon.

I returned to the drawing. There was still quite a bit of shading and detail work to do. I erased a little errant pencil mark and began shading under the bush, accounting for the light coming from the fire I hadn't drawn yet.

God, I couldn't believe the pictures were out there. This was horrible. School would be even more intolerable than before.

I tried to put it out of my mind and threw myself into work for another hour, focusing on the areas that needed darker shading so I could get my frustration out by pressing harder on the pencil. Caleb had long since left. Mom came in.

"Honey, this is already so good. You've got a lot ahead of you, don't you?" she asked.

She wasn't wrong. "Yeah, but it's fun."

"Come to Walmart with me, Nic."

"I'm working."

"Come on, we never go anywhere together. I just want to spend some time with my daughter."

The guilt trip. I was such a sucker for it. "Fine."

On the drive over, she asked, "So really, what was with the makeup last night? I was so surprised."

"Oh, God." I put my face in my hands. The thing is, Mom wore makeup like any middle-aged American woman. Which was fine. Her choice. "I didn't want to. They guilted me into it. And now there are pictures out there for everyone to see!"

"Honey, it's not that bad." This wasn't convincing. I'd inherited her easy-target status, but not her optimism.

"You don't know that. It'll be all over the school by Monday."

She sighed as she turned the car into the Walmart parking lot. "I'm sorry."

"It felt horrible."

I'd told her many times I don't want to wear makeup and she was always fine with that.

"Like it wasn't you?"

"Exactly." At least she understood, sort of. Mom got me pretty well, for a mom.

She pulled into a parking spot and stopped the car. Then she looked over. "You know how I feel about things. You should always be true to yourself. People will like you better for it."

"Yeah, I know." I didn't look at her because I knew she had way more faith in the success rate of that approach than I did. I'm not sure it worked for her, either, however. I knew she'd still been bullied all through high school.

Once we got inside, we split up so I could go look at the books, figuring we'd meet in the frozen food section in a few minutes. It wasn't like I could buy anything, but I liked to look.

On the way there, I stopped at the cell phone counter and was looking at a Samsung. I messed with the screen for a couple minutes before I heard, "Can I help you, sir?"

I jerked my head up to see an old dude in the official blue vest facing me from behind the counter. My face heated and emotions swirled as they always did when I got called sir, but I didn't say anything. What was the point?

His expression didn't change from bored, and I turned around and walked across to the books. I was reading the back of a sci-fi book—of course I loved imagining a world as different from this one as possible—when I heard a male voice say, "There sure are a lot of lesbians around here."

I stupidly looked over and saw two boys from school standing next to the cookbooks, smirking at me.

Of course, I blushed yet again and turned my head back toward the book. They laughed and strutted away, and I tried to continue looking at the books, but it was hard.

All because I don't try to look like a pageant star or something.

I mean, it was the same in middle school, except when I tried dressing a little more like a girl in eighth grade. I still got made fun of for being fat, but it was like once they got over the novelty of making fun of me for wearing normal clothes, I got credit for trying in the fashion department. But the next year, I couldn't do it anymore. I hated it so much.

But maybe I was just in denial. Maybe everyone saw

something in me that I couldn't see, and I really was a lesbian. I mean, my only friend was a girl, and we were close. Maybe I was secretly in love with Sam and didn't even know it myself. Which would mean all the guys I thought I liked were … what? Beards?

I put the book back and headed over to the freezer area.

"You okay, honey?" Mom asked.

I guess I still looked bothered about the lesbian comment, so I shrugged and looked away. I didn't know if there was any truth to it.

The thing was, comments like that were frustrating because, what would be the problem if I was a lesbian? Who cared—it was the twenty-first century. But then, since I didn't think I was, it was enraging for a different reason.

We picked up several frozen meals and some chicken and fries and headed to the register.

Just my luck, the guys who'd made the comment were one lane over. Who knew what took them so long to get to this point—all they had was a twelve-pack of Coke—but they were intentionally talking all loud about ugly girls in Tulsa.

Sigh. It was nonstop.

Mom was oblivious to it, or at least she ignored it, which was her modus operandi for everything bad. Ignore, ignore, ignore. Don't give them the satisfaction of seeing you upset, or of getting the reaction they're trying to get out of you.

She casually moved between me and the guys, so I guessed she did notice.

We didn't talk while we were standing in line. The guys still hadn't made it to the cashier by the time we left, and I heard them complain about the slow line as Mom pushed our cart out.

Finally, once we were outside, Mom said, "Nic, I'm going to be working extra hours from now on." She'd been part-time since she started four months ago. "Starting on next week's schedule, I'll be doing a lot more evenings."

I nodded, not sure how this would impact me. "Okay."

"I need you to help more around the house. Cleaning."

Ah, that was it. I crossed my arms. "Are you asking Caleb and Dad, too? And Izzy?" She'd better not only be asking me because I was the oldest girl.

"Of course I am," she said, giving me the side-eye. She brought the cart to a stop and opened the back of the minivan. We had an old Toyota Sienna that had seen better days, but there was no way we'd be upgrading now.

I helped her load the food into the van as she listed all the things I would be responsible for. Vacuuming. Cleaning my room. Cleaning the bathroom Caleb, Izzy, and I shared.

It was going to suck. Why did everything have to suck?

Chapter 16

After we got back from Walmart, I headed upstairs to paint some figurines or something. But before I could get started, an idea hit me. The whole ride home, I'd been obsessing over the makeup thing last night and the lesbian comment today and whether there was some truth to it. I decided to try to figure things out.

I went into my room, climbed up onto the bed, and sat cross-legged in front of my laptop. I googled "LGBTQ."

I'd never understood what the Q meant, but apparently it could be either "queer" or "questioning," the second of which fit me at the moment, since I was googling it.

But otherwise, things were confusing. I mean, the real question was, was I a lesbian?

There were a bunch of quizzes to answer this question. But they looked cheesy so I didn't take them. I wanted information from a reputable source, not some cutesy quiz. Who would make a cutesy quiz about whether or not you were a lesbian, anyway? They must be a joke.

I found some good articles that talked about how it's

often confusing because you might wonder if you're attracted to a girl you're friends with because you really like her. But maybe you just want to be her, not be with her. I read this one article that talked about how all the sites that tried to explain things gave differing and contradictory information, which was true. But what I ultimately came up with for the one true test was whether or not you wanted to go down on the girl you supposedly liked.

So I thought about that with Sam.

Okay, no. Just no. I'd never even seen that part of her, but the answer was clear—I didn't want to.

I'd spent the night at her place a bunch of times, but she had two twin beds in her room. Getting with her had never occurred to me in all those times.

I could never do that. It sounded kind of gross.

But then I thought about blowjobs, and they were totally gross, too. Of course, I'd only ever seen three penises in my life. Dad's and Caleb's each once, by accident, and one other I didn't want to think about. That was a dark time.

He was an asshole. I was just a little kid, and he kept cornering me in my own house and messing with me. I'd always wondered if that was why I was so weird.

Anyway. Who knew? Maybe I'd feel different if it was someone I liked. And if I was old enough to have a clue what was going on and consent.

Which of course led me to think about Zach.

Okay, now, I had trouble picturing Zach's penis, even though the idea was sort of ... I guess I could say, interesting. I mean, the idea of giving him a blowjob didn't appeal, but maybe I simply wouldn't like those. Not everyone did, right?

Hell if I knew.

Fuck.

Still, it seemed like I was less disgusted by the idea of Zach's penis than Sam's girl parts.

But then, maybe I was a lesbian but I just wasn't attracted to Sam specifically.

Gah.

Maybe I was even asexual. That was a thing, too. But then, would I want to kiss boys? Because I did. I'd never wanted to kiss Sam.

I googled, "why do I hate being a girl?" which was interesting. The article I found pointed out that it might simply be that I hated being considered inferior, which made sense. I did hate that. And also, a lot of girls were uncomfortable with the attention their newly developed bodies got. Sixth grade had been a fucking nightmare. I was a B-cup by Christmas, and everyone thought it was hilarious. Several times, boys grabbed my boobs. And when I reported it, they were just told to stop "teasing" me. Not assaulting me—teasing. But I wasn't going to cause a scene, and it was too embarrassing to tell Mom, so nothing changed. It tapered off in seventh grade, and by eighth grade they'd stopped. And fortunately I hadn't grown much since then, so I wasn't huge now.

Still, being a girl did bite.

But anyway, it wasn't just those reasons. The rest of the article talked about trying to figure out which gender you identify with. Maybe I was transgender. Clearly, I didn't identify with girls. I never really had.

When I was ten, a friend and I were playing, and for some reason, spitting came up, and she'd announced, "Girls don't spit!" I'd made this big production of spitting on the ground. Just saliva. Then I'd said, "See, girls can spit." I thought I'd made this profound point.

She'd thought it was hilarious.

Another time the same kind of attitude got me humiliated. We'd been in music class and about to start casting our musical, where the main character was male. I pointed out on principle that a girl could play the part, too, and the teacher came in right then and forced me to audition for the part. I seriously cannot sing, so that had truly sucked.

Was I trans?

I couldn't imagine what else it could be. But I also didn't know how to know for sure.

Chapter 17

Sunday morning, we did the forty-five-minute trek to Tulsa to go to the mall. We parked by Penney's and walked through the mall to Dillard's first. There were loads of people and lots of noise and I stared at the fountain as we passed it, people sitting all around it.

Once we got to Dillard's, we headed to the juniors section. Izzy was tall and well into the lower sizes. She was growing so fast. I worried about her developing young, too. I didn't know how she'd take being manhandled by all the boys. But maybe it wouldn't happen to her.

One could hope.

Maybe I should talk to her about it. Warn her. Tell her to tell the teachers and make a big deal about it, poo-pooing be damned.

I started looking through the jeans—I still barely quali-fied for juniors sizing, thank God. Then this woman came up to me and said, "Excuse me."

I looked up and saw a middle-aged saleslady in a white and green dress. "Yeah?"

"Oh," she said, putting her finger to her lips. "Never mind. You are in the right spot."

As she walked off, I realized she'd probably thought I was a boy lost in the wrong department. Idiot.

I found a few pairs to try on and glanced over at Mom and Izzy. They were looking at these shorts. I wondered if Mom was stressing about how short they were. She'd never had to go through that with me.

I headed into the changing room and pulled off my jeans.

This gave me a glimpse of myself in the mirror. I hated my legs. There'd never been a gap between my thighs, that was for sure.

I pulled on the first pair, the tag scratching me as I pulled them up.

They were alright, maybe a little baggy in the waist but they fit okay elsewhere. I'd started putting on the second pair when I heard my name.

"In here," I called.

"Okay, good," Mom said.

"I like this one," Izzy said.

"We've got to see what it looks like first, honey."

I had the second pair on and checked out my butt in them. I guess it wasn't the worst butt on the planet. At least it wasn't flat. The jeans fit well enough.

I heard shuffling in the next dressing room. "Mom, how does this go?" Izzy asked.

Mom must have gone in there to help her.

I tried on the last pair of jeans and stuck with the second pair, leaving the others on the bench. Mom was standing outside the other changing room so I handed her the jeans and went in search of the one shirt I was allowed to get.

When we were at the register, Izzy started showing me

all the stuff she'd picked out. Girly stuff. A little lace, some pink, and definite bling.

"What did you get, Nic?" she asked.

I held up the jeans and a red t-shirt.

"How come you never wear skirts?"

Mom glanced over, head cocked to the side like she was wondering herself.

"You know why. It's not me." Even if it wasn't for how they looked, skirts made me feel exposed.

"But why not? You're a girl, too."

"Only anatomically," I said. But if I was trans, would I want to do something about that? What did the surgery involve, anyway? Did they give you a transplanted penis or what? I knew hormones were involved, but beyond that, I was clueless.

Izzy's brow furrowed. But she left it alone, obviously guessing I couldn't explain it to her.

On the car ride home, Izzy made me sit in the back row with her because she wanted to tell me something. Once we got settled, and Mom pulled onto the main road, she whispered, "I have a secret boyfriend." Then she giggled.

"A boyfriend? Really?"

Her eyes went wide. "Shh! Not so loud!"

"You don't want Mom to know?"

"No, only you."

"Okay, so tell me about this boy," I whispered back. "He better be nice to you."

"He is. He called me and told me I was pretty today. He said he wants me to be his girlfriend but it's a secret."

"Why a secret?"

Her grin grew wider. "Isn't that cool?"

"Sure, Izzy."

"Isabella," she whispered.

"Sorry. That's great, Isabella. Keep me posted." She didn't want to talk about the secret part, which I thought was a little weird for a ten-year-old. Not that I'd necessarily know.

"Don't you want to know his name?"

"What's his name?"

"Jake!" She said it loud enough that she covered her mouth in surprise, which made me laugh.

She continued grinning and leaned back in her seat.

After that, I thought back to the shopping experience and how it was like I was separate from my whole family. There were the normal ones, and there was me. One girl, one boy, one me. Was I really doing things wrong like so many people thought? I just didn't know how to be anything but me.

We stopped by Sam's on the way home and picked up the keyboard. Sam's mom chatted with Mom and Izzy played with their cat while we went upstairs.

There were a few moving boxes around and the magnitude of the situation hit me in the gut. She was leaving. It was almost the worst thing that had ever happened to me. But I needed to be cool. It's not like she could do anything about it.

She had the box for it leaning against the wall, but the keyboard was still sitting on the stand.

Be cool. "I still can't believe you're giving me this. You're too nice."

She shrugged. "I really never play it anymore, anyway. Let's box it up."

I held the box while she maneuvered the keyboard into it and we folded up the stand and the little seat she used with it.

"I can't believe you're leaving." Suddenly, I wanted to cry. Here I was, taking this thing that had once mattered to her, but she'd moved on. Like she would probably move on from me.

Sam frowned. "I know. I don't want to. It sucks. And I feel bad for you, too. We really need to work on OSIN."

"Yeah. That we do. But there's no time left …"

"Yeah." She sounded down and I didn't know what to say.

"I guess we'd better take it downstairs. They're probably wondering what we're doing."

She laughed. "You grab the stand and stool."

We got everything downstairs and into the car. I waved at Sam as we were backing out.

"I'm sorry she's moving, honey," Mom said.

I couldn't even say anything. I still wanted to cry.

"Are you sad?" Izzy asked.

"Yeah. She's my best friend."

"I'm sorry, too."

"Thanks."

Once we were home, I dragged everything upstairs and threw the new clothes on the bed. I set up the keyboard next to it and sat on the stool in front of it. I was again excited by the possibilities it represented.

It might turn out that I had this hidden natural talent. Maybe once I mastered the keyboard, I could move on to guitar. I could almost see myself on a stage, grinding away on a lengthy solo, fingers flying over the fretboard.

I smiled and turned the keyboard on. I plugged in my headphones and played a few keys.

Hideous noise.

Okay, so I had a ways to go. But music had to be the key. I'd have more in common with more people. It could be the thing that turned the tide for me socially. It wouldn't matter if I were trans or not. I believed in the music.

Chapter 18

I was on my way to the stairwell to meet Sam, Ryan, and Lizzy—OSIN was on—and this guy I'd known since second grade called across the hall, "Hey, Nic, are you going to start competing in beauty pageants now?"

My face burned. The pictures from Friday were making the rounds. After he was out of hearing distance, my brain unfroze so I muttered, "Fuck you," which felt good.

Once I got to the stairwell, Sam was already there with her hamburger.

"Hey. So what is up with those pictures?" She jokingly glared at me. "You didn't mention anything yesterday."

I sat against the wall next to her and closed my eyes. "Yeah. It was too embarrassing."

"What happened?"

"Well, I was over there and they pestered me and ... I don't know. I just gave in." I grimaced and shrugged.

She gave me a light punch on the shoulder. "You are such a sucker. You need to stand up for yourself more."

I put my face in my hands, wallowing in the burn of

the humiliation and desperation I felt, even though I wasn't telling Sam how bad it was. I felt sick to my stomach thinking about it. "I know." The whistling! God.

"It was so weird seeing you like that. I mean, you looked good, but not like you at all."

"I know. It felt really wrong."

"But really, you're too nice." She plucked the pickle off the burger and dropped it in her mouth.

I looked over at her and unwrapped my burrito. "I don't know that I'm nice. I think I'm a little antisocial."

"Nah, I don't think that's it. You're just extremely shy."

"But I don't even like those girls. I mean, they're fine, but they're so boring. God, who cares about fashion?" I took a bite of the burrito.

"So you have high standards." She bumped my shoulder with hers. "They're brainless followers, that's all."

"I guess." I finished chewing and said, "Oh, do you know what Alyssa said once? It was a little while ago, but still."

"What?"

I chuckled. "She was carrying on about how she's going to go to UCLA and how college is so great because you don't ever have to go to class."

Sam snorted. "See what I mean? Brainless."

"I was like, uh, I don't think it works like that."

"No shit. Plus she doesn't do well in school, anyway."

We were quiet for a moment, until I said, "I don't think Ryan and Lizzy are coming."

"I think you're right. It's not like they're the most engaging people, anyway." She smirked.

"Right? They're probably somewhere else making out."

"Most definitely." She took a bite of her burger and

when she finished it, said, "So my dad's leaving this Sunday."

I shook my head. "I can't believe it. It's happening." I put my hand on my stomach to calm the new fluttering.

"I know." She looked off in the distance before turning back. "Oh! I almost forgot. I convinced my mom to let me go to a party this Saturday. I'll just stay at your place and Zach can pick us up. I'm guessing your mom won't mind?"

The mention of Zach had my mind whirling anew with possibilities. Maybe soon we'd be going out. Just four days away! "I don't think she'll care. But you're sure Zach will take us?"

"Yeah, I saw him in the hall this morning and asked him. He said he doesn't know of a party yet, but one will come up. And even if one doesn't, we can all hang out at his. So it's cool. Just check with your mom."

"Will do."

"Awesome. Maybe you can chat with Zach." She waggled her eyebrows.

I was grinning and had to tamp down my enthusiasm or Sam might figure out how much I liked him. I just wasn't ready for that kind of conversation.

"Also, we've got that art club meeting Wednesday. You need to try to mingle more, okay?"

I nodded. She wasn't wrong.

"It will be good practice for Saturday night."

"Yeah."

In an earnest voice, she said, "I know you can do this, Nic. You need to try a tad harder, that's all."

That wasn't quite fair. I *was* trying. I simply couldn't get it right.

"Operation Social Interaction for Nic is still live," she said. "Full steam ahead."

Chapter 19

Wednesday, I was in math next to Carlos, with Kyle chortling away on his other side and going on about the pictures. Carlos looked uncomfortable, though he half-smiled. Apparently, they were the funniest thing Kyle had seen so far this year. I just wanted the class to end so I could get to the art club meeting and try to make friends. I really did want some new friends. And I had a lot more in common with other art kids than with the average kid.

I stared at the board while Mr. Martinez went over some more equations. I wasn't able to concentrate on account of Kyle and my nuclear cheeks announcing my humiliation to the entire room, but I was trying my best to write down everything that mattered.

I glanced down at my notes and realized I'd left off an entire line of the equation, so it made no sense whatsoever.

Why did I have to care so much about what people thought? Why specifically did it bother me so much that people had seen me with makeup on?

It felt almost as bad as being seen naked would be. Maybe because it revealed what I was by reminding everyone what I wasn't. I wasn't a makeup-wearer, even though I was a girl, so I had to be the other thing—a freak. A lesbian, of course.

I wondered why nobody thought of me being trans. We weren't *that* far from Tulsa, and I was willing to bet there were some trans kids there. It was a city, after all.

Anyway, I thought the lesbian assumption was why Kyle thought the pictures were so hilarious. But he knew I wasn't gay, since I'd turned up on Carlos's doorstep. I don't know if he considered the possibility that I was bi. I guess the point was that I was dumb enough to think that even in my natural state, I should be good enough for Carlos.

Idiot.

Finally, Mr. Martinez wrapped up the lesson and let us go. I didn't look at Carlos or Kyle and escaped without further verbal reminders of my shame.

I found Sam at her locker, and we headed over to the art classroom for the meeting. It didn't start for another forty-five minutes, but the whole point was to get there and talk to people.

We climbed the stairs, and I remembered racing down these to get to the bus the day Zach drove me home. I closed my eyes for a second and suppressed the grin that was threatening to escape when I thought about how great Friday would be. Mom had agreed to let Sam stay and for us to go to a party. She seemed a little nervous about it—it was my first party, after all.

Never mind that Caleb had gone to a couple already. Mom was just more worried about me, because I was a girl, I guess. More reason to hate being one.

Not to mention that it was messed up that they were trying to protect me *now* Where were they when Dad's friend was messing with me?

Sam opened the door into the room, and the sound of

a dozen voices spilled out. I tucked the dark thoughts away, and we maneuvered around the tables nearest the door to get where everyone was. People were standing over by the pottery wheels because there was more open space. The shelves with all the ceramics pieces were on the other side.

"Hey, Sam, check out my pot," I said. I pointed to this giant piece of bisqueware. It was about eighteen inches high, and Ms. Tolliver hadn't been sure it would survive the kiln, but it had. I was proud of it.

"Wow, that's awesome. Is that coil on the bottom?"

I nodded, and we went over to inspect it. The bottom six inches was a big circular bowl, then I put vertical slab pieces on top of that in a narrowing cylinder, and finally some more slab pieces that narrowed even more until there was a mouth-shaped opening at the top, but it opened to the side rather than up. It was a bit wacko.

"Is that a bong?" this guy asked.

"No," Sam said. "It's not."

Oh, God. I hadn't thought how it would look. I flushed. I was such an idiot.

"I love that pot," someone else said, and I turned to see Mia, the girl in my class who I'd spoken to at Key Club last week.

"Thanks. It's nothing like your stuff." Then I glanced at Sam. "You should see what she makes—she actually creates small flowers out of clay. It's amazing." It was true. She'd made this one pot with decorative delicate petals around the rim.

Mia smiled. "Thanks."

Sam said, "That's really cool. Is there one here?"

Mia showed her one of them, and we admired it.

"Oh, look," Sam said. "There's Andrew. I'm going to go talk to him." She disappeared across the crowd, which left Mia and me. This was probably a part of OSIN.

Despite wearing more makeup than she usually did, Mia looked like a little girl to me. It baffled.

We chatted for a while—she wasn't too hard to talk to, though we stuck to art, except for when she mentioned her boyfriend. When she talked about him her eyes glowed a bit. He bought her things all the time, including the charm bracelet she was now wearing. I wondered what that would be like. Not that I'd want jewelry. But having someone who liked you enough to buy you presents might be cool.

I didn't know if I was doing a good job participating in OSIN, but at least I wasn't being a complete wallflower.

Ms. Tolliver went to the front of the room to start the meeting. Among other things, she talked about the art contest. We were responsible for the fundraising, and we were going to be selling chocolate. Which would suck. I hated going door to door. But since I was hoping to win something in the contest, I figured it would only be fair that I do some of the legwork.

When it was over, we all meandered out.

There was a black BMW with tinted windows idling in front of the sidewalk. I saw Mia's face light up as she bounded over to it.

She was getting in just as we passed, and I glanced in and saw a buff black-haired white guy with sleeve tattoos on both arms looking pissed off. He didn't look like the kind of guy I would have pictured Mia with, for some reason. He looked dangerous, and she seemed so nice. Plus, I would have at least thought the guy would be happy to see her.

If Zach were picking me up, would he be happy to see me?

Chapter 20

Friday morning on the way to class, I got a text from Sam about the plan for lunch.

—*eating with the band crew*—

That meant I wasn't welcome. Those guys were like that. I tried not to take it personally.

—*and my mom changed her mind about the party. i cant go cuz my dad is leaving sunday*—

—*no way!!*—

—*i know, really sorry*—

—*that sucks*— It so did.

I'd been trying to think of a plan to maybe even try to make a move on Zach.

God, I hated her mom. Then she texted again.

—*but i bet Zach will still pick u up. u should go anyway*—

—*…*—

—*do it!*—

I looked into the classroom with all the kids and sat in my regular seat in the middle.

Did I have the nerve? It wouldn't be easy, that was for sure.

If I had any hope of having a real life, I would have to step out of my comfort zone. But could I take that big of a step right now? I mean, God. Was I that brave?

—*thinking about it*—

—*let me know. ill tell zach*—

She usually saw him in the hall in the morning or before sixth period.

I put my phone in my pocket because class was about to start, my hand shaking a little from the idea of going with him alone.

If I went, Zach was a nice enough guy that he'd probably feel obligated to talk to me since Sam wouldn't be there. Of course, I couldn't know that for sure, which might mean I'd end up alone all night. And I'd be dependent on him for a ride, so it wasn't like I could just up and leave if I wanted to.

Plus, Evan would be there, which would be potentially unpleasant, especially on the ride there and back. And what if Zach got drunk? I'd have to either ride with him or call my parents, which would be embarrassing. They'd never let me go to another party.

By the time the class was over, I'd gotten a burst of bravery. Although it would be terrifying, I would have to step out of my comfort zone to be with Zach. My hands still shook a little when I picked up my stuff.

Once I got my lunch and went to my stairwell spot—it was simply easier to not have to deal with other people—I sat down and texted Sam.

—*ok, ill go*—

I waited for a moment.

—*yay! ill tell him when I see him. ill give him your number*—

—*cool*—

I was smiling to myself when Mr. Martinez came down the stairs.

"Where's your friend?" he asked, cocking his head.

"In the cafeteria." I felt like a specimen on display.

"Isn't there someone else you could eat lunch with?"

I shrugged, not sure how to respond. Once again, an adult didn't approve of my choices. It was getting so old.

Still, I had the party to look forward to. And Zach.

Chapter 21

Saturday afternoon, I hit a bad note on the keyboard and flinched. I had it set up with earbuds plugged in so I could do whatever without the whole house knowing how much I sucked. Because man, did I suck.

Really, it was probably Zach's fault that I kept hitting bad notes because I couldn't concentrate. I kept thinking about him. I kept wondering what it would be like if we ended up alone in some corner tonight. Would he kiss me?

If he didn't, would I have enough nerve to kiss him first?

Let's be real—no. But he had to like me, the way he'd been acting—looking at me in the mirror, being so friendly, and so on. So I still held out hope.

I pictured that entrancing grin of his and how he looked at me when he was talking about the blue hand. He genuinely thought it was cool, and it seemed like maybe he even thought *I* was cool. That made my heart swell.

This seemed like a sure thing.

There was a knock at the door and Izzy called my name.

It was good to have my thoughts interrupted. I set the earbuds on the keyboard. "Come in."

She came in like a tornado followed by glitter, wearing her favorite pink shorts and a shirt that said "Brainy Princess" across the front.

At least there was the "brainy" part. She had some good aspirations. Otherwise, ugh. What was with little girls and princesses? How we came from the same parents, I'll never know.

"Hi, Nic."

"Hey, Iz."

"I'm going to let that one go because that was short for Isabella, right?"

I laughed. "Of course." I was never going to get used to this. For ten years, she'd been Izzy.

"I got my new box!" she said.

This was perfect for getting my mind off Zach. Thank God for little sisters.

Then she scowled. "My last one."

I hadn't talked to her about my idea. "How much is it every month?"

"Twenty-five." She sat down in the middle of the floor, and I sat across from her. She opened the box and began spreading the contents out in front of us.

"Well, I have a proposition for you. I *might* be willing to make up the difference for you."

"Really?" She clapped her hands together.

I looked down to see a bunch of square pieces of thin wood, some metal parts, and paint. "Yeah. But you'd have to do something for me."

"What?" She shook with excitement.

"Clean my room." Mom wasn't super strict about it, but it was one of the chores she'd recently highlighted.

"That's it? That's easy." Izzy was a neat freak already.

"Yeah, but you have to keep it up. Once a week."

"Okay, deal." She stuck her hand out.

I laughed and shook it. "Deal."

She grinned at me, her pink braces showing.

"What is all this?" I asked.

"It's a clock." She held up two long and thin black metal pieces. "See, these are the hands."

"Oh, right." I pulled out the instructions and read through them while she fiddled with the pieces. There was a battery pack with a metal rod sticking out of it that the wood pieces—which had holes in them—were supposed to be stacked on. The point was you could angle them in different directions to make your own custom clock.

My phone rang, which jarred me because it was weird. Sam was the only one I ever talked to, and she always texted first.

"Aren't you going to get that?" Izzy asked.

"No." I didn't recognize the number, even though it was a local number.

I picked up some of the pieces of the clock and we stacked them on the rod. Then she started moving the pieces around in different configurations, her lips pressed together in concentration.

Out of the corner of my eye, I saw a popup on my phone indicating that there was a message. A little more unusual, so I checked the voice mail. My heart started up double-time when I heard Zach's voice on the message.

"Hey, Nic. Wanted to plan for tonight. Call me. Later."

Okay, that was weird. We could do that via text.

Wait, did he want to talk to me? There went my heart again.

Holy shit.

"Who is it?" Izzy asked.

My insides were about to burst from excitement, which I knew was an overreaction, but I couldn't help it.

"Nobody." I felt weird. I didn't think I could tell her.

"You look really happy."

She was right. I was grinning crazily now. I tried to squelch it and utterly failed.

She giggled. "Come on, I want to know!"

"Okay, fine. Just this boy I know."

"A boy called you! Oh my God, Nic! I'm so jealous." Her knees bounced up and down.

"Izzy, it's no big deal. And you shouldn't be jealous. What about Jake?"

Her face lit up even more. "He's so funny! Maybe you and me can both have boyfriends at the same time."

Wouldn't that be nice. The thought made me smile even more.

"I think he really likes me," Izzy said. "Everyone says so."

"I thought it was a secret."

She giggled. "He's mean to me sometimes, and that's why everyone says that."

"Mean to you how?"

She must have sensed my alarm. "It's not a big deal. Like sometimes he calls me names. Or acts like I smell."

"How does he do that?"

"He holds his nose when I walk by. Only when he's with his friends."

Ah, that made sense. I knew from watching the kids around me that boys that age were especially idiotic. Some of them liked girls, but it was the worst thing in the world for that to be known.

"He's not worth it, then. No boy has the right to be mean to you, even if he likes you. Because if he really likes you, he wouldn't be mean to you."

She frowned. "I don't know. He's not very mean."

"Come on, you know better. It's important to have self-respect."

She looked away and I said, "Let's work on the clock."

"Okay." She smiled again. "It's still so cool that a boy called you!"

We moved the wood pieces around for a bit, trying to find a good configuration.

I was, of course, desperate to call Zach back, but I had to calm down first. I knew enough about this kind of thing to play it at least a little cool. You might *be* desperate, but you shouldn't *look* desperate.

"What's he like?" Izzy asked.

The massive grin on my face had faded. "Oh, you know. Nice."

"But what's he *like*? Is he cute?"

"Yeah, I guess. But you know it's not all about looks."

"Adam has really cute hair." Izzy said.

"Who's that?"

"Just this boy in my class. But he's stupid. He goes around making fart sounds with his armpit."

I laughed. At least by high school most boys had stopped doing that.

We shifted the pieces some more until we thought it looked cool.

Then I was ready. I was sure I could speak in a normal voice. "I'm going to call him back real quick."

"Nic," he answered.

"Hi," I sort of squeaked. I hadn't noticed how deep his voice was before. I mean, he was a guy so that was to be expected, but I liked it.

"What's your curfew? Nice signal, asshole."

"What?"

"Sorry, I'm driving," he explained. "Curfew?"

My heart sank. The driving was why he'd called instead of texting. "Eleven-thirty."

Izzy sat there grinning and watching in fascination, which made me feel weird, like a specimen again.

"Cool. So I'll come by at about six forty-five, okay?"

"Sure." My pulse was speeding up again despite my best efforts to cool it down.

His laughter came through the phone all husky. "You sound nervous."

I guess my "sure" had been wobbly. "Yeah." Why couldn't I come up with something more than one-word answers?

"Thought so. You need to get out more, don't you?"

"I guess." I laughed nervously. "Yeah."

"It's cool, I'll make sure nobody bothers you. I'll be like your big brother."

That was nice—I liked the idea that he'd look out for me. It was kind of sweet. But I hoped he didn't think of me as a sister.

"I better get going, Nic. See you tonight."

"Bye."

I clutched the phone and noticed my hand shaking a tiny bit again.

"You're smiling again," Izzy observed.

"He's nice."

"Do you *like* him?" She reached over and grabbed my hand.

"No!" God, I could never admit it. It was too hard to say.

"You *do*!" She grabbed my other hand.

I disentangled myself. I didn't want her to notice me shaking. "Izzy, I don't want to talk about it."

"Isabella," she said, sounding disappointed.

"Okay, sorry." I took a deep breath and then snapped a

quick picture of the clock. "Let's take this apart so we can glue it back together."

"Fine."

It had sounded like Zach was looking forward to tonight. Why else would he have called instead of just sending a quick text later—"your house, 6:45," would have worked. Why the need to make the plan right now?

This was so cool. He had to like me.

I helped Izzy squeeze the glue on in the right places and we got the first piece on the base. Then I let her go with it, as she was doing okay.

Was he thinking about me, too? What would he think about? Somebody told me that I had a nice nose once, but I doubted that was it. My boobs? Not small, but not giant. Though I was supposed to have nice hair, too. I didn't do anything to it, but it was long and smooth naturally. Some boys liked hair, right?

I didn't really have any idea. All those experiences other girls had with boys in middle school had been inaccessible to me.

I was wondering what I'd do if Zach touched my boobs tonight when Izzy asked, "Now what?"

Crap. I needed to stop thinking about him. I didn't want to build this up into a big thing only to find out I'd been wrong all along.

That would be awful. Another Carlos scenario.

I looked down. Everything was in place. "Just need to let it dry, then you can paint it and put the hands on."

"It's so cool. Can I leave it here?"

"Yeah." I got up and put the clock on top of the dresser before heading back to the keyboard.

Izzy stood by the door. "Will I get to meet him?"

"What? No!" She'd probably give something away. How mortifying that would be.

"Why not?" She sounded hurt.

"Not tonight. Another time." Like after we'd been dating a while.

Izzy smiled and skipped out of the room and I sat at the keyboard, dreaming of everything good that could happen tonight instead of practicing.

Chapter 22

I'd been practicing for a while on the keyboard when Mom came in, looking pensive. "Honey, I've thought about it, and I think since Sam can't go, I don't want you going to that party tonight."

My heart nearly stopped. "What? I have to go!"

"Why?"

I couldn't tell her. I couldn't even tell Sam.

"I know you're disappointed, honey." She was frowning like she didn't like saying it.

I squeezed the sides of the stool and grappled for something I could say to convince her. "Mom, come on. Zach's going to be there."

"That's just it—I don't really know him well enough. With Sam, I know you'd look out for each other, but how can I trust a boy I hardly know?"

"Please?" The desperation was ripping my stomach apart.

"I'm sorry. I need you to be safe." Her brow was furrowed.

"I can take care of myself!" God, here we go again. If I was a boy it would be no big deal.

"It's not that I don't trust you, honey," she said in a placating tone, "but girls need to look out for each other at parties."

"God, Mom. It's not like I'm a real girl. Nobody would want to drug *me*."

She narrowed her eyes. "What do you mean?"

"Never mind." I held my hand to my stomach to calm it.

"You're still so young. The world can be a dangerous place."

"Come on, I'm about to get my license." My pleading tone embarrassed me.

"I have to leave for work. We can talk more later." She pulled the door shut as she disappeared into the hall.

Oh my God. She was ruining my life.

I was stunned, and my eyes stung. After a couple breaths, I couldn't hold back the tears.

This was so fucking unfair. I moved over to my desk and stared at my figurines, wanting to break them. All I'd have to do is bend the metal a few times on anything that stuck out, like a sword or a staff, and it would go. I could hardly see them through my tears.

God, I hated crying. Once it started, I was out of control. My face would show it for hours. Now I would have to spend the whole night in my room.

I moved back to my bed to keep myself from breaking anything. And after the worst of it passed, I texted Zach to cancel. This made me start all over again, though, especially when he texted back.

—*thats 2 bad chica. maybe next time*—

I couldn't tell if he cared.

But then I thought about the fact that he'd called me

"*chica.*" Nobody had ever called me by a nickname before. At least, one that wasn't disparaging.

That made me feel marginally better. I mean, maybe this wasn't my only chance with him.

But it didn't totally stop the crying.

After I'd lost about a gallon of snot, I thought about working on the keyboard again. But then it occurred to me that I'd never get to go to a party since Sam would be gone soon, and Mom still wouldn't "know Zach better." It was hopeless. This turned me into a blubbering mess again, and I never got to the keyboard. Everything was so pointless. Why did I ever get my hopes up?

At least I'd see Sam tomorrow. Maybe I'd even tell her how much I liked Zach.

Chapter 23

I helped Sam pack up her bedroom Sunday afternoon. This meant preparing her various art pieces for packing by the movers that were coming Friday. We had newspaper spread all over the floor with drawings on them, which we'd been spraying with that fixative. On the can, it said to ventilate well, and the room smelled a little like alcohol, even though Sam had put a fan in the open window aiming out. It was kind of funny since the AC was still running. You could feel heat seeping in around the fan.

"How many more of these do you have?" I asked.

She laughed. "Almost done."

She unrolled another one—a nice study of a castle in Scotland that she must have done recently—and put it on top of some empty newspaper and sprayed it.

After spraying the last two, we each collapsed on one of her twin beds, avoiding the papers at the foot of each.

I bounced my legs against the side of the bed. "Hey, what did you end up doing with your figurines?"

"I didn't tell you? I'm keeping them."

"Ah." I lay with my eyes closed. "Cool. Why not sell them?"

"Sentimental value, I guess. Maybe we should pack them now."

"We should."

Neither of us moved and after a moment, we both cracked up at our laziness.

"Okay, for real, now," she said forcefully.

We both sat up at the same time. Despite the fan, I think we might have been a little high from the fumes. I felt off. Woozy. I guess we should have ventilated better.

But then we crawled into the tiny finished attic that was behind her closet. It was our painting area.

We gathered the various figurines and loaded up the boxes with protective foam and then wrapped the figurines in paper. After we had them mostly done, Sam asked, "Have you tried to see if Carlos and Kyle might be potential friends for you?"

My stomach twisted as I relived the horrible moment that Carlos first looked at me at his house, and I felt my cheeks flame. Luckily, Sam wasn't looking at me right then. I didn't know how I could tell her about that. It would be so humiliating.

"I don't know, I think Kyle's kind of a jerk," I said. "He made fun of me over the makeup pictures."

"Oh. I always thought he was okay. Shows you never know. Not like he's a hottie, himself."

I shrugged. The thing was, Sam used to be as much of a loser as me. No friends. Targets on our backs. Things changed in eighth grade. I didn't understand what had happened, except she became popular among the band kids overnight. Nothing like that had ever happened to me. It wouldn't have been with the band kids, but you'd think maybe the art kids.

But no.

The only thing we were still the same on was boys. She'd never had a boyfriend, either. We didn't talk about it, even though I was pretty sure she'd liked a few.

I hadn't told her about my last conversation with Zach because I didn't have the nerve, and I still didn't. Even though this was the perfect opportunity to bring it up. It would be admitting too much—even to Sam.

I heard the bedroom door open and her mom said, "Sam?"

We crawled out, Sam in front, and her mom stood there looking at us both on our knees on the floor. She sniffed the air and said, "What have you two been doing in here? Is that pot?!"

She looked back and forth between us, eyes narrowed. It was weird how much Sam looked like her, pale skin and straight blonde hair.

"What?" Sam asked. "No! God, Mom. It's that spray stuff for my drawings. We're venting it out the window."

"Do not take the Lord's name in vain, Samantha." Her mom pursed her lips and looked at me through still-narrowed eyes. She didn't like me because she thought Sam and I were "too close," which I thought was her way of accusing us of being together. "I think it's time for you to go, Nic. Please call your mom."

Chapter 24

I went home and after eating dinner, I messed around with the keyboard for a while. I was still terrible but it seemed like I was getting better. I'd found some stupid easy songs to play online and worked on learning them.

So I was playing "Old McDonald Had a Farm" and "Yankee Doodle" like a pro.

I was very glad for the headphones. Can you imagine how bad it would have been if my brother had heard me playing "Twinkle Twinkle Little Star"? He would have told everyone. How humiliating if people knew I was trying to learn that.

I was glad he didn't even know about the keyboard at all.

A little before nine, I took my earbuds out and noticed a weird sound. Pretty quick, I realized it was yelling. I ran over to the door and listened. Were my parents fighting?

I'd literally never heard them argue. Bicker, yes, but actually fight? No. I pressed my ear to the door to hear better. I still couldn't make out what was being said.

Then I started to pluck words out. "Bill." "Savings account." "Cable."

Okay, so, money. My stomach clenched. Was it getting worse?

I sat back, head spinning. Would we end up moving? We had a nice two-story house built in the '80s. I mean, it wasn't as big as Sam's, but it was a decent size. My neighborhood had a lot of houses with pools and stuff like that, though we didn't have one.

Moving would be okay if it involved changing school districts. It would give me a fresh start.

It had gone a little quiet, but then there was more yelling and Caleb came running up the stairs and shouted, "You're ruining my life!" before slamming his door.

I needed to do something to get my mind off all this crap. Sam moving. Money problems. It all sucked.

I opened my backpack up to finish up some history homework I'd been avoiding all weekend and sat at my desk, moving some of the figurines and Testors paint bottles back to make room. I held up my favorite blue—dark and metallic—to the light so I could admire it before pushing it back into the corner with the rest, clinking them all together.

After a few minutes of work, I thought about the art contest. I hadn't worked on the dragon drawing since getting the keyboard, but there was plenty of time. I should plan my projects at school to maximize my entries. A little bit of everything. I could only enter one per category, and I wanted to enter a lot of work. Even thinking about it had me excited—I knew I could win something, which would make me competitive for art school.

A knock sounded on my door.

"Yeah?"

Mom came in. Her face was red like she was about to

start crying. I would have felt bad except that I was still pissed at her about last night. I mean, nothing bad would have happened with Zach there. And something *good* could have happened.

"Hi, honey."

I just looked at her.

"I'm letting you know that we're getting rid of all the cable except basic." She looked like she wanted to talk, but I didn't. "I know you don't watch a lot of TV, but you should know."

"Okay."

She slipped back out the door, and I went to lie on my bed, thinking about Zach. I wondered what it would feel like if he touched me. And where? My hand? Which one? Would I want something else? I didn't even know. When was I going to find out?

Izzy knocked on the door and called my name.

"Yeah?"

She came in, her eyes wide with fear. She crawled onto the bed and nestled against me. "Why are they fighting?"

"What'd they say to you?"

"No more cable. But why were they yelling so much?"

"Money." I squeezed her hand.

"Are they going to get a divorce?" Izzy's voice was tight.

"I don't think so." I hoped not. I couldn't even imagine what that would be like.

Chapter 25

I was waiting for Sam in the stairwell Monday, desperate to talk about the text I'd gotten from her on the way to school.

—*were not moving until December!*—

I mean, that was awesome. More time for OSIN. And obviously more time with my best and only friend.

So when she got there and had a girl with her, I had mixed feelings. I really wanted to talk to her about the not moving.

The new girl had a long auburn braid and walked with a slight limp. She had on makeup, but only a little, so maybe she wouldn't judge me too much.

Sam introduced Chelsea to me.

"Are you a sophomore?" Chelsea asked in a friendly voice while Sam sat down next to me.

"Yeah. You?"

She nodded and looked around, possibly confused by the setting.

"We just sit on the floor," Sam said.

"Oh, sure," Chelsea said. She sat on one of the steps.

Maybe she'd work out. Even if my conversation skills needed some work.

But they were talking about band now, so I listened and ate my pepperoni pizza. For once it wasn't too greasy. Chelsea played the trumpet, which was sort of cool. She looked like she'd be a flute player. All innocent. I thought of trumpet players as more boisterous.

After a while, Chelsea put her hands on her thighs and leaned forward to step down. "I guess I'm going to go to the library. I need to get something for history."

"Alright." Sam crumpled her burger wrapper.

"Nice meeting you," Chelsea said to me.

"You too."

Once she was gone, Sam bumped my shoulder and grinned at me. "Could you believe my text?"

"No!" Now we could talk about it. "What happened?"

She shrugged "They fought a little Friday night. I heard something about not wanting to take us out of school mid-semester. She told me this morning we're not going until right before Christmas."

This was an incredible relief—I felt almost happy. Maybe they'd end up calling the whole thing off.

"Oh, by the way," Sam announced. "I'm pretty sure I can convince my mom to let me go to a party this Saturday."

"Really? Mine'll definitely let me go if you're there. She doesn't trust Zach alone." Again, the irony of her not trusting *this* guy when he was probably the only decent guy in school.

"That's funny. He's so nice." She arched an eyebrow. "I wonder if she'd let you go on a date with him."

I blushed and picked at the crust on my pizza. "Shut up." If only he'd ask. "I have no idea."

"I'll talk to him this afternoon. Let's plan on it, and I'll work on my mom this week."

"Yeah, okay."

She checked her phone and held it up for me to see. Time to go.

I went to my next class. What was the likelihood of success for OSIN now that Sam was staying so much longer? I was feeling lighter than I had in awhile. When I got to art, I pulled my drawing and colored pencils from the cubby and sat down next to Mia. She was wearing a long-sleeve shirt, which was weird. She was one of those girls who seemed to want to show as much skin as humanly possible, within the limitations of the school dress code. Or pushing the boundaries of it.

"Hey," she said.

"Hi." I'd seen her a few times since the art club meeting and she'd been friendlier since then.

Mia had her block of clay in front of her and pushed her sleeves up before taking the wire cutter to slice off a hunk of clay. Her fingers and hands were so small, it was no wonder she could do such delicate work.

Me, I had hams for hands.

She managed to keep her brightly painted fingernails in nice condition despite all the clay work she did. I thought they were fake like my mom's.

Her shirt was one of those stupid ones with the shoulders cut out, and I could see there were three small purple bruises on her skin. I stared longer than I should have, and she looked at the spots herself. She quickly focused back on her new pot that was just taking shape.

I didn't know what to think or say so I got to work on the landscape I'd started last week.

Chapter 26

As I was heading out to the bus after school Monday, I saw Zach in the hall. That was a little unusual, and I took it as a good sign from the universe. But it seemed especially good when he saw me, smiled and waved from the other side of the hall.

And even better when he said, "Hey, you. I never see you after school. You want a ride home?"

Here was my chance! My heart went crazy.

Still, I managed more than three words. "Sure, that would be cool, if you don't mind."

"No problem at all. Is Sam around? I could take her, too."

"She has a dentist appointment today."

"Let's go, then."

I held onto the straps of my backpack to still my shaking hands and followed him out, taking careful steps to get through the crowd.

"You take art, don't you?" he asked. "That's where you made that hand?"

"Yeah." I needed to say something else but my mind was blank.

"That's cool. My older sister works as a graphic designer."

"Really?" I wondered if I'd meet her if we started going out.

"Yep."

We got to his car and he unlocked it and rolled down the windows. This time I noticed he had one of those tree-shaped air fresheners hanging from the rearview mirror. I couldn't smell it, though. All I could smell was boy deodorant from when he leaned over to get his sunglasses from the glove box.

My mind spun as I scrambled to come up with something else to say because it was my turn to speak. "So, what does your sister work on?"

"She works at an ad agency in New York."

"Oh, that's very cool." It was also intimidating as hell. Could he be interested in me if he was the kind of guy who had a sister living in New York? Was he cosmopolitan or whatever himself? I certainly wasn't. I'd never been anywhere except Arkansas and Texas.

He backed out of the spot and we joined the crush of cars trying to get out of the parking lot.

"That's too bad about Sam moving. You guys seem really close." He tapped his fingers on the steering wheel.

This made me feel a rush of relief again. "Actually, she's not leaving yet. Not until December.

He looked over. "Really?"

"Yeah, really."

"You must be happy then."

I nodded. "I am."

God, I was such a bad conversationalist. Why couldn't I think of anything else to say? Other people didn't have any trouble thinking of stuff to talk about. I wanted to ask him if he wanted to hang out some time, but now I couldn't even open my mouth.

"So, why are they moving?" he asked as he pulled onto the main road.

"Her dad got a new job. I think he lost his before and was looking for something, and what he found is in Scotland."

"It's still kind of crazy that she's moving all the way over there. 'Across the pond.'" He chuckled so his eyes crinkled, and it made me laugh.

"It is crazy. He's a chemical engineer—you'd think he'd be able to find something, at least, in America."

"You mean like Argentina?" he teased.

"*North* America."

Zach shrugged. "He might have some family connection over there."

"Maybe, though she never mentioned anything like that."

This turn of the conversation made me relax back into the seat, because it was easier than trying to come up with something to say. And it was flowing. Maybe I *could* ask him to hang out.

I looked over at him and was trying to organize the words that were rampaging through my brain. Should I say, Do you want to hang out some time? Or, What do you do on the weekends? Or, Do you like movies? That one sounded good. "Do you—"

"Sam's an artist too, isn't she?" he said at the same time.

I exhaled. Off the hook. "Yeah, she is."

Another time. I would definitely ask him.

Chapter 27

I picked up my cold drink from the counter at Orange Julius and sat next to Sam in one of those tiny uncomfortable metal chairs on Friday afternoon. The store was on a corner of a shopping center, so there were loads of people to watch, flowing by like a footrace in slow motion.

I sucked on my drink—an original orange one. I loved them so much I could never get myself to try something else. I watched a couple teenagers walk by holding hands.

A little twinge of envy twisted my heart, but then I realized it might not be long before I knew what that felt like.

That idea was intoxicating.

"What do you think of Evan?" Sam asked. She looked at me sideways.

Did she not notice how he acted around me? "Oh, you know, he's okay. Though not very friendly."

"He's always nice enough to me. I think he's cute."

I looked back at her, surprised. That was the first time she'd ever admitted something like that to me. We didn't talk about boys, at least, not in great detail. Sam had never told me about liking anyone.

It was another perfect opportunity to bring up Zach, especially since he was friends with Evan. I tried to summon the courage to do it, and utterly failed.

But Evan was such a douche—how could she like him? I mean, he openly blanked me every time we were around him. How could she not notice?

"What, you don't think so?" she asked when I didn't respond.

"No, he's alright." He wasn't bad-looking at all. Wavy almost-black hair and super-dark brown eyes that always looked intense, but that might have been because he was always looking at me with extreme disgust. Otherwise, he was kind of built-up, like he worked out. Which was unusual for a band dork.

Objectively, he was cuter than Zach. Still, I knew who I preferred.

"Do you think it's weird? Is that why you're not saying anything?" Sam asked.

"No, it's not that. But he's kind of a jerk to me, don't you think?"

"Really? I haven't noticed." She frowned thoughtfully.

But she'd noticed Zach looking at me? That must have been super obvious, because Evan's dirty looks were blatant, and she'd missed those.

"Well, he sometimes makes comments you probably don't hear. He says I'm fat."

She frowned deeper. It was hard to deny that I was fat, but it wasn't like I was obese. The problem was that I was really tall so I just exuded bigness. Even when I was a little kid, I was never twiggy like most kids were.

"Maybe you're imagining it. I think he's nice."

I looked away, pissed off. I knew what I'd heard at Key

Club. But I couldn't say anything. What if she ended up mad at me? Even the thought had me panicking a little.

"Anyway," she said. "Did you start your paper yet?"

"For English?"

"Yeah."

"Nope. I'll do it this weekend."

"Yeah, me too." She nodded absentmindedly.

I took another sip of my drink, finishing it off.

The moment to mention Zach had passed.

"You finished?" I asked.

She shook her head. "Are you mad at me?"

"No." I shouldn't be. She was never anything but nice to me, and was actively trying to help me get more friends. But it hurt that she hadn't noticed the way Evan was. "You ready for tomorrow?"

"Yes! I'm so excited. Zach's picking us up at 7:15."

I nodded, excitement building in my own chest. A whole night with Zach. He'd surely feel at least a little obligated to spend time with us. I couldn't wait.

"What are you going to wear?" Sam asked.

"Oh, I hadn't even thought about it."

Sam laughed. "Me neither, not until just now. We are not normal teenage girls."

"No, we're not. But probably jeans, and I'll have to find a good t-shirt, too."

"Weight Watchers!" I thought I heard, and I looked up to see a group of guys who were college age. One of them was pointing at me.

"What?" Sam said.

"I said, it's a live ad for Weight Watchers. She looks like the before picture."

They all laughed and moved on, though Sam called, "Fuck off!" at them.

Then she looked at me and said, "Assholes."

My cheeks burned, and I could feel my tear ducts waking up.

I willed myself not to cry.

"Don't let them bother you. Who cares what a bunch of wasters think?"

"Yeah." Me, that's who. Crap.

"Anyway," Sam said. "I'm going to wear jeans, too. I think I'm going to wear my Foo Fighters t-shirt."

"Oh, yeah, that one's cool." I knew I sounded flat, but I was distracted.

"Just forget about them, Nic," she said.

I was definitely trying.

Just think about good things. Like the party Saturday. That would be the day my life would change. I would make myself talk to Zach.

Chapter 28

Saturday night, Zach picked us up and drove us to the party, giving us advice all the way there. "This is about socializing. You guys need to make sure to make the rounds, especially you, Nic." "Don't take a drink from someone you don't know." "Stay away from the bedrooms unless you want to see something you don't want to see."

We got out of his car, and my heart started pounding like crazy again because this was my first real party, and I was here with the guy I liked and who appeared to like me back. Admittedly, it wasn't just us, but since Sam liked Evan, it might as well have been.

I'd ended up in a Doctor Who shirt and my best jeans. And purple Vans. It wasn't going to get me anywhere with the general crowd, but I figured Zach already knew what I looked like.

Sam managed to look kind of cute even though she was dressed basically like me. I guessed being thinner and smaller made her inherently cuter.

We could hear the music well before we got to the door

of the large, white house. The lower floor of the house was finished in a very light stone, and the top half was wood.

The foyer was big and full of people moving around, and the music was even louder inside.

It was, in a word, overwhelming. I already wanted to cower in the corner.

Now my heart was racing for a different reason.

Zach was talking, and I turned to stare at him dumbly.

"A drink?" he asked.

Shit, my mouth was hanging open. "Sure." I shut it.

He disappeared off to the left while Evan went straight ahead into the pulsing crowd.

"We're here," Sam said, smiling at me.

"Yeah, we are. It feels weird."

"Oh, it's okay. You just need to be a little braver. Try to talk to people. Most of the time, people will talk back."

I wasn't sure she was right.

We were still standing there like a couple noobs when Zach reappeared with three red Solo cups. He was holding two by the rims pinched between his fingers. He handed the other one to Sam and held the others up for me to take one.

I liked the idea that he'd sort of touched my beer. It must have sloshed up on his fingers when he walked over.

Was that weird? I had no idea.

Except for that thought, now I felt almost normal. I was a kid at a regular high school party.

I followed them into the living room, where everybody was.

Okay, so this is what I saw: skin and hair and flashes of color, everywhere.

I was clearly not handling it well. I lost Sam and Zach in the crowd and wriggled my way to the wall. On the way, I encountered the couch, which had two separate couples on it seriously making out. I found myself staring for a few seconds, both fascinated and jealous. One of the guys had his hand on the girl's boob.

I wondered if Zach would be like that. And would I like it?

It was impossible to know.

I kept going past the couch and past some more people.

I took a sip of my beer and found it disgusting. I'd had sips of my dad's beer, but never more than one, and now I remembered why.

Okay, I should try to mingle, probably. I mean, I couldn't rely on Sam to do everything. But God, I didn't know how to start.

I stood there for quite a while, the sweat from the cup eventually running over my fingers as the beer warmed.

It would be even grosser now.

This football player gave me the once-over, and the disgust on his face gave away his assessment of me, but he just turned back to his conversation, which was a relief.

Of course, then I felt conspicuous in that location, so I moved down the wall a little, toward the kitchen.

This was disappointing. Where were Zach and Sam? I felt totally abandoned. I know Sam wanted me to talk to people, but she had to know it would be impossible on my own. She could have at least introduced me to some people or something.

Just about the time I realized I was resoundingly bored and kind of frustrated with Sam, I saw her break through the crowd. Her face lit up when she saw me and she barreled toward me.

"There you are! I've been looking everywhere for you!" Her face was a little red and she might have been slurring a little.

"I've been right here the whole time," I said.

She leaned up against the wall right next to me. "You're being a wallflower. Almost literally."

"I know. I keep looking at people talking and trying to visualize myself joining the conversation, but I can't figure out how it would go."

She stepped away and turned toward me. "Come on, there are some people you can meet." Her voice wasn't even.

"Are you drunk?" I was stunned. It hadn't occurred to me that Sam would get drunk.

She shrugged. "I've had a couple beers."

"Whoa." I hadn't thought she would drink. I mean, I figure you have to take a beer or risk looking like an alcohol prude or whatever, but this was a surprise.

"Come on," she said.

"Where's Zach?" I asked.

She didn't answer, so I followed her into the crowd, past some upperclass girls and then the football players. We landed with a group of kids I didn't know, though they looked like lowerclassmen, at least.

A couple of them looked at me as we squeezed into the circle. Nobody said hi, but they were in the middle of talking about a movie I hadn't seen, so I just listened. I knew Sam had seen it because she jumped in. I tried to pay attention to how that worked. Basically, when there was a tiny lull, she said her thing. It didn't seem that complicated, and I didn't know why it was so hard for me.

But my hands were still shaking, and I was afraid I'd start sweating.

Then, some giggling girl came and grabbed Sam by the elbow, and I was left on my own in the group. Finally, finally, they moved on to a movie I had seen. So I formulated a clever comment about it, but there never seemed to be a lull. I noticed that actually, sometimes people just kind of talked over each other, but I didn't have the nerve for that.

When an opportunity came, I summoned the courage and said my thing. However, my timing was bad and the other people didn't stop talking. The only people who looked at me were the ones standing next to me, and they both looked surprised, with wide eyes, before turning back to the group.

Fail.

I slipped away because I was sweating by that time. I was also still holding the stupid, warm beer. I took another sip and found it positively revolting, so I headed back to the kitchen. I was surprised and happy when I got there to see Zach over in front of the window, and then I noticed he was chatting with Sam. Relief washed over me.

They didn't notice me until I got over there. Zach pushed Sam's shoulder as they both laughed about whatever he'd said and then they looked at me.

"Hey," Zach said, still wearing that enchanting smile. "Having fun?"

"Sure," I lied.

"What number is that?" he asked.

Sam laughed. "She's not drinking anything."

"Is that the first one I got you?" he took it from me—I was happy to let it go—and took a sip. "Mmm, warm beer."

I loved that he'd drink after me.

"You can't possibly like that," Sam said.

"Well, it's beer," he said with a laugh.

I wanted to ask how many he'd had, because he was supposed to drive us home at some point. I hoped soon.

"Don't worry, I'm not drinking much tonight, either, Nic. Driving and all that."

I needed to chill out. I smiled.

"Remind me what time you guys have to be back?" he said.

"Eleven-thirty."

We all pulled out our phones simultaneously and noted that it was almost 11:00.

Zach nodded and slipped his phone back into his pocket. "Let me go find Evan so he knows we're leaving soon." He headed out of the kitchen.

That left Sam and me. She smiled, looking a little lost in her thoughts.

"What?" I asked.

"Nothing."

"What were you guys talking about?" Why had he spent no time at all with me? Was I wrong about him, or was it something else?

"I don't know. Stuff. You, a little bit. Did you know his sister's an artist?"

"Yeah." But they talked about me? "What did you talk about, about me?"

"Art and stuff." She put her arm around me, and I stiffened a little. She wasn't usually this tactile. I crossed my arms to relax and she said, "He's so nice."

Zach reappeared with Evan in tow.

The whole ride home, I was nervous about my parents figuring out Sam was kind of drunk. They had to be watching for it. I mean, everyone knew what went on at high school parties.

Zach dropped us off, and I was disappointed to note that he hadn't looked at me once. Had I misread him?

I couldn't see how.

Anyway, when we got in, Sam kept it together, and we made it upstairs without incident. My mom had the air mattress made up for her so we changed and got into our respective beds. I figured we'd talk about the night, but she was asleep seconds later.

Which left me alone with my own thoughts about the party. Not a disaster, but a massive let down. Nothing good had happened.

Chapter 29

Sam and I waited on the steps outside the side door next to the garage for her mom the next morning. She was a little green and cradled her head in her hands.

"You better get a grip, or your mom's going to know something's up," I said.

"God, why did I do that?"

"How many did you have, anyway?" I thought she'd had more than Zach had.

She groaned. "I think just three."

"Maybe too much for your first time."

"Clearly."

I watched her mom pull around the corner and into the driveway. Not that Sam had noticed—she was still looking at her feet.

I bumped her shoulder. "Head up."

She dragged her head into a normal position, stood up slowly, and pulled her duffel over her shoulder before shuffling to the waiting car.

I hazarded a glance at Sam's mom and found her glaring at me, too. She had this way of hiding it behind a tense expression, where you might just think she was grumpy. But she hadn't always looked at me like that. It had gotten worse the longer Sam and I went without being girly-girls. I think once she realized it was a lost cause, she was eternally pissed at me. Like I dictated Sam's choices.

Sam got in the back, and I waved at her as they drove off.

When I got back inside, Dad was getting a beer out of the fridge and asked me if I wanted to practice driving in a bit.

I didn't *want* to, but I knew I *needed* to. I wasn't comfortable driving yet, even though my birthday was in a few weeks.

"Nic!" Izzy called and came running in from the den.

"Yeah?"

"Come upstairs! I want to tell you something."

I eyed the drawing on the dining room table—what I'd done so far did look good—before following her upstairs. We went to her room. And oh, my God, the pink. Pink everywhere.

"Jake called and told me I was pretty again today!" She sat on her bed.

"I thought he was being mean to you?"

"No, he's nice. He's so cute!"

"Really? What's he look like?" I sat next to her on the bed.

"He has long brown hair and dark eyes and always wears nice shirts."

This made me chuckle. I wondered what a "nice shirt" on a boy was to Izzy. "Sounds cute."

"And he's so funny!"

"That's cool. But really, if he's mean to you when other kids are around, he's not a good guy. You should get rid of him."

Izzy frowned.

I was probably being a little harsh. "It's up to you, but don't let some boy disrespect you just because he's cute and funny."

She nodded thoughtfully.

"I've got some stuff I need to do now so I'm going back to my room, okay?"

I started practicing on the keyboard. I was making slow but steady progress on everything. Things were looking up. Now I needed to ask Zach to hang out the next time I saw him. Somehow I had to find the courage, because I *was* going to ask.

Chapter 30

All Monday morning, I couldn't wait for lunch with Sam because I wanted to talk about Zach before heading off to study for a math test. I'd finally decided to come clean about how much I liked him. Maybe if I told somebody, it would be more real, and I'd have no choice but to talk to him.

I had just gone into the stairwell when Sam burst through the door.

"Oh, my God!" she said, wide-eyed with a huge grin across her face.

"What?" I asked, unable to suppress my own smile.

"Zach asked me out!"

It felt like my heart stopped beating, and I almost fell over, I swear. And then it was like every feeling I'd ever had had been sucked back into my chest, while the blood drained from my face.

"What? Why?" I asked stupidly.

"I guess because he likes me!" She laughed, sounding more like a typical girl than she ever had before.

"Oh." I summoned up the bleakest of smiles. "What'd

you say?" I held my breath even though the answer was obvious.

"Yes!"

I nodded. Of course she'd said yes. Zach was nice to both of us, not only me. Now I felt like I'd been run over.

"It's so weird—I thought he liked you!"

I forced another painful smile.

"Aren't you excited?" Sam asked. "Finally one of us is going to go out with somebody!"

"Yeah, it's great." I thought I might puke and held my stomach. "I was just going to say, I can't stay long. I need to go to the library." I had to get away from her. "Just remembered I have a math test."

"That's cool. I'll go with you."

"Oh—okay." What could I say? My throat was tight. I couldn't eat the burrito I'd brought. "I guess I'm going to go now."

"What's the rush? Let's at least eat before we go there." She sat in her regular spot against the wall.

I stared at her, unable to process what was happening.

I'd been wrong *again*. Of course he'd never liked me. He was only looking at me because he was baffled at how somebody could be so ugly.

Or maybe he was trying to figure out how to get me out of the car.

How could I have been so stupid? How could I have expected a normal nice guy like Zach to like a weird girl like me, especially when I was probably trans anyway? If I was. I still had no idea.

But those times he volunteered to drive me—what was that?

"Are you okay?" Sam asked through a mouthful of burger. Then she reached over and touched my arm. "Wait. You didn't like him, did you?"

Without thinking, I recoiled from the touch. Then I managed to say, "Don't be stupid. Of course not." I looked away.

"You *did*. Oh my God. Why didn't you tell me? I won't go out with him."

I took a breath. This wasn't her fault. I had no claim on Zach. "No, Sam, I didn't like him. I'm just surprised. A little jealous, that's all."

She looked at me through narrowed eyes, obviously trying to decide if she believed me.

"Aren't you going to eat your burrito?" she asked, eyes still narrowed.

"I'm not hungry." I sounded mechanical. My entire body was burning with humiliation, and I was about to cry. "I'm going to go to the bathroom."

"I'll meet you in the library, okay?"

"Okay, sure." I concentrated so as not to stumble through the door, and blindly made my way to the nearest bathroom. I don't think there were many other people in the hall, but I couldn't say for sure. My heart was racing, and I was queasy and even a little dizzy. I made it into a stall and fell onto the seat, face in my hands.

I didn't want to cry. It would be obvious. And I needed to get to the library or Sam would wonder what was up.

Oh, God.

How could I have been so stupid? I'd actually thought …

My stomach roiled so badly that I stood up and faced the bowl because I really thought I might spew. I braced myself against the stall walls and willed my stomach back under control.

Stupid. I was a total joke. No one could possibly want to go out with me. I was a pariah.

The first time I figured that out was in art class in

seventh grade. Art hadn't always been a sanctuary. One time the teacher left the room and Keely, this super-popular girl, said so everyone could hear, "Nic, Mack wants to ask you out but he's too shy. Do you want to go out with him?"

I wasn't a total idiot. Mack was one of the most popular boys in the entire seventh grade. I knew he didn't want to ask me out. But the whole class was listening, and I knew they expected me to be embarrassed and cower and say nothing. Mom's approach.

So I said, "Yeah? Sure, whatever."

Nobody even laughed, it was so unexpected. Nobody said anything. Keely herself didn't know what to say. She'd left me alone the rest of the class.

But anyway, the point was that I was laughable as a romantic partner. How had I forgotten that? Besides, wasn't I trans? Who dated trans people? I really didn't know how that worked. Would they have to be gay guys? But then I wouldn't have all the right parts, so that wouldn't make sense. I had no idea about this.

Was I trans, anyway? It didn't feel quite right.

I gripped my stomach and sat back down and tried to calm myself.

Once my breathing was even again, my heart didn't feel like it would explode, and my stomach had settled, I left the stall.

I looked at myself in the mirror, even though I normally tried not to. Because, ugly. But I had to make sure I looked normal for me.

I didn't, not really. My face was still white, and I looked freaked out. I hoped Sam wouldn't notice. I was pretty sure she believed me about not liking Zach. No one else would notice, for sure.

So I washed my hands and left.

The hall felt like a tunnel of doom. It didn't take long to get to the library. I took a deep breath and went in, but I didn't see Sam anywhere.

Then I heard a familiar voice and turned to see Zach. And Sam. Talking. With silly grins on their faces.

I died all over again and mechanically headed to the nonfiction section.

How was I going to survive this?

Chapter 31

Just my luck, in history that day we went to the library to do research for a paper. And the chairs and tables he had us sit in were all in sight of where Sam and Zach had been talking.

So, constant reminder.

I had some books on my table, but I was just staring straight ahead. I couldn't think, much less read and analyze something.

God, I was so stupid. How could I be that oblivious? And arrogant? To think someone could like me. Right. Me. The local freak. Imagine if people thought I was trans, too. It would be even worse.

I had my notebook out, too. I drew a fancy sword and started detailing it with an ornate hilt and even embedded gems. This wasn't a practical sword, but in my head it could cut a person in half, anyway.

"How's it going, Nic?" the teacher asked, his fingertips resting on my table while he stood there looking down at me and my drawing.

"Fine." I sounded so flat, almost dead.

"What topic are you working on?"

"I don't know." I'd forgotten the options already.

"You need to come up with something. You shouldn't be wasting this time."

"Why does it matter?" I started sketching out a trebuchet.

"If you don't do it now, you'll have to do it on your own time."

"Maybe I won't do it at all. I don't see how it makes a difference one way or another." I began working on the first wheel.

He sat down in the chair next to me. "Is something wrong?"

"Ha. No, everything's great. Grand. Awesome."

He looked at me with that condescending concern some teachers manage. Like, they're worried, but they think our problems aren't real problems, so we should just get over them.

Honestly, I thought they were more worried about breeding a school shooter than about how I felt. But I would never do anything that horrible to other people, even if half the adults around me might imagine I could.

"Do you have friends you can talk to?"

I chuckled bitterly, bile forming in the back of my throat. "Not really."

"Listen, I don't want to tell you how to live your life, but you should consider changing the way you present yourself. Being unique is fine, but people aren't always sure what to make of people who step too far out of the norm. You might be happier if you make some changes."

I stared at him, my ears ringing. "So, what you're telling me is that, if I conform, I'll suddenly be happy, and everyone will love me. Mm-hmm, sure."

He sighed. "Nic, get to work on your project."

"Okay." I detailed the throwing arm part of the trebuchet.

He walked away, and I wondered if I would really not do the project.

Chapter 32

I waited for math to start, with only about half the class there. I thought about how at least not everyone knew about the whole Sam and Zach thing. Or at least, if they did, they didn't know about my involvement. The humiliation of everyone knowing I'd been foolishly pining after him for months—a year?—would be unbearable.

Idiot.

I looked up at the sound of people moving close and accidentally made eye contact with Carlos, who looked away. Kyle's face slipped into a smile right behind him, and I stared at my desk, burning with humiliation again.

Yes, it would be worse if anyone knew I liked Zach. Only two other people knew about Carlos, and that was bad enough.

I mean, if Sam had known how I felt about Zach, I guess it's possible she wouldn't have said yes when he asked her out, and I could hardly be mad at her for it since she didn't know. I held no claim on him.

But I was so glad Zach didn't know. God, that would be so awful.

"Put your books and notes away," Mr. Martinez said.

Oh, shit. I'd again forgotten about the test. I'd studied a little last night, but I'd been so fixated on working up the courage to ask Zach to hang out today that I hadn't spent very much time on it.

And then today, I'd spent my lunch hour in the bathroom and then concentrating on not crying or puking in the library.

I put everything under my desk except for my pencil and eraser. Hopefully I could do what was needed.

Mr. Martinez passed out the sheet, and I looked it over. It didn't look too bad. I should be able to do everything okay.

I started off with the section on irrational numbers. These were all easy ones—no, of course the square root of two was not a rational number, but four was.

You know what else wasn't rational? Me. It was insane to have thought Zach could like me.

I set my pencil down and closed my eyes to focus on keeping calm and breathing evenly and quietly, because I could feel excessive emotion coming on.

In the library, Sam had seemed so happy. Had she liked him all along, too?

Okay, maybe if I concentrated on the test I'd feel better. I opened my eyes and looked at it again. Just polynomial arithmetic from here on out. This wasn't hard, just time-consuming, because you had to show your work in case you messed something up. I'd had Mr. Martinez last year for geometry, too, and knew he was good about partial credit.

I worked the first one, getting halfway through before thinking of what Sam and Zach would get up to on their date. Would he kiss her?

Argh. Of course he would. When?

I gritted my teeth and muddled through the rest of the question. Then I got going a little and whipped through the rest. I looked at the clock and there were still fifteen minutes left, so I took the test up to Mr. Martinez and sat back down, left to my own horrible thoughts.

Being in my head sucked.

Carlos and Kyle took their tests up, and I avoided looking in their direction. Finally class ended and we filed out.

I headed to my locker to grab my backpack and then headed toward the bus. When I pushed the outside door open, I almost ran smack into this older boy who'd been about to open it himself.

"Whoa there, man," he said. Then his eyes narrowed as he studied me for a moment while I tried to get around him. "Wait, are you a girl?" he asked.

A couple other boys who'd been watching this whole exchange laughed, and I blushed and squeezed past him and out toward the bus.

Why did I always have to blush? Why couldn't I just be like, "Fuck you," and carry on?

I hated being me.

Chapter 33

Monday night was the worst. I went straight to my room when I got home, and out of habit sat down at the keyboard, which I realized I could never look at again. I crammed it into the back of my closet behind some boxes.

How could Sam do this to me?

It didn't matter that I hadn't told her—she should have known. And why had she believed me today, anyway? We were best friends, after all.

I tried to do some figurine painting but faced the same problem. Everything reminded me too much of Sam.

I also had to avoid social media, because what if Sam posted stuff about Zach on there? It would kill me.

I didn't know why she hadn't texted me yet. I figured she'd want to text or even talk.

Was she busy texting with Zach.

I went to pee at one point and accidentally looked in the mirror.

I looked seriously bad. I mean, I was my normal ugly, but then I was also extra pale, and my eyes were swollen as if my face knew I was going to cry.

Which is exactly what happened when I got back to my room. I couldn't get back out of bed.

Eventually, Izzy knocked on my door for dinner, and I realized Sam hadn't got in touch with me yet, which seemed weird. Izzy left me, and I went into the bathroom again. My eyes were red and swollen. Great.

If I didn't go down, there'd be questions, though. So I headed down. I could hear Izzy talking about something that had happened at school. Some kid broke his arm at recess, it sounded like. She seemed excited about this.

There was a casserole on the table that Mom had made and Dad had heated up. Dad wasn't much of a cook, but he could operate the oven.

Izzy was still going on about the kid, who'd apparently cried. Her fork was waving in the air. She talked with her hands like I did. As I pulled the chair out next to her, she looked over.

"What's wrong?" she asked.

I stared at the casserole and sat. "Nothing."

"Why were you crying?" Izzy asked.

"I wasn't." I served myself a piece—it looked like some hamburger and potato thing, with cheddar cheese.

Izzy stood up and hugged me, which made me feel both better and worse. I was about to cry again so I muttered, "Enough. Thanks."

I looked over at Dad, who was focused on his plate, probably glad to avoid a conversation about emotions. Out of the corner of my eye, I could see Caleb smirking, though he said nothing.

I seemed to have killed the mood because everyone was quiet.

So I ate and disappeared upstairs, where I couldn't stop myself from crying the rest of the night. It's how I fell asleep. Full of dread for the next day.

Chapter 34

Tuesday morning I somehow dragged myself out of bed, all crusty eyes and raw cheeks. I was tempted to try to stay home, but I didn't want to draw parental scrutiny upon myself. So I powered through getting ready, then through the morning classes, and headed to lunch.

I went through the line and almost got a hamburger, but it reminded me too much of Sam, so I got a piece of pizza.

I had decided would eat at a table for once, but then Sam saw me before I found one.

"Let's go to the stairwell," she said, clearly wanting to talk, judging from her excited tone.

What could I do? We went to the stairwell.

We sat in our regular spots, and I started eating my pizza while staring at the floor, wishing I could sink into it.

"We saw *Super Z* last night," she said.

My heart hurt. "Oh yeah? I hadn't realized it was out yet." I'd read the book but didn't pay a lot of attention to movies.

"Yeah, it was good. But Nic, he held my hand!"

"Yeah? Cool." Torture. I dropped the pizza onto the plate.

The door opened, and I looked over and saw—to my horror—Zach.

Both their faces lit up with glowing eyes, and he said, "Hey," while staring right at her. I wasn't even there.

But then he looked over and said, "Hi, Nic. How are you?"

"Fine," I muttered while he sat on Sam's other side.

They stared at each other some more. Honestly, I'd never seen two people mooning over each other before, but that's what this was.

Then he laced his fingers through hers.

I looked down at my ugly fingers and wiped at a grease spot with my napkin.

Sam said, "I was just telling Nic about *Super Z*."

He asked, "Are you going to see it?"

"I don't know." No, not a chance because it will remind me of you two. "The book was probably enough. Was it true to the book?"

"Mmm, not really," Sam said. "They changed a lot."

"I never read it," Zach added.

They continued talking about it, and I tuned them out, not able to unsee the way Zach's thumb moved back and forth on Sam's hand.

It felt like there were a hundred knives trying to escape from my stomach. I couldn't take it anymore. I stood up and announced, "I've got to go."

They both looked up, surprised. I guessed they'd forgotten I was there.

"Okay, see you later," Sam said. She sounded like her normal self.

"Bye," Zach said as I pushed the door open.

Once away from them, I could breathe a little better, but I was still feeling like I might die. Just fall over from a broken heart.

Chapter 35

Wednesday, I managed to avoid Sam and Zach.

I felt bad about it and also missed her, but it was necessary for my sanity.

On my way to art class, I saw Alyssa of the makeover across the hall in the crush of kids. She saw me, and we made eye contact, but she didn't say anything.

Like I should have been surprised.

Once I got to class and sat down, Mia smiled at me.

Maybe she could replace Sam as my best friend. We had at least one thing in common.

Then she looked at me, and I realized I was staring and quickly averted my eyes while my cheeks warmed.

Now she probably thought I was a freak.

I went over to the cubbies where we kept our stuff and grabbed the colored pencil drawing I was working on.

It was a desert landscape I was doing based on a full-page photo from a magazine. There were some small scraggly bushes in the shot, but mostly it was dunes with the sand gradations to recreate. I could relate to it, with the apparent simplicity of the scene masking all sorts of other stuff going on underneath. The drawing was challenging but I'd been enjoying it. At least until Monday.

Still, I was sure I'd be able to enter this in the contest. I was planning to do a charcoal drawing eventually, but I needed to pick a subject. They were usually people or objects. Maybe I could do a stylized dragon. I could sketch one out in pencil first and then work it in charcoal. That could be cool.

I wondered what Mia was going to enter since we were allowed to bring stuff we worked on outside of class. I didn't know what she got up to at home. She spent most of her class time in pottery, probably because there was free use of a kiln. And free supplies, too.

Would Sam enter something?

Just thinking of her made me ache again. How was I going to survive this?

Besides, she wouldn't even be here. I don't know how I could forget that.

"Are you okay?" Mia broke into my reverie.

I stared at her a second, trying to reorient myself. "I'm fine."

"You look a little gray."

"Not having the best week." Once again, I'd misinterpreted a boy's behavior. And this time the reminders weren't limited to two classes a day.

"Maybe working on your drawing will help. It's coming along nicely." She smiled again.

Okay, maybe she didn't think I was a total freak.

I started back on the drawing, thinking about the dragons languishing at home. I should work on that again. Anything to keep my mind occupied.

I'd hoped to finish the landscape drawing this week, but it wasn't going to happen because I couldn't do anything. I just stared at it, picturing Zach holding Sam's hand. Then I had to deal with two of my favorite people in the world in math class before I could finally go home.

I sat down at the dining room table for the first time in a while and looked at the drawing. There was some dust on it that I had to brush off. I should have covered it. But it seemed okay. No harm done. Thank God.

I took stock. The only piece that was completely done was that little shrub. The next one I did would be on fire, right next to it. I started filling it in, but nothing I did was any good, and I had to erase several times.

My phone dinged. I checked it and saw a text from Sam. My hand gripped the case, and I dropped it on the table.

I stormed over to the cabinet and yanked a trash bag out of it to lay it over the picture. I set the pencils and other tools on top of it to hold it in place.

There, that was better. Now I could go upstairs and ignore Sam's texts while lying on my bed feeling horrible.

Chapter 36

Somehow, against everything I wanted, I'd been convinced to go to another party Saturday night with Sam and Zach. And of course Evan. A guilt trip combined with no energy to fight back. I didn't expect anything good to happen. I just wanted to get through it.

Sam now sat in the front with Zach, so it was Evan and me in the back. We got in at the same time when he switched with Sam and in the process of leaning over to fasten our seatbelts, we bumped heads. He jerked back and glared, like I'd somehow ruined his life. I knew he was thinking how horrible it was to be touched by such an ugly girl. He probably was all offended because he assumed I must like him, which I definitely didn't, but I knew that's what he thought. Evan had himself plastered to his door. There'd be no double-dating here, for sure.

I was glad I was sitting behind Zach this time, because I couldn't look at him in the mirror and miss the fact of him looking back. Of course, now I was staring at the back of his head, instead.

At least I could do that without anyone knowing.

Sam and Zach chattered away in the front about I don't even know what, because I was trying not to listen.

When Zach parked the car, I felt none of the excitement or even nerves I'd felt only eight days earlier, when everything seemed poised for greatness. I was numb. Even my feet felt dead. We trekked down the sidewalk, Sam and Zach holding hands and Evan and me single file behind them.

My heart started speeding up as we neared the house. The nerves were back. I suspected tonight would be a repeat of last week, where I'd been hiding out the whole time. I hoped it wouldn't be worse than that.

We came into hearing range of the music, making me even shakier. But then we got to the door and went inside.

Evan dove into the crowd, unable to get away from me fast enough.

"You guys want beers?" Zach asked.

Maybe if I had one, things would go better. Just one. So I nodded.

"Yeah," Sam said. "Just one, though. Nic and I can share."

"Um, actually, I think I'm going to try to mingle. I'll take my own." I shuffled my feet.

Sam looked at me like I'd gone crazy and Zach took off.

"What? I'm supposed to be trying, right?"

"Yeah. I'm just surprised. So how've you been this week? It feels like I've hardly talked to you."

By design. I'd wondered if she'd notice. "Mm, yeah, I guess I've been keeping myself busy. I started on the dragon drawing again." Technically true, even if I'd made no progress.

"Oh, that's cool. It's going to look so awesome when you're done."

"I hope I don't mess it up. Sometimes I wonder if it's a good idea to leave it out, too. With Izzy and Caleb and their friends coming and going."

"I'm sure it's fine. Izzy's into art and Caleb's not *that* much of a jerk."

That was true. Izzy loved it, and at one point, Caleb and I had even been close. When we were both little. We were only a year apart, after all.

But then he turned into a total guy, who I, of course, couldn't understand.

Zach returned with the beers, and I took one and took a quick gulp. Gross, but, liquid courage. And I needed some of that. Plus some distraction from reality.

Zach took off and Sam said, "Come on, let's go."

"I'll go try to mingle," I said. How the hell was I going to do this?

She narrowed her eyes for a second, then followed Zach.

I wondered if she had forgotten about OSIN.

I took another sip and failed to suppress a grimace. There were a couple of couches in the living room covered with people and of course loads of people standing around, talking and laughing and having a good time.

What would it be like to enjoy socializing? I could deal with being around people, but if there wasn't some purpose beyond socializing—like we were there to discuss the art club or volunteering or whatever—it was painful. It felt like there was a wall between me and everyone else that I couldn't get past. Socializing for the sake of socializing was a nightmare.

And that's what parties were. What had I been thinking, coming to this?

I was still standing in the foyer, so I had to move when the door opened. A couple boys came in. One was—oh, wonderful—Carlos, whose shocked face when he saw me gave him away before he started looking anywhere but at me. But the other was a guy I'd never seen before. He was in these holey black shorts and green flip-flops, with a wrinkled purple t-shirt completing the ensemble. He had black hair but pale skin.

That's the kind of guy I should like, if I was ever going to let myself do that again. I should have some sense of leagues, and who else was in mine. Even though Zach's a little on the chubby side, he was still really good-looking. I never had a chance. But this guy clearly didn't care about appearances. He wouldn't expect a girl to be all made up perfectly.

My brain shifted while I watched them round the corner into the kitchen. I came to my senses.

The guy hadn't looked at me, so he couldn't have known what I'd been thinking, thank God. It was idiotic. He'd never be interested. No one would.

I finally moved out of the foyer so I was standing barely inside the dining room. There were people standing around the table in there, but it wasn't as crowded as the living room and they seemed to be happy to ignore me.

I had drunk a few more sips when I noticed three kids —a boy and two girls—in the corner of the room looking at me. I looked away, but now I was tuned into their conversation.

"Isn't that the girl who let her friends do a makeover and then didn't learn from it?"

God, Facebook again. My unpainted face heated.

"Yeah. Nic." They were all still looking at me.

The guy snorted. "Of course she goes by a guy's name."

"Well, her real name is Nicole."

Did they think I couldn't hear, or did they not care?

I was frozen in place at that point. Because if I walked away, they'd know they'd gotten to me. But I was starting to feel panicky, because I wanted to get out of there.

Instead I took a shaky sip, paying more attention to the cold of the beer than the foul taste, and looked at the window. All I could see was the white wooden blinds.

What was the big deal, anyway? Why was it such a crime to be female and not made up? My hands started shaking. Why were girls expected to perform all this body modification just to be considered minimally acceptable?

My aversion to wearing makeup was so strong. But other girls and women didn't seem to have such issues. Even if they complained about it sometimes, they didn't seem to truly mind. Could it be that I really was a boy in the wrong body?

It didn't feel quite right, though. When I looked at boys, I didn't feel any kinship. I felt either dislike—most boys were total shits—or some kind of attraction. So what was it? I simply wished it was possible simply to have no gender, because that sounded like a relief.

The trio cleared out, and I was left more or less in peace.

People came and went through the dining room while I nursed my beer. After I'd had about two-thirds of it, my heart was no longer beating so fast. I hadn't been wondering who else was talking about me. Instead, I'd just been peacefully drinking my beer, not fretting. I even felt like I was floating a little.

I decided to go in search of Sam. Where had she got to? I missed her, especially when I thought about her leaving.

I went out the back of the dining room, ending up in the den. Maybe the other one was the living room. If those were different things. I'd never been sure. It was kind of dark in there, with only one floor lamp to light the whole room. Kids seemed to be dancing to the music, which I saw must be coming from the fancy entertainment center built into the wall. I started a circuit around the room, looking for Sam.

I had to squeeze past people, but I made myself go on, eventually making it around. She wasn't in here.

I moved into the living room, straining my eyes with the transition to bright light. I did a circle around this room, too. I nearly ran into Evan, who sneered, "Watch where you're going." I didn't even care. I kept going, but still no Sam.

So I headed back into the kitchen. There were a few kids in there, and I decided to dump what remained of my warm beer into the sink.

"What'd you do that for?" this junior boy exclaimed.

"It was warm," I said.

"Coulda gave it to me."

I moved out of there and back into the living room because I'd seen an open sliding door. Maybe there were more people out there. I wormed my way through the crowd and out the door.

I was on a big redwood deck. There was lighting all around, though it wasn't particularly bright. Occupied lounge chairs ringed the deck.

It was kind of a nice night. It was the time of year it could still be hot during the day, but cooled off at night. I stood for a moment, experiencing it. It smelled crisp, and I knew fall was coming. My birthday, too.

Then I looked over to the right at one of the chairs and spotted Sam's butt. It took me a moment to make sense of the scene. She was basically lying on top of Zach, and they were making out.

I stumbled back from the shock. How had I forgotten about Zach? About Sam and Zach.

The burning started behind my eyes, and I ran in the other direction, finding some steps down into the yard. But as I ran off them, I slammed into someone in a purple shirt.

I had to grab the handrail to keep from losing it, and I looked up at Carlos's friend. "Whoa there," he said.

I just sort of sobbed and continued past him. I made it around the side of the house, to where the trash bins were. Nobody else was there because it stank. So I was able to regroup a little.

I wiped my eyes. God, it was humiliating when people saw me cry. It used to happen so much, though I'd gotten better at controlling it. All through elementary school, I was a crier, and I despised it. All the teachers acted like I chose to do it, when I would have done anything to avoid it.

Sort of like now.

How was I going to get through this night? How was I going to get through this life—alone?

Chapter 37

In art class Monday, Ms. Tolliver gave us a new assignment, a self-portrait, in colored pencil or pastels. "I have mirrors if any of you don't want to or can't work off a smartphone photo."

"Which media are you doing?" Mia asked.

"Pencil," I said. "I still haven't gotten used to pastels."

"Me neither, but I'm going to give them a shot. I like how they look."

"I bet you can do it. They can definitely look more dramatic than pencil, but I'm not shooting for a masterpiece here."

Mia smiled and I went over to get the pencils out of my cubby.

I took a picture with my phone, and sketched a light outline of my face with a pale peach color I'd be using as the base for my skin.

I tried to look at it as an arbitrary object, because this was torture. Having to look at myself. I couldn't stop the refrain in my head: ugly, ugly, ugly …

It was infuriating. Why couldn't I think about bunnies or something?

That whole "Look in the mirror and tell yourself you're great!" thing was so foreign to me. I could never do it. It was a lie, and I knew it.

But still, it was annoying to have to work on a project that involved constantly thinking about my appearance. No chance I'd be entering this in the contest. My face hanging on a wall? No way.

I looked at the photo. Was this a girl's face? How could you tell if someone was male or female without makeup or signs of facial hair as a clue?

Whatever.

I inspected the photo with my artist's eye. The light wasn't very good in it so I would have to improvise a bit.

My ears looked funny. In this particular case, I don't mean ugly, just that ears in general look funny when you study them. They were going to be tricky to draw. I outlined them anyway to get the general shape, which seemed okay.

Just as I started outlining my nose, a couple boys brushed past me. One of them said, "It's too bad there's going to be a permanent record of her ugly face now."

The other one laughed and of course I blushed.

Mia looked over at them and said, "Shut up, Brian. Don't be such a jerk."

"What, I only speak the truth." They went back to the other side of the room after getting stuff out of the supply area.

Mia looked at me and rolled her eyes. "Just ignore them."

I shrugged but the knot in my throat loosened. Brian was one of the assholes who'd grabbed my boobs in middle school. But as he'd said, that was the cold, hard reality. I mean, it would be nice if people didn't feel the need to be so fucking honest all the time, but I couldn't exactly refute it.

I worked on sketching my neck, which was bigger than it should have been. At least I'd looked up when I took the picture so I didn't have any discernible double chin. Still, ugly.

Chapter 38

I got home after school Monday and started working on the dragon drawing, which felt good and got my mind off Sam and Zach.

I'd hardly made any progress when the door to the garage opened, and I heard Izzy's voice.

"I told you, it looks great, honey," Mom said.

When I saw Izzy, I couldn't hide the surprise on my face. She'd gotten a major haircut.

"See! Even Nic hates it!" she said.

"Nic doesn't hate it," Mom said, looking pointedly at me.

"No, it's cute, Izzy." It was really short. I was thinking they called that style a bob.

"Isabella," she said with a giant frown on her face.

"What inspired this?" I asked.

Izzy crossed her arms and Mom said, "A boy cut her hair at school."

"What?" That made no sense at all.

She mouthed, *Jake*, which made me narrow my eyes. That jerk.

"What actually happened?"

Mom shook her head and said, "Someone put gum in her hair and then he offered to help get it out, and instead just cut her hair."

"Mom, I want to tell Nic something."

"Okay, that's my cue," Mom said. She dropped her purse on the kitchen counter and started rummaging through the pantry.

"You don't have to work tonight?" I asked.

"Nope. I'm going to make a real dinner."

"Cool."

"Nic!" Izzy said, apparently impatient for me to listen to her.

I turned to look at her. Her eyes were wide, but they looked a little red and puffy, like she'd been crying earlier.

"Your hair looks cute, you know."

"I hate it. But guess what!"

"What?"

"I told Jake he could stuff it."

I laughed. "Stuff it?"

"Yeah, I told him to get lost, that we were done. And I said it in front of his friends, and he was so embarrassed."

"That's awesome. What a jerk. Why did he put gum in your hair?"

"Why do boys do anything?" she asked.

"Very astute, Iz. I'm proud of you. Did you tell Mom?"

"No, just you. There's no point now, it's so over."

"I'm glad. He was no good for you."

"I know. If only I'd listened to you earlier." She sighed. "Whatever happened to the boy who called you?"

Oh God, gut punch. After a long moment, I managed to say, "He was no good for me, either."

Or more the other way around. I was no good for anyone.

Chapter 39

In math class, Carlos and Kyle were goofing around with each other like the day I'd thought Carlos had been flirting with me.

God, what an idiot I was. Over and over.

But then it pissed me off. Who were they to judge? Especially Kyle, who was fatter than me and had terrible acne. If I was ugly, he was ugly, too.

Why were people so obsessed with how girls looked? Hardly anybody really knew me at all because it was all about appearances. Appearances, appearances. Everything was so fake.

Out of nowhere, I had the coolest idea for the self-portrait. A hand pulling my face off ... to reveal something else. What could it be?

The idea made me feel better, as it would be really original. It might be worth entering it in the contest because it would stand out.

After class, I had started toward the art building to pick the drawing up when I saw Sam and Zach. Sam stopped me.

"I've got to get to the art building and make it back to the bus," I said, trying to take off again.

"I can give you a ride home," Zach said. "We're going that direction."

I didn't want that, but how could I say no? "Okay. I just need to get something over there first. I'll find you in the parking lot."

When I got to the art classroom, Ms. Tolliver caught me and we had to chat for a minute before I could leave with my drawing and pencils. Eventually I got away and strolled along the gravel driveway toward the main build-ing. I didn't feel like hurrying—I didn't want to see them again, especially together.

I cut through the building to get to the student parking lot on the other side and emerged back into the sun. I couldn't see much but I meandered over to where Zach usually parked. My eyes adjusted, and I glanced down the last row and saw Sam leaning against the side of his car, Zach straddling her. They were, of course, kissing.

I desperately wanted to leave, but the buses were gone by now. If I disappeared, I'd have to wait until my dad could get me, and Sam would wonder what my problem was.

I was just going to have to figure out how to deal with this.

The likelihood of that decreased as I walked toward the happy couple. They didn't notice me even after I stood in front of the car for a moment, looking back toward the school. I glanced back and his hand was in her hair. I cleared my throat.

Nothing.

God, I wanted to die.

What was the protocol here?

I leaned on the front of the car.

Apparently they felt the car move, because I heard Sam say, "Hey."

She came around the front, still smiling, and we all got in.

I rode all the way home with my arms crossed, trying to make myself smaller and more invisible. I was invisible to Zach, who didn't see who I really was at all. He was only aware of the ugly facade. He was nice to me because of Sam. He'd probably always liked her.

I planned out my self-portrait modification in greater detail and finally had a solid idea of what would go behind my real face.

As soon as I was at my desk, I made room for the drawing and laid it out.

I sketched out a hand and fingers gripping the left side of the chin and then added another face behind and to the upper right of the original face. This way it was like the hand was pulling a mask away from the real face, the one in the back. I needed to finish the normal face first, so I worked on detailing that.

When Izzy came to get me for dinner, I didn't even go down because I couldn't stop drawing. She had to come in to see what I was doing before going down herself. After a couple hours, I had the face done, so I worked on the hand.

Now to the fun part. For the real face, I first gave it red eyes and then used black and purple to make the skin odd looking. I added in very dark purple stripes. It looked like a weird tiger face.

Actually, what it looked like was a demon's face.

I wasn't sure how that had happened. It's not like I was saying I was a demon inside, but the point was, nobody knew, did they? Nobody knew shit about me.

They just knew what I looked like, which meant nothing. It says nothing about what's inside me.

Chapter 40

Wednesday before Key Club, we decided—or Sam and Zach decided—we'd stop by a sandwich shop for dinner first. Sam and Zach were ahead of me and as soon the sandwich maker had their orders moving down the line, he turned to me and said, "What can I get you, sir?"

Again with the heat in my cheeks.

And Evan snorted behind me, making no effort to control the laugh that came afterward.

Sam and Zach must have heard, but nobody said anything, so I ordered my six-inch Italian like always. Toasted on flatbread.

I don't know if the sandwich guy still thought I was a boy by the time he put it in the oven, and it wasn't like he was dripping with testosterone or anything, himself. The girl who put all the toppings on and rang us all up didn't call me sir, so that was something.

Sam picked a table, and I followed her, getting stuck with Evan because Zach, of course, had to sit next to her. I thought Evan would fall off the end of the bench, he scooted so far over. We unwrapped our sandwiches.

"Are either of you doing the food drive?" Zach asked before taking a bite of his sandwich.

Evan looked at me.

I nodded. "I was planning on it."

"Nope," Evan said.

It was awkward enough that I think even Sam and Zach noticed, so we ate in silence after that.

But once we were done, Sam said, "Nic's working on this really cool drawing of a couple dragons."

"Yeah?" Zach asked, his arm thrown across her shoulders. "What's it like?"

"It's a fight scene. They're fighting at the top of a mountain."

"Oh, that sounds cool. Do you have a picture?"

I shook my head. "It's not far enough along yet. I just started it."

"We should probably go," Evan interjected.

Just like before, all the way over there, Evan was pushed up against his door like I had the plague.

This was how it would be from here on out.

At least until Sam left.

Would Zach even continue driving me after that point? I might not need him to, since I would have access to my dad's minivan. I could probably borrow it Wednesday nights. But then, would I even want to continue with Key Club with Sam gone? It wasn't like I'd made a bunch of friends there. Nobody would miss me if I quit.

Then an evil thought occurred to me: would things change after Sam left? Could Zach change his mind about me?

I couldn't help but get a little flutter of hope in my belly.

But that was idiotic. He would never like me. He obviously never had. I had to get that insane set of grossly misinterpreted memories out of my head.

Chapter 41

I survived the rest of the week, even though I didn't think I would. Friday night I parked myself in front of my dragon drawing and really went at it. I got the first burning shrub done but not the smoke since that would be going in front of the back dragon, and I'd need to account for the impact that would have on its appearance.

I looked up when my dad walked past to go sit in his favorite chair in the den and read his newspaper and drink his Milwaukee's Best beer.

I got back to work on the second shrub.

Caleb came downstairs, in his jean shorts and t-shirt as always. He went into the kitchen and drank some orange juice, then he yelled so Dad could hear, "I'm going out."

Dad shook the paper and folded it. "Be home by eleven," he yelled back.

"Eleven? What the hell, Dad. The movie I'm going to runs later than that. I'll come back after it."

"Caleb, come here." Dad sounded kind of irked.

Caleb sighed loudly, but not so loud that Dad could

hear, and went out to the den. He flicked the back of my chair as he passed.

Such a dick.

"I'm here," he said. "What."

"Caleb, what is with your attitude lately?"

"I don't have an attitude," he scoffed.

As if. "Lately" meant the last two years. It was hard to remember what he was like before that—when he was still my nice little brother.

"Caleb. You're late for curfew half the time and have been skipping your chores. If you don't get yourself back on track, you're going to end up grounded. Now, your curfew's eleven tonight."

"Dad, come on. The movie ends at 11:10. Can I please stay out until 11:30?"

"No."

Whoa, go Dad.

"I can't believe this."

"Do your chores and come home on time, and maybe next week you can stay out later. You should try to be more like your sister. She has fewer restrictions because she plays by the rules."

Oh, thanks, Dad. God. Parents had no idea about the social dynamics of teenagers.

Caleb snorted. "I'm not going to be anything like her. I want to have actual friends."

Dad opened the paper back up and started reading.

I was used to Caleb's betrayal by now, but it still worried me. Was it going to be repeated with Izzy?

Caleb turned and stormed out the side door. He said something after opening it, and then suddenly Logan's dad was standing in the kitchen looking at me. He set a twelve-pack of beer on the counter.

"Hi, Nic," he said. "How's it going?"

"Fine."

"What are you working on?" He came over and stood next to me to inspect the drawing, ruffling my hair. "Is that a dragon fight?"

"Yeah." I hated that he thought he could just touch me. All because I was a girl.

"Why don't you draw things like flowers and cats? Why always so gruesome?"

This gave me that sinking feeling. How I'd like to simply fade away to nothing. Here was another adult who thought I was living my life wrong. I wasn't girly enough for anyone. "Because I don't like flowers, and I do like fantasy. Dragons are cool."

"Okay, if you say so." He looked up and headed into the den. "Mark!"

Dad finally noticed him. "Pete, hi. How's it going?"

Pete went out there and sat in Mom's chair, on the other side of the end table from Dad.

God, imagine what everyone would think if I announced I was really a boy.

Not that I would. That wasn't it.

Anyway, screw that guy. This drawing was going to win me the contest. I started filling in the background dragon's chest while they chatted about whatever. Sports and shit.

Then Pete brought up the vacation the group was planning over Christmas break.

Please say no, Dad.

Dad said, "We can't do it right now."

Thank God.

"Look, if it's money, I can spot you. We'd love for you guys to be there."

After some back and forth, Dad nodded thoughtfully. "I'll have a chat with Nina."

"Great." Pete stood. "I've got to get going."

"Okay. We'll see you next week."

"Yes. I'll kick your ass again." Pete laughed. Dad was terrible at poker.

Pete breezed through the dining room, squeezing my shoulder on his way out.

Of course he did. Jackass.

Chapter 42

"Don't forget to signal," Dad said Saturday evening.

"We're in a parking lot." Signaling in our minivan involved moving the signal lever up and down because the turn signal didn't blink anymore, and Dad hadn't gotten around to getting it fixed.

"You're practicing. You wouldn't normally drive up and down parking rows."

I laughed. "You obviously have never been Christmas shopping at the mall."

"Okay, smarty-pants," Dad said through a chuckle before getting all serious. "Listen, Nic, Christmas isn't going to be like it usually is this year."

I tried to slow the minivan down and hit the brake too hard, so we jerked to a stop. "Sorry." I looked over at him. "Are we going to Texas with the group?"

"I don't know yet. I'm not going, either way."

"That's okay about Christmas, though. We don't expect to be spoiled."

He patted me on the shoulder. "You're a good kid, Nic.

Now, for some more practice, I want you to make a three-point turn between the two parking spaces under those two street lights."

I executed the turn in the minivan perfectly—even braking softly—and we went on to practice more boring driving up and down the rows of the lot around the elementary school.

Dad made me park a few more times in arbitrary empty spots.

I was so bored, I asked if we could go over to the testing center to practice parallel parking again.

We'd used its parallel parking test site before. There weren't a lot of real parallel parking opportunities in Emerson. Plus, I didn't think he would have trusted me to try in this thing. You could hardly see out the back.

"Tomorrow, in the daylight. For now, let's go pick your mom up."

"Is she ready?"

"She just texted that she's finishing up."

I put the car in park and started to get out when Dad said, "Why don't you drive? Get some more practice on the road."

"Really?" I was apprehensive about it. I mean, that was dumb, because when I was driving for real it would obviously be on the roads.

"Yes, really. You need to get used to it, especially in a bigger car."

Mom had a smaller one, but it was a standard, and I hadn't learned it yet, so the minivan would be my only option until I did.

I made my way across the parking lot to the exit and pulled onto the street. I headed east, which meant I had to deal with a stoplight at the top of this ridiculous hill. I would never, ever come this way in Mom's car even after I learned how to drive it. It even made her nervous.

Finally, I pulled into the City Flame parking lot. I found a spot with no cars next to it and pulled in.

Dad laughed. "Scared of the other cars?"

"Well, this is a van."

"It's not that big. Try parking between two cars. That spot over there." He pointed to one.

"Fine." I did as he said, feeling good. I could do this driving thing. And then we sat.

And we sat. And sat some more. It was good that we were both comfortable with silence, because I didn't have anything to say at the moment.

"Did you text her?" I asked.

"Yeah, she's not answering. Go inside and see what she's up to?"

"Fine." I didn't want to, because what if someone I knew was in there? She'd been a stay-at-home mom before starting there and I wished she'd picked something less embarrassing. Why couldn't she work in an office? My dad was a college-educated CPA, after all. All their friends had office jobs.

But I got out and headed across the dark parking lot and pulled open the wooden door.

I looked at the host station but she wasn't there. Just this tall, skinny kid barely older than me.

He looked confused for a second and then said, "Can I help you?"

I was already looking past him at the bar, but she wasn't there, either. I figured she'd be rolling silverware somewhere.

I glanced back at him and he was staring at me, still trying to figure out what I was doing there. "Is Nina around?" I asked.

His shoulders relaxed, and he said, "Sure, I can get her."

I sat down on the green bench and waited.

The door opened again and there was shuffling as a bunch of people came in.

"Look who it is," a male voice said.

I saw Mike, one of the kids who'd tormented me since second grade. A boob-grabber.

Great.

"Did your girlfriend stand you up?" he asked, making all the others snicker.

I noticed the host was back at his station, and he had menus in his hand for the group. As soon as they were gone, my mom was standing on the other side of them.

She was looking at me quizzically. "Hi, honey."

"Can we go?" I said and abruptly stood up. I pushed the door open and sort of stormed out.

As soon as we were on the sidewalk, she grabbed my arm and asked, "What did he mean? Do you have a girlfriend?"

"What? No!"

"Are you sure? You know Dad and I would love you no matter what."

"Mom, I'm not gay! Jesus. He was being a dick." I started walking to the car.

"It was just such a specific thing to say."

I stopped in the middle of the lot waiting for her to catch up. "Everybody thinks I'm a lesbian because I'm not girly enough. That's all."

"If you're confused, it's okay, too." She tilted her head and smiled at me.

"I'm not confused!" Okay, I was, but I really, really didn't think I was gay. "Can we go?"

"Okay, honey. But you know we love you just the way you are."

"Mom, I'm not five."

She hooked her arm through mine, which was a little weird, and said, "I know that." When we got to the car, Dad was smiling at us. He probably thought we were bonding, but I was too busy being mortified.

Chapter 43

Monday was a long day. I had lunch with Sam and Zach again because I couldn't figure out a way to get out of it. They made out some, though Sam kept pushing Zach off. She mouthed "Sorry" once. I sat against the wall and closed my eyes, fighting the desire to simply go away. I didn't want to exist anymore. It was too hard. I was tired. Everything was hard. Being me was hard, trying to be someone else was hard. Impossible, even.

By the time math rolled around, I just wanted to go to sleep and wake up when I was an adult.

About halfway through class, a woman poked her head in the doorway. I didn't know her name, but she was the school counselor.

She looked down at a clipboard in her hand before calling, "Nicole Summers."

What? I looked around in confusion. Carlos and Kyle were staring at me, a smirk on Kyle's face. What did she want from me?

"Nic," Mr. Martinez said, "go on."

I got up, still confused.

"Grab your stuff," she said.

"What'd you do, Nic?" Kyle muttered under his breath.

"Nothing," I whispered.

But I was wondering the same thing.

The woman gave me that forced smile adults sometimes have around me. Like they don't approve but need to pretend to be nice, anyway.

Had something happened to Dad? Was it Mom?

"Hi, Nicole."

Ugh. I hated my name.

"I'm Mrs. Taylor. I'm the school counselor."

I nodded. Surely she'd say something now if there was a problem with my family. But the woman didn't say anything else on the way to wherever we were going, which was weird. And it had me even more worried. Maybe it was so bad she wanted me sitting down first.

I was starting to sweat a little from the stress by the time we got to her office.

Caleb wasn't in there so I relaxed a little. So, not something with my family.

I followed her into the closet-sized room with a small metal desk. On one corner, there was a large plant of some type that had spilled over the side and was trailing down the desk leg.

"First, I have to ask you—do you have any weapons on you or in your locker?"

"What?" What was she talking about? "Why would I have weapons?"

"I don't know. Do you?"

"No."

She motioned to an uncomfortable-looking wooden chair with frayed orange upholstery. "Have a seat."

I sat, even more unsure about what was going on now.

She sat behind her desk and folded her hands. "Do you know why you're here?" Her voice contained a challenge.

"Uh, no. Is my family okay?"

She furrowed her brow and tilted her head. "They're fine. This is about you, not them."

I nodded, thoroughly confused. What the hell was going on?

She pursed her lips as she pulled something out onto her desk and pushed it toward me. "Do you recognize this? A student was concerned about it."

There sat my self-portrait. A burst of pride went through me, and I admired it for a moment, before it occurred to me that this made no sense. "Why do you have that?"

I reached out to pick it up but she pulled it back.

I thought of the weapon question and things started to come into focus. Still, I said, "I don't understand."

"Nic, we have to take things seriously here."

Heat crept into my face as I realized what was going on. "You think that is a threat?"

"Is it?" She tucked it back in her desk drawer.

"No! Jesus, no. You think what, I'm the next school shooter?" This was horrifying and my stomach twisted. They all hated me.

"Nicole, we have to be very careful in today's world."

"No one is in any danger from me."

"You don't want to hurt other people?"

"No." I shifted in the chair, which was indeed uncomfortable.

"So what does it mean?"

What did the drawing mean? I didn't totally know since I hadn't really thought it through. "It was just an idea I had. People don't always know each other."

"But you're saying you're a monster underneath." She laced her fingers together and rested them on the desk.

"Why are you assuming that it's a monster? It could be a purple superhero."

"Is it?"

I shrugged. "Sure."

"It has red eyes."

"Laser vision."

She blinked a few times. I stared back.

"Okay," she eventually said, "your father is on his way." She went into the other room.

I waited in that stupid chair, feeling like an idiot. Why hadn't I thought more about things? I didn't have to make it a demon-like face, did I? I don't know what else I could have done. A clown face? I had no idea.

Finally Dad got there, his face all worried.

This was humiliating. I didn't even know what the woman had told him, because I hadn't heard the phone call. "I need to get stuff out of my locker," I told him.

"Okay, let's go."

We walked downstairs, and I grabbed my backpack and loaded it up. We headed to the parking lot.

"How do you feel about going out for Italian?" he asked when we got to the minivan.

"Cool." I was afraid he'd ask me to drive, but he didn't.

We were quiet all the way to Olive Garden, and once we were seated and had ordered and they'd delivered our salad and breadsticks, he finally said, "What's going on, Nic?"

I shrugged and dished out salad. "What did they tell you?"

"Not much. You drew something that scared them?"

"God, they're such idiots." *Fucking* idiots. "No. The

drawing meant nothing. It was cool. If they give it back to me, I'll show it to you."

He took a bite of a breadstick and studied me.

"Dad, would you not tell Mom about this? You know she'll freak out and overreact." This was true.

"Are you sure you're okay? You've seemed quieter than normal lately."

I knew this was dipping into some uncomfortable territory for him.

"Is it because Sam's leaving?" he asked.

"Yeah." That would work. "It's just hard. We've been best friends for a while."

"I'm sure it's hard. But you'll find more friends."

Not so far. And we had a whole operation underway to accomplish that. Of course, it couldn't be going worse. Zach, a guy I'd thought could be a friend, even more than a friend, preferred Sam. Things were unraveling.

"Yeah," I said. I wanted the food to arrive so we could focus on that. Still, I was pretty sure I'd convinced him not to tell Mom about the drawing, and this would all blow over. I hoped so, anyway.

Chapter 44

Friday afternoon was typical except that I was unusually tired. I'd had trouble sleeping, but had no idea why. Mom hadn't said anything all week, so I thought things were okay.

It was a long ride home because I just wanted to lie down. Once I got to the house, it didn't even register that my parents' cars were both there until I saw them inside.

What were they doing home?

They sent my brother to his room—Izzy wasn't home yet—and I stared at them.

Mom's face was tense. "Let's go to the den."

I complied and fell on the couch even though neither of them sat down. God, had Dad told Mom? My pulse raced. Was that what this was about? "What are you guys both doing here? What's going on?"

"Look, honey," Mom said. "The school called, and they're very concerned about you in light of the drawing."

"I told everyone it wasn't a threat. What's the problem?" I couldn't keep the irritation out of my voice.

"They're worried that it's a cry for help."

"God, it's so stupid. So, what are you going to do?" I asked. I couldn't believe the school had called them again. I thought I had everything under control. I'd had to see that woman a couple more times, but whatever.

"Honey, we just want you to be happy."

"Ha. Good luck with that." I crossed my arms and wanted to cry. "Did they tell you what the picture is?"

"No, only that it looks like a threat of violence," Mom said.

"Why is it such a crime to be weird, huh?" I asked. "Tell me that."

"You're not weird, Nic!" Mom exclaimed.

I rolled my eyes. This was a conversation we'd had repeatedly. At least Dad was okay with us being weird. He believed in owning it.

"You just march to the beat of a different drum," she continued. "That's all."

"So what's happening, then? You didn't both skip work to tell me I'm not weird."

"No." She threaded her fingers together. "We've made an appointment with a psychiatrist for you next Thursday."

"What?" A shrink?

What was the point? It wasn't like they could change any of the things in my life that sucked. "I don't want to see anyone."

"It's not up to you, honey," Mom said. Dad was still over there looking awkward. Rubbing his beard.

I had another heart-stopping thought. "Can I still take my driver's test on my birthday?"

"Of course," Mom said quietly. "You're not in trouble. We only want to get you the help you need."

This was beyond humiliating. I jumped up. "I'm going to work on my drawing."

Mom nodded. "That's a good idea. Art is good for the mind."

"My mind is fine!" Or was it? I had no idea.

God. What did they really think of me?

Chapter 45

"You're about six feet from the curb," the driving tester said as he shut his door. "Try again."

My hands shook as I pulled forward again and lined the minivan up as well as I could next to the pylons. I had to get this right. It was my freaking birthday, two days before I had to see the shrink.

I glanced over at the guy again. He and I didn't like each other. He had this shaved head and was big, burly, and gruff. He also looked uncomfortable in his brown dress pants.

"Any day," he muttered.

The thing was, parallel parking a bigger car is kind of hard, especially when you're in the car with a judgmental jerk. So I went for it and got half in when I realized I had the angle wrong. I started forward to correct it, but the guy would have none of it.

"That's it. Go on and circle the block."

It was a good sign he was having me continue, right? He probably wasn't going to fail me.

I signaled to turn right out of there, doing the whole

up-and-down thing on the signal.

"Is that what you did when I checked it?!" he practically yelled.

I cowered a little. Dad had told me not to do the signal thing when the tester was in the car because it might draw attention to it. But when the guy had gone around the minivan checking that it was roadworthy, he'd had me turn the signal on, and I'd done it the way we always did so the light would come on and off like it was supposed to.

I glanced over at him, and he was shaking his head in apparent disgust.

"Should I go?" I asked. God, I wished this guy wasn't such a dick and would just tell me what he wanted.

"Yes," he snapped.

I circled the block and approached the testing center. This was it. I'd be getting my license. Or would I? I hated having no idea.

"Go ahead and turn in and park," he said.

I pulled into the spot carefully and we sat there for a second with him writing something down. I squeezed the steering wheel.

"Did I pass?" I whispered.

"I'm giving you a 69," he said gruffly.

Oh no. "Is that passing?"

"You need a 70 to pass."

My heart sank. I hadn't passed. How could I have failed? How could he do that to me?

He opened the door and slid out. "You can take the test again next week, but get that fixed. And practice your parallel parking." Then he shut the door, and I had to fight my burning tear ducts.

He tapped on the window impatiently. "Come on."

Humiliating. I followed him in, and he gave me the

paperwork indicating my failure and made me sign something.

Then I went back out to the waiting area and Dad smiled at me and said, "How'd it go?"

"He failed me!"

"Oh no, what happened?"

I was pissed at Dad. "How could you let me take the test with the signal broken like that?"

"Was that why?" he sputtered.

"Yeah." I didn't see the need to mention that I'd failed the parallel parking twice, too, because I was convinced it was the signal—and me tricking him with it—that pissed the guy off. "He said I could retake it next week, but you need to get it fixed first."

"Nic, I can't get it fixed by next week. It will have to wait until next month."

No! I was supposed to be able to start driving around today. This sucked so hard. We were still standing in the middle of the waiting area in the testing center. One lady smiled at me sympathetically.

"Come on, let's go," he said. "You want to stop for ice cream?"

Like I was some little kid.

"I don't care." I truly didn't.

He put his arm around my shoulders and squeezed, then let go and we headed out into the sun. At least it wasn't hot anymore, being near the end of October.

We stopped at Baskin Robbins, and I got mint chocolate chip in a waffle cone, which did not make me feel better. Dad and I didn't talk on the way home because I was still pissed at him. I finished the ice cream up just as we pulled into the driveway.

Dad reached over and patted me on the shoulder. After dodging Mom and Izzy, I went upstairs. I should have done some work on the dragon drawing, but I didn't feel like it.

Although I tried not to cry, a few tears rolled down my face. I mean, this was something I'd waited a long time for and worked for, and that jerk had intentionally made me one point shy of passing. He'd done that on purpose. It was mean.

My phone dinged with a text from Sam.

—did you pass?—

—no—

—what?—

I explained, and she agreed the tester was a jerk. But then she started going on about Zach and I couldn't take that. I told her I had to go, set the phone down, closed my eyes, and threw my arm over my head. That's the very moment Izzy chose to knock on my door. When she saw me lying there, she just lay down next to me. She was warm and quiet.

That's what I loved about Izzy. She knew when to talk and when to stay quiet. I had no words to give her.

Chapter 46

Thursday, Mom and I waited in the shrink's office after filling out the paperwork about my medical history and how I was feeling right now. The theme seemed to be summed up in one question: Had I felt down, depressed, or hopeless?

This short, bald man with ears that stuck way out came out from a door beside reception and gave us a smile that seemed genuine enough. "Come on back."

I reluctantly got up and headed in that direction.

"You, too, Mom," he said.

"Oh! Okay." She dropped the *Sports Illustrated* she'd been holding for some reason—she hated sports, so it was weird—and followed me.

He stuck his hand out and introduced himself as Dr. Holmes and shook both our hands in turn. I hadn't shaken a lot of hands before, but his felt weak.

First we went to this office with another couch that matched the ones in the waiting area. Mom and I sat next to each other while he sat in a rolling chair close to the couch.

My heart rate was getting up there again, and my hands were shaking. I was afraid I would start sweating. I wanted to leave.

"First, I wanted to talk about what you are hoping to get out of this therapy, and then we will talk about options. Then you'll take a battery of tests, Nicole, while you and I will talk a bit more, Mrs. Summers. I've reviewed the paperwork you filled out."

Mom nodded but I didn't move. The paperwork she'd filled out was also about my feelings and behavior.

Like she knew anything real about my life. She didn't even know about Zach. At least, not that Sam was with him or that I'd liked him.

Dr. Holmes continued, "I want to understand more about your goals. Why have you chosen to come in now?" He was looking directly at me.

"My mom made me," I said drily. "The school freaked out because of a drawing I did, so they said we had to."

Mom looked at me. "I haven't seen it, but it appears to be of herself as a demon."

I rolled my eyes even though I was starting to sweat. "Everyone is totally overreacting to that, and you don't understand it at all, anyway. It's not a demon."

"I'd like to see the drawing," Dr. Holmes said. I noticed that he was wearing brown pants and black shoes, which is one of the fashion no-nos I actually remembered.

"It's at the school," I said. Thank God for that.

"Do you have a picture of it?"

"No." I did, but no way was I showing it to this guy yet. He'd also totally overreact and judge me, too. I got the judgment vibe off him.

He got back to goals and they decided that my goal should be to be happier and to learn how to interact with people better so I could have more friends, since my only friend was moving in two months.

That was all them.

"Does that sound good to you, Nicole?" he asked.

"Doesn't seem like I have much choice."

Then he sent me to this little room that had nothing but a white table and a blue plastic chair. It didn't look as cozy as the couches. Also, what, was I five? It was a kiddie table.

"There are a variety of tests and questionnaires for you to fill out, Nicole."

God, I hated that stupid-ass name. It was so not me.

"The first is timed, so I will give it to you and leave you here. I'll come back after half an hour to give you the next test." He took my phone and pointed out a clock on the wall—a Mickey Mouse clock. Then he shut the door, and I felt a twinge of claustrophobia.

I'd recognize an IQ test anywhere, and that's what it was. I'd taken one in seventh grade, after I'd found out that I'd tested high enough to go into the gifted and talented program when I was in second grade. But my teacher had decided I didn't have the right temperament for it, so they'd left me in the normal track. I had been pissed when I'd found out in seventh grade, and made them test me again mid-year, so I'd gotten into the class for the spring semester.

And I can tell you, some of those people in there weren't that smart, so it still ticked me off.

I worked away at the test. Identifying patterns and so on. Stuff I do every day while trying to figure out how social interactions work. For some reason, the social patterns eluded me, but the others were easy.

Then Dr. Holmes came back and took that one away and gave me some other tests and questionnaires.

"These aren't timed, but I'll be back in half an hour. That will end the session for today."

It took very little time—maybe fifteen minutes. One was another intelligence-type test, but the rest were obvious mental health screening questions. I thought about lying on them, but I didn't.

What would he do if he found out I didn't feel like a real person? Would he say some kind of fluffy crap that would piss me off? If he told me what was most important was to be myself, I might punch him. I was so sick of being fed that lie. Because that's what it was. Nobody appreciated kids being themselves. Not adults, not other kids, nobody.

What about maybe being trans? I didn't get the feeling this guy could help me figure it out. No one could. God. It would have to be me.

Would he ask if I'd ever been sexually abused? Did I have the nerve to say yes? Once it was said out loud, there'd be no taking it back. Would he tell me that was why I was the way I was? Would he want me to change? Should I change?

Chapter 47

Mom and I were sitting on Dr. Holmes's couch the next Thursday afternoon, waiting while he retrieved my file from the front desk because they'd given him the wrong one. With a week to imagine the worst, I was dreading what he'd say about my tests. I tapped my fingers on my knees.

She side hugged me, even though we weren't sitting that close.

He came back in, in his brown pants and black shoes.

"Sorry about that," he said as he sat in his task chair that was in front of the couch but off to the side a bit. He pulled some of the papers out of my file and attached them to the clipboard.

"No problem," Mom said.

"First, I'd like to go over a few things. We won't go into the details of your questionnaires, Nicole, because that's private information, but I would like to go over the other tests. First off, the first test lets me know that you have a high IQ."

Out of the corner of my eye I saw Mom smile and

look at me, but I didn't look back. This shouldn't be news to her. She'd supported me when I worked to get into the gifted program in middle school.

My stomach started doing this fluttery nervous thing. Was he going to reveal something to Mom? I had no idea, but I didn't have a good feeling about this guy.

He started going on about IQ and blah blah, and I simply tuned him out, though Mom looked rapt.

Eventually, he finished with that and said, "Okay, Mrs. Summers. I'd like to talk to Nicole alone now."

This increased the fluttering in my stomach. Mom got up and left me alone with this weird guy. What was he going to ask now? My stomach twisted.

After some basic pleasantries, he asked, "Did you want to start seeing a psychiatrist?"

That wasn't what I expected. "No. My parents are making me." I leaned back into the couch.

"Your parents are making you. Why do you think that is?"

"I said last week. I drew a picture that scared the school."

Dr. Holmes crossed his legs and clasped his hands around his knee. "Right, the picture of the demon. Did you bring a photo of it?"

I shook my head. "No. Also, it's not a demon."

"You didn't. Okay." He smiled. I don't think he meant it to be, but it was kind of a creepy smile. Like his mouth didn't match his eyes or something. "So, tell me about your friends."

"Sam's very smart and a good artist and plays the oboe and other instruments."

He looked at me expectantly. "What about the others?"

"There aren't any," I said.

Mentioning Sam reminded me of the horrible stairwell

lunch I'd had with her and Zach today. With just the three of us there, they'd totally started making out. I mean, what the hell? I was *right there*. It felt so weird, and I wanted to leave but didn't know if I should, but then I didn't know if it was weird to stay. I mean, I'd gotten there before them, so it seemed wrong that I would have to leave.

He cocked his head. "You only have one friend. How do you feel about that?"

"It's fine." Of course, it wasn't, but what was the point in talking to this guy about it? He wouldn't understand. Adults never did. It was always my fault. I wasn't doing life right.

"It's okay with you. Why do you think she is your only friend?"

I shrugged, tapping my leg with my fingers. "I don't know."

"You don't know."

What was with this guy repeating everything I said? "No, I don't know."

"Did you used to have more friends?"

"I don't know, I guess. More kids were okay to me earlier on, like in elementary school or whatever." This was making me feel ill, thinking about all this crap.

"They treated you okay. What about middle school?"

"Not really, until Sam in seventh grade." I hated my history.

He shook his head. "Not really."

The repeating was getting on my nerves.

"How did you handle not having friends? Who did you eat lunch with?" he asked.

"Nobody. I went to the library."

"You ate lunch in the library."

"No, I didn't eat."

"You skipped lunch?" He looked surprised, probably wondering if I got fat some time after that.

"Yeah."

"What changed with Sam?"

"I knew her in sixth grade, but we didn't get to be friends until seventh grade."

"Since seventh grade. Have you ever had a boyfriend?"

"No."

"You haven't. Why not?"

I clenched my teeth hard enough that my jaw hurt. Jesus, stop repeating everything I say. "Boys think I'm ugly."

"I'm sure boys don't think you're ugly."

Besides the annoying repetition, this whole line of questioning was weird. Wasn't he going to ask me about things like my actual childhood? Wasn't I going to have to avoid telling him about the evil, perverted friend of my dad's?

"What about your family?" he asked.

"What about them?"

"How are your relationships with them?"

I shrugged. "My parents are fine. My sister's sweet. My brother's a jerk." It was all true, even if it was the dumbed-down version.

"You like your sister. What's she like?"

"She's a typical ten-year-old girl, all into clothes and trying to be older. She wants to wear makeup but Mom won't let her yet."

"She wants to wear makeup. Why do you think that is?"

"She's just normal, that's all." God, what if she did do what Caleb had done and abandon me in the worst way?

"Are you allowed to wear makeup?"

Here we go again. "Do we have to talk about makeup? I don't like it so I don't wear it."

"You don't like it. Okay. So your brother's not very nice. Was he always that way?" He wrote something down.

"No. We used to be friends. He's only a year younger."

"Friends." He smiled. "That's nice. What happened?"

"He became a teenager."

Dr. Holmes's smile widened, though I hadn't been joking. That's what happened. That's when his priorities shifted, and he realized I was not his cool sister, but instead I was a loser, and if he didn't disassociate himself from me, there would be social consequences for him. I was a liability. I wondered if Izzy would do the same thing. I hoped not. I'd be out of high school by the time she hit it, anyway.

"What is your parents' relationship like?"

"With each other?"

He nodded. "Yes."

"Fine. They get along." I had to struggle to not roll my eyes.

"They get along with each other." He wrote on his clipboard again. "Are they affectionate?"

"What?"

"Do they display physical affection with each other?"

"Uh." Gross. Like I wanted to think about that. But I did, and not really. They never kissed in front of us. And Mom slept in Dad's office because he was a terrible snorer. They had a bed set up in there. I mean, they'd obviously been affectionate with each other at least three times, but I really didn't want to think about it. "No."

"They're not affectionate? You never see them kiss?"

"No." Why was he asking this, anyway? What did this have to do with me?

He nodded and then off went his pen again.

Weird.

"I'd like to revisit the fact that you only have one friend. Why do you think that is?"

I sighed. "Because people don't like me. I'm a social leper. Associating with me is socially dangerous." It wasn't just my brother.

"You're a social leper. What does that mean, exactly?"

"Like I said, if someone talks to me, they risk other kids judging them."

He furrowed his brow like he was confused.

"Also," I continued. "I don't have much in common with most kids. I'm not religious so the Bible kids don't like me, and I don't want to drink or do drugs, so I can't be friends with the rest of them."

"Not all teenagers do those things."

Really? What teenagers did he know?

"I think we need to work on a plan for you to change your social strategy."

"Why?" Good luck with that.

He looked at me without expression. "For now, the session is over. I look forward to seeing you next week."

I nodded, stood, and hightailed it out of there.

He hadn't answered my last question.

Chapter 48

A couple Saturday afternoons later, Zach picked Sam and me up. We were volunteering for a few hours at our food drive at Walmart for Key Club.

It was nice to be in the car without Evan getting intimate with the door so he could be as far away from me as humanly possible. But I missed Zach's rearview mirror looks again. My heart ached remembering the hope I'd felt from those looks.

He dropped us off by the front entrance, where we already had two tables set up, on either side of the doors, with a giant cardboard bin set up next to each. Five well-made-up girls manned the two tables.

"Thank God," the skinny one said. "I'm so bored." She was wearing a tight miniskirt with a light sweater. She grabbed her purse and came out from behind the left table, followed by the girl who was with her.

"Hey," Sam said.

The girls started off and Sam said, "Wait, is there anything we need to know?"

But they were gone. They hadn't even looked back.

The three girls at the other table gave us that down-the-nose look I was used to and one said, "It's not hard. Just ask people to donate canned or boxed foods."

Sam nodded and I followed her to the chairs behind the table.

The other girls were all semi-popular, but they must also want to get into good colleges, or else they wouldn't be doing this volunteering.

I looked up and saw Zach walking toward us. He must have parked and was planning to stay. Great. I didn't know he was volunteering with us. Now I'd have to deal with all the intimate whispering. God, it was physically painful being around them.

"Hey!" Sam said, smiling at him as he came up. He kissed her, which seemed unnecessary since they'd done that like three minutes earlier. Then he dropped into the third chair there. I looked away.

I glanced over at the perfect girls at the other table. One was studying her fingernails while the other two had their heads close together as they whispered something.

I pulled my phone out because Sam and Zach were talking about the movie they'd seen last night.

I pretended that a game on my phone was fascinating as I worked on a puzzle in order to ignore everybody else. Then this woman came out and placed a plastic bag full of cans in the bin by us, and I remembered what we were there to do.

Another woman came through with a kid in tow, and I looked at her and intended to say something about the food drive, but then I chickened out. For some reason, I felt self-conscious with the other girls watching. Sam wasn't paying any attention because she and Zach were in some intense-sounding conversation.

So I ended up smiling at the woman, then turning all kinds of red after she looked at me funny.

I smiled at several more people as they came in.

Then one of the other girls decided to get proactive. She stood at the end of her table and said, "Hi, would you like to donate to the food bank?" which wasn't particularly inspired, but it was better than what I was doing.

I continued smiling at people until one lady came out with two bags of macaroni and cheese. I guessed she thought poor people needed fluorescent food.

I was staring at that when this other woman asked, "Can we donate money?"

"Huh? Oh. I don't know." I looked at the table and spotted a plastic jar with a hole cut into the lid. "Yes!" I said.

She laughed at my awkward enthusiasm and dropped in a twenty.

As she left, she said, "Have a blessed day."

I hated that phrase. It was so annoying. For one, I wasn't sure what that meant. I mean, people could be blessed. That would mean things generally went well for them. I, on the other hand, was not blessed. But if a day was blessed, what did it care? Would that just mean that everybody in the world that day was blessed for the day? That was clearly not true. Some people were going to die today, just like every other day.

Sam and Zach's conversation grew more intense. Zach sort of yelled, "Fine, if that's what you think." His chair scraped as he got up and stormed away.

All three of the other girls were staring at Sam, who was blushing herself, for once. For a millisecond I was glad, then I felt like an asshole.

"Are you okay?" I muttered.

"Fine," she said, looking away at Zach.

What if they broke up? Was it possible he might want to go out with me then? I'd have to wait until Sam was gone, just to be decent, but then would she care? I didn't know the protocol here.

Of course, then I felt like an asshole again.

"Would you like to donate to the food bank, Rob?"

I looked up to see the girl across the way smiling in a way that was meant to be sexy at a group of guys from school, including one who'd called me a lesbian before.

He motioned toward me. "How do I know she's not going to eat it all herself?" he asked with a sneer.

Shame hit me like it always did. Sam glared at him and the two girls giggled, and the standing girl said, "Don't worry, it's safe with me." She hadn't missed a beat.

Wonderful.

Why did I care what these jerks thought? I shouldn't. I knew they were cosmic trash. Yet still, I did care. I hated that.

To take my mind off it, I thought about what Sam's and Zach's fight could have been about. Would they break up? It would be a relief to not have to see him around so much.

Chapter 49

Mom and I were waiting at the shrink's office that next Thursday. It was already almost 3:20, which was stressing my mom out because it had been scheduled to start at 3:00, and she had to be at work at 4:30. She was going to be late. Or more realistically, I'd just have to cut the session short. Thank God.

"I don't understand this," she said. "Don't they know we have time restrictions, too?"

I shrugged. I wasn't looking forward to this appointment. If it was anything like the last time, he'd be repeating everything I said, when he wasn't making stupid assertions about teenagers. It had been a couple of weeks since I'd been in because he didn't have an opening for last week, but now I was on the books for this time slot every Thursday.

Finally, this little kid came out and left with his mom. Mom huffed when Dr. Holmes didn't come out right away. A couple minutes later, he asked me to come back.

"How was your week, Nicole?" he asked as soon as we were situated.

"Fine."

He nodded. "I'd like to get back to what we talked about two weeks ago."

"What?"

"Your trouble making friends."

Of course. I sighed. "Okay."

What kind of crazy shit was he going to say this time? Kids aren't judgmental? They pay attention to inner beauty?

"Did you have any good friends in elementary school?"

"Uh … I had a friend from third grade to fifth grade, but she turned against me in fifth grade." Man, thinking about that shit still hurt.

"She turned against you how?"

"Well, we were friends—just the two of us—but I guess she wanted to be friends with the cooler girls. The girls in the class formed a club that only my friend, me, and this one other girl weren't in. The other girl's mom had died a few years earlier so she was always kind of excluded from things, though I think it might have been self-imposed. I wasn't too worried about this club, but then one day some of the girls in the club cornered me in the bathroom and made these disgusted noises and told me my friend had told them that I had brown streaks in my underwear."

"Brown streaks in your underwear?"

"I tried to point out that even if it were true—and it wasn't—that she was way more messed up than me to be going through my worn underwear. But it didn't take. She was in the club. Then she went out of her way to tell them all these other things about me and I became the main target of the club."

"You were targeted." He nodded and wrote something down. "What did you do about it?"

"I ate lunch by myself and then spent all recess sitting

at the bottom of the steps where we lined up to go back in." Shame bloomed as I remembered. Then I got mad. "Even some of the teachers got in on the fun."

"Teachers? How?"

I shrugged. "They hated me because I was fat and shy and let the kids openly bully me." I remembered Mrs. Black in particular.

"When I was in fourth grade, I had surgery on my hips and was on crutches for four months. In fifth grade, I ended up back on them, and this one teacher didn't believe I needed them. She even told me that one day in front of other kids."

I'd written a story for her class about this boy on crutches who overcomes his obstacles, and when I stupidly volunteered to read it in front of the entire class, kids laughed at me, and she didn't tell them to shut up. She'd let them laugh.

"You said teachers, plural."

"The P.E. teacher hated me because I was fat. She yelled at me in front of everyone when she was subbing in math class one day, because she thought I hadn't done what she'd told us to do, even though I actually had. It was really embarrassing."

"How do you know she disliked you because you were overweight?"

"A couple years earlier, she told me I wouldn't be so fat if I exercised more." Joy. It still embarrassed me to remember back. She'd said it in front of a whole group of kids.

"Hmm. That wasn't nice." Amazing that he agreed. I'd half-expected him to point out that it was probably true.

"No. I ran around and rode my bike and everything, just like everyone else." I really had. I didn't know I was chubby back then.

"You were active," he said. Then he smiled weakly and asked, "Did you try to make friends with any boys that year?"

"No. They didn't like me then, either."

He nodded. "The boys didn't like you."

God, what was with the repeating everything I said? It was fucking infuriating. "No, they didn't like me."

"Tell me more about middle school. What about sixth grade?"

Sixth grade. I wasn't telling this idiot about the boob-grabbing. What else happened then? I struggled to remember, which must mean it had been nothing too bad. "That was the year I met Sam. We weren't friends yet, but we knew each other. Otherwise, kids left me alone."

"They left you alone. How did that feel?"

"It was a relief after the girls' club year."

He nodded and wrote something on his notepad. "I want to revisit the fact that you don't have a boyfriend."

No. I did not want to discuss this. My stomach was already hurting.

"Would you like to have one?"

I felt myself blushing, like I was a child. God, I was such a loser. "I don't know."

"You don't know."

"It doesn't matter what I want, they aren't interested," I deadpanned. Of course my mind went to Zach. He and Sam had made up over whatever they'd been fighting about—she'd never even told me—so I was trying not to think of Zach that way.

"And why do you think that is?" He tapped his pencil on his notepad.

This was so irritating. I shifted on the couch and steeled myself for a fight. "I told you before—I'm ugly."

"I thought you might say that. It's not true, you know."

Like the opinion of some old guy counted. "Look, it's objectively true. I don't meet the American standard of beauty. I don't look anorexic, and I don't wear makeup. Beauty is a yes or no kind of thing. Either you have it or you don't, and I obviously don't."

He stared at me for a moment, clearly trying to think of something to say. "I disagree," he finally said.

I just looked at him.

"Hardly any women meet that impossible standard of beauty, and that doesn't mean they are ugly. Beauty is in the eye of the beholder."

I looked at my knees in my black jeans and tried not to gag or laugh out loud. It would have been bitter.

He continued. "You just need to be yourself, and people will like you. Nobody likes all other people, but you don't need everyone to like you."

Such bunk.

"Have you ever thought of wearing makeup?"

This shit again. "Yes, I've thought about it, and no, I'm not going to do it. I hate makeup. I don't see why girls should have to modify their bodies simply to be accepted as human. Boys don't. They get to be hairy and smelly and sloppy and everyone loves them anyway."

"I don't think that's the right way to look at it."

"Are you aware of the origin of makeup?" I gave him my conclusion about sexually aroused babies, and he looked at me like I was deranged.

That can't be a good thing from a shrink.

He recovered and said, "We've talked before about your drawings. I'd like you to bring pictures of some of them for next time, okay?"

I nodded, not looking forward to it.

We finished up the session a couple minutes later.

When Mom and I left, we hoofed it to the car.

"How was it, honey?" she asked once we'd gotten out of the parking lot.

"I don't like him. He repeats everything I say."

"Oh, I'm sure it's not that bad. I think psychiatrists do that sometimes to make sure they understand what you're telling them."

"It's worse than that." But I looked out the window because it was clear she wasn't going to believe me. Which meant I'd have to keep putting up with him.

Chapter 50

Dad got the minivan blinker fixed, and we went to the testing center again on Monday.

I went up to the counter to check in for my appointment.

The guy working there glanced up. "Last name?"

"Summers."

Then I went to wait with Dad. They had these flimsy metal chairs with maroon padded fabric seats, which could have come from Walmart. There were some other people waiting, including a boy about my age. I studied the tile floor.

I watched a brawny man come in from a side door and head to the counter. "Where's my next one?" he asked the guy there.

"He's there." Then he pointed at me.

God. Someone else thought I was a boy. This was bullshit, but it still made me feel like I wasn't even a real person. I closed my eyes to let the frustration pass.

Would this bug me so much if I actually was trans?

Wouldn't I like being mistaken for a boy? This felt like a revelation—I hated being mistaken for a boy, so I couldn't be trans. So what was I?

"What's his problem?" Dad muttered to me, rubbing his beard in annoyance. Not that he would say anything. He was as confrontation-averse as Mom.

The tester picked up some paperwork and read off it. "Summers."

I followed him out but stopped at the counter for a second. "I'm not a boy, you know."

The guy looked up and stared for a second but said nothing. He didn't even look sorry.

My heart was racing from the encounter, though. Maybe not the smartest thing to do before the test.

At least it was a different guy from before.

It ended up going okay. I failed the parallel parking, but I didn't get in trouble for having a crappy car. The guy gave me an eighty-two. I didn't care, as long as it was at least seventy.

I was grinning stupidly when I went back inside to Dad, who was engrossed in an issue of *Sports Illustrated*.

"You passed?"

I nodded, still smiling.

"That's great, Nic." He stood up and patted me on the back. "I'm also impressed you corrected the guy at the counter. You're normally so shy." He looked over at the guy in question. "What an idiot."

"Yeah. Let's go." I wasn't even sure why I'd done it. Except, I wasn't a boy. I wasn't.

"Do you want to drive home?"

I shrugged.

I felt far more adult than I ever had. It was a nice feeling, even though I didn't really feel like I'd accomplished anything impressive. Everybody got their license at some point.

Still, I had freedom I hadn't had before.

Chapter 51

The Sunday after Thanksgiving I drove to Taco Bueno—which is a better version of Taco Bell because they have this awesome free salsa bar—to eat and work on some art. I was relishing the freedom of having a car. Or, kind of having one. Having access to one.

I could only afford a couple tacos and a Coke, but I loaded the tacos with salsa. While I was eating, these four guys—college age—came in and were being obnoxious and disruptive dudes. Saying things to each other loudly, slapping each other on the back. One guy jumped over the line barricade for no reason.

I was uncomfortable because these were just the kind of guys who would go out of their way to harass me for being me. But I kept my head down and tried to fight my rising pulse.

I minded my own business and finished eating, then pulled my sketchbook out and started working. I sketched the restaurant, then moved on to do one of my left hand, sort of randomly. I liked how hands looked, even if mine weren't my favorite. Zach's were better.

The whole time the guys ate, they continued to carry on an ongoing scene. Everybody who came in while they were there looked at them in surprise before realizing nobody was actually fighting, they were simply being douches. I stayed uncomfortable, clutching my pencil and eyeing the door. I wanted to leave, but I'd have to walk across the room and when I did, they'd target me. I felt it in my gut. I didn't feel like taking it today.

When they finally left, they turned left outside, toward where my van was. But then I saw a big SUV peel out a minute later, so I relaxed and continued working. I was also the only customer in the restaurant at that point.

I drew the girl working the register because she had awesome spiky hair. I wished I had the guts to do that. I was too chicken to cut my hair. If people thought I was a boy with long hair, imagine it that way.

I got a refill on my drink, then drew some more.

Eventually, I packed up my stuff and went out to the minivan.

On the windshield, under the wiper, was a little yellow piece of paper. It had to be from the guys—my car had been the only other one in the lot when they left—and I dreaded what it would say. It was about four inches square and had several things written on it, some around the edge like a border and some in the middle.

HEY GIRL FAG, 1-800-KILL-YOURSELF made up the border. Then in the middle was:

DIE

UGLY

FAT

DYKE

My hands instantly shook, and it spread all the way up my arms so my whole body was shaking, too. I struggled to get the door open. My heart raced as I got inside and tossed the note inside the car. I wanted to cry, but that wasn't the only reason I was shaking.

I'd experienced a lot of bullying, but this one was truly scary. I mean, we hadn't even had an interaction. All the hatred in that note for simply sitting in a restaurant, minding my own business. I was glad it was the middle of the day and I wasn't near a dark alley where a bunch of guys were waiting to punish me for not being like everyone else.

Chapter 52

My next shrink appointment was on the first day of the month that Sam would leave. December. This was a shock, even though I'd obviously known it would happen. It still made me sick to my stomach.

He was running late again, and Mom was pissed off by the time he came out to get me.

The first thing he wanted to do was look at the pictures of my drawings I'd dutifully brought on my phone. I also brought my sketchbook, which had a lot of different things in it. Lots of dragons, but also some mundane still lifes from my room and such.

I handed him the phone first, and he swiped through them, one after the other. I'd put them all in one album so he wouldn't stumble across other random stuff. Not that there was anything exciting on my phone. No funny selfies, for sure.

At first I was only half looking at him, but then I noticed his expression. You'd think as a shrink, he'd be good at masking his feelings, but it was obvious that he didn't approve of my drawings. Dragons, knights, some battle scenes. I don't know why I liked to draw fantasy stuff even though I mostly read sci-fi. I should probably have started drawing space stuff. I guessed it would freak people out less.

But then again, that wasn't what I wanted to draw, so what the hell. I wouldn't change just for stupid society's approval. It wasn't like I was out starting fires or torturing kittens. Mine were victimless transgressions.

He finished with the phone and started flipping through the sketchbook. He looked a little less disturbed at that, except when he saw the studies I'd done of medieval weapons. Swords, maces, a halberd, an ornate battle axe, a trebuchet. Then he stopped and stared at the sketch I'd done of my built-in desk, because I'd drawn it down to detail.

"Are these fantasy figurines?" he asked.

"Yeah."

"Do you play Dungeons & Dragons?"

"No." I wouldn't tell him that it was only because Sam and I never could find anyone willing to let us join their group. "I just paint the figurines."

"You just paint them. Okay." He kept flipping through the sketchbook.

He was putting all that bullshit gender crap on me. He was freaked out that I drew dragons and knights and weapons. And was interested in D&D. Which must mean I was a satanist. It's what people thought.

Stupid people.

I wondered again what he'd say if I told him about the molestation. Would he be like, "This explains everything, you weirdo!"

I didn't want to hear that. I didn't want the way I was to be because of something bad that happened to me. Because who I was felt so real that it would be hard to accept it was the damaged version of me rather than the real one. It would mean maybe I *should* have changed. To be who I really should have been.

If I wasn't a boy—and I knew I wasn't now—what was I?

God, it was all messed up.

Though I don't know what I was worried about, though. I wasn't going to tell him about the abuse, and he obviously wasn't going to ask. I mean, if he wasn't clued in enough to ask on his own, how would he react if I just told him? He'd obsess over it and think it explained everything that was wrong with me.

He handed the book back, and I set it next to me on the couch.

He rested his ankle on his knee. "You are obviously quite talented."

"Thanks."

"Are you interested in violence?" he asked, evidently trying to sound casual.

"What? No. God, why does everyone think that?"

"You draw weapons."

I shrugged. "I think they're interesting. You might ask me if I'm interested in history, since they're part of that."

"Are you?"

"Maybe." Not remotely.

He pursed his lips like he'd read my mind. "Do you own any weapons?"

"No," I scoffed. God.

"No weapons. Have you ever been in a physical fight?"

"No."

"No fighting." He looked at me with narrowed eyes.

This guy didn't get me at all.

"Can I see your sketchbook again?"

I handed it over and he flipped through it again. "It's very unusual for a girl to draw weapons."

"I'm not a typical girl. So what?"

He blinked at me a couple times. Then he asked more about violence. He wasn't going to let this go. It was painful, but time ran out, and we left.

Mom went on about how pissed she was that he was always running late. She dropped me off at the library where I was meeting Sam, and headed to work.

Sam was already there at a table in the back. We said hi, and I plopped into the seat across from her.

She sighed.

"What?" I asked.

"I'm sick of Zach. He always wants to make out, and we never do anything fun anymore."

Oh. That was a problem I wouldn't mind having.

But I was being a terrible friend. "I'm sorry. Have you talked to him about it?"

She sighed. "I don't really know how. It's like he just assumes it's what I want, too, but I'm bored."

"Don't you like it?" Wasn't it supposed to be awesome?

"In small doses. Plus, I think he's kind of a wet kisser. Not that I have anything to compare it to, but I think so."

"Oh." I wondered what she meant.

And then I wondered if they'd really break up, and what it would mean for me. Was I an asshole for thinking that? I wasn't sure.

Probably I was. But did it even matter?

Chapter 53

Ever since the day I got my license, I'd been thinking about the fact that I knew now that I wasn't trans. But I hadn't figured out what I *was*, so I finally decided to google it again. I sat on my bed and pulled out my laptop. Maybe I'd have more luck this time.

I did. I stumbled across a question on a site where the girl said she didn't feel like a girl or a boy—and that rang true to me. I mean, I still liked Zach, even though he was with Sam, so I thought about him. I was more comfortable with the idea of his penis than the idea of having my own. I'd kind of wished I was a boy all through my life, but it was more about dealing with society's bullshit expectations than a physical thing. I didn't feel any real connection to boys the way I imagined real boys would.

Then I hit gold—I found the term "gender nonconforming." I had a hard time really understanding exactly what it meant. The Wikipedia page talked about it like it was a disorder that could or should be treated, while at the same time, it sounded like something that was a choice—a choice to not conform. But that wasn't what it felt like to me. It wasn't like I was rebelling. It was like I couldn't play a girl. It was just wrong.

Either way, from what the page said, it sounded like I might end up depressed and even suicidal in the future. Great.

I kept digging. There was also the term "gender nonbinary," which might or might not be the same thing as gender nonconforming. I guessed gender nonconforming was more about how you acted and gender nonbinary was more about who you really were. But that made it sound like a choice again.

I leaned back on my hands, the laptop in my lap. I didn't feel like I had a real problem with my body—other than the fact that it was fat. Even my boobs didn't really stress me out. They had in sixth grade, but now things had leveled out and they were normal-sized. So was I nonbinary? Did I want to make people stop calling me "she" and "her" and switch to "they" and "them?"

I almost laughed out loud. That wouldn't go over well at Emerson High, for sure. I'd get more attention and everyone would refuse to use the right pronouns, just to be the assholes they were.

But I wasn't sure that's what I wanted, anyway.

Someone on one of the forums said they had asked themself what they would do if society didn't exist.

That was easy for me. I wouldn't change anything about my body, but it would be so awesome to be a person without all the stupid trappings of girl-ness.

Though I could do without a period, for sure.

But anyway, it was a moot point since society *did* exist. And I did have a female body.

Oh my God, I was so confused. I probably should join

the forums and ask my own questions, but while even shy people usually felt safe in the anonymity of the internet, I didn't feel that.

Would I ever be certain of anything?

Chapter 54

The next week, Mom started feeling sick on Monday—the flu or something—and Thursday morning she called the shrink to cancel my appointment because she didn't think she could leave the house. They told her that we'd still be charged even if I didn't come because we were canceling with less than forty-eight hours' notice. I still couldn't drive her car, so she was stuck taking me. She was so pissed, coughing, sneezing, and even cussing mildly all the way there.

Then she sat in the waiting room doing the same thing, minus the cussing. The other woman there glared at her and Mom was mad enough that she explained herself. The woman huffed and clearly tried to not breathe the same air. No sympathy there.

The woman hightailed it out of there once her son came out from the back, and I went in to talk to the idiot. Late as usual.

It went pretty much like I expected. More stupid conversation about nothing of substance, except how I was doing life wrong. Perceiving everything wrong, presenting myself wrong, everything wrong.

I wanted to tell him that I was gender nonconforming, only to see what he'd say, but I never said anything.

I could hear Mom coughing all the way from the waiting room. After a while, the time was up and I went out to the waiting area.

Mom had apparently had a conversation with the receptionist, because the next thing I knew, we were both back in his office.

"I can't believe that you insisted"—she coughed—"on me bringing Nic when I am this sick." She had a serious case of man-voice.

"You are sick," he parroted. "I am sorry about that."

She continued, "You are always running late, and we have to wait"—she sneezed and sniffed—"causing me to be late to my own job, but you can't even make allowances for someone who's sick."

He nodded sympathetically. "You have to wait for the appointments. I understand your frustration."

"I don't think you do. You have no respect for my time." Go, Mom.

"I'm sorry you feel I have no respect for your time." His hands were on his crossed leg.

Mom sort of lost it, for her. She was shaking and said, way louder than I expected, "What is wrong with you? Why do you keep repeating what I say?"

He was quiet for a moment, and then Mom got up and I followed her out. Even before we got to the car, she said, "We aren't going back to that jackass."

I was so happy. "I'm sorry you're sick, but I'm glad you finally see what he's like with the repeating."

"I didn't believe you. It's infuriating."

"Yeah."

It was. And it was over. I was officially shrink-less.

"But honey, you know we'll have to find someone else. I am worried about you."

Okay, only temporarily shrink-less. What jerk would they find for me next?

Chapter 55

Sam's last day came too fast. It was the Wednesday before Christmas. We were lying on the two beds in her room. It was weird to see all signs of her gone. We were now in this generic furnished house, with cheesy boring landscapes hanging over each bed. Her large, hard-sided suitcase was by the door. She had all these stickers all over it. Different bands and other stuff.

Sam's parents had a property manager and were going to rent out there house. So maybe they would all end up coming back.

I could hope. I stared at a cobweb in the corner.

Their flight left midday tomorrow.

"I'm sorry we didn't find any new friends for you," Sam said. "I believed in OSIN. I guess people around here suck too much."

She wasn't wrong. "I'm thinking again about applying to OAMS." The state's math and science academy.

"You totally should. It would be a fresh start. Plus I'm guessing it's mostly geeks there instead of jocks and preps. Maybe things would go better for you."

"Yeah, that's what I've been thinking." I fiddled with the hem of my shirt, pulling it down. "But they don't have a great art program."

"You're good enough that I wouldn't worry about that. You just need to keep working on your own, and you'll get better and better."

"It might be hard there."

"Come on, you barely try in your classes and you still make A's. You'd do fine."

"I guess."

"And they do have art there, right?"

"Yeah, as an elective." I'd done the research.

"So you spend a little more time in the art room than everyone else. No big deal."

"True."

We were quiet for a bit.

"What did you decide about Zach?" I finally asked. She had been going back and forth about whether to break up now or wait until she was gone. She was sick of him and didn't see the point of trying a long-distance thing. Either way, he would be a free agent soon, and I wondered if he'd act interested in me again. Then I felt really guilty.

"I'll just wait," Sam said.

I laughed to cover the guilt. "Chicken."

"It's true. I don't know what to say. I've never had to break up with anyone before."

"Yeah."

After a moment, Sam said, "So, I think you should plan to visit me. Maybe in March. By then we'll be in our house or whatever."

"Really?" The thought had never occurred to me. I thought she'd be gone, and that would be that.

"You should. I already asked my mom, and she said it was fine."

"During Spring Break?"

"Yep."

I figured I might as well call Mom right then. I explained the situation.

"Honey, we can't afford it."

"Come on, please, Mom."

"I'm sorry."

I hung up. "She says we're too broke."

"Oh. That sucks."

I wanted to cry. Sam had gotten my hopes up, and Mom had dashed them. Or maybe I wanted to cry because Sam was leaving, and I might never see her again. Or because I didn't have any other friends. Or just because I was ugly.

Chapter 56

Friday, a couple days before Christmas, I drove to our dinky mall to get presents for everyone. I had no idea what I would get, so it was going to be a chore.

Friday was also the day after Sam had left.

I was feeling horrible, to be honest, which made searching for a parking spot even more of a drag. I mean, I didn't have a single real friend in the whole country now. It was surreal.

I stumbled across an empty spot, with no other car in sight. Also surreal. I did not whip into it. No, I had to go super slow to get the minivan safely between the two cars. For once, luck was with me—they were both small.

As I headed inside, I thought that maybe Zach was sort of my friend. I figured he'd still drive me to Key Club. Though now that I had my license, I could use the mini-van, so I might not even ask. I figured I'd just play dumb and see if he planned to pick me up. But would he be mad at me after Sam dumped him?

There were people *everywhere*. My heart was going a bit faster than necessary because of all the crowds and chaos. I passed a sunglasses kiosk, which was three deep with shoppers, and headed to the department store. I would get my dad a plaid shirt for work. Dad had given me some money for gifts.

I got there and then swam through the crowd to get to the men's department. I found a nice shirt—one I'd wear, really—and got Dad's size and then stood in line for ages. When I got to the front, the cashier said, "Good evening, sir."

It twisted my stomach every time. "I'm a girl."

"Oh."

He rang me up in silence, and I paid with cash and then left. The awkwardness was palpable. He never even said anything. How hard would it be? Something like, Sorry, I just saw someone tall and assumed. Anything. God.

Then I headed over to the gag gift place to get some stupid thing for my brother. After perusing the options—I picked up a bottle of lube before realizing what it was—I settled on a pair of Batman flip-flops. They were perfect because my parents would think it was a thoughtful gift since he was into Batman, but I knew he'd hate them. They were too cutesy.

Now I had to figure out something for Mom.

She was impossible. She already bought what she needed, and I didn't know what else she wanted. I walked the place, slowly passing store after store in the flow of people.

A scarf?

Eventually, I stumbled upon one of those accessory places and squeezed inside to the scarf display. Nothing jumped out at me.

I sucked at giving gifts. Out of desperation, I picked a pink and black checked flannel scarf. I mean, it didn't scream, Mom!, but nothing else did either. Maybe I could get her some earrings, too?

I tried to get to the earrings but it was difficult, and I ended up going around another rack, only to find I was still blocked.

"Are you going to pay for that?" this snobby-looking girl asked me. Her name tag said, Britnee.

"What? Yes. I was trying to get to the earrings." What, she thought I looked like a thief? Because I didn't look like I belonged here?

"It looked like you were about to leave with it."

"I wasn't." But now I was pissed. I tossed the scarf on top of a rack of wallets and walked out.

"Well," she huffed.

Whatever.

Now I was seriously mad. I didn't know what to get Mom, so I wandered over to Walmart because I needed to get some school supplies, too.

Once I made it to the right aisle, there were of course a lot of people to navigate around. I saw pink notebooks and ones covered with basketballs or baseballs. Where were the normal, neutral things? Why did everything have to be so fucking gendered? This only upset me more.

I dug through the stack of pink notebooks and found some green ones and blue ones, so I snagged those. I found some red folders. Finally, I checked out and stepped back into the mall.

Now I still had to find something for Mom. I guessed I could go back to the department store and see if they had anything there I could afford.

Maybe I could get her a small bottle of perfume.

It was a fight to get to the perfume counter, but I managed it. One of the women behind the counter looked at me and then moved on to someone else at the other end.

"Excuse me," I said to the other woman when she finished helping a lady.

Her brow furrowed for a millisecond before she put on a fake smile. "Can I help you?"

"I need to get a bottle of Obsession."

She went through the options—they had several gift packs that came with other stuff like hand lotion and whatever—until I got overwhelmed. "Can you ... uh ... I've only got thirty bucks."

"A single bottle is ninety dollars."

My eyes widened in shock. That was almost my whole budget. "Oh. Never mind."

I fled the counter and instead looked at the wallets. My hands were shaking from being around so much feminine stuff. It was like it was coming to get me.

The wallets were all $100 and up, too. God. I had no idea it was so expensive to be a normal woman.

Okay, so I'd have to go somewhere else. There were some of those discount stores nearby. Maybe one of them would have something I could afford. I was fed up.

Now I just had to successfully extricate the minivan from the parking space. I would head over to the discount store first, and then the arts and crafts store to get Izzy something next. That would be a madhouse, too, but more fun than this place.

Chapter 57

In the end, I think my parents' friends paid for us to go on the trip over Christmas with them, though Dad didn't come because he couldn't afford the vacation days. Mom drove us down to Dallas the Monday after Christmas. We did this caravan thing, getting split up once we got into town.

We planned to regroup at the hotel.

"I'm going to find Logan," Caleb said once we had everything in our room. They were sharing a different room.

"Don't disappear," Mom called from the bathroom where she was unpacking her toiletry case.

Then he was gone, thank God. Izzy crawled onto the bed she and I would share and spread out to take up as much room as possible.

"You didn't go with him?" Mom asked after emerging from the bathroom.

"Are you kidding? I hate Logan." I pushed on Izzy until she scooted over, and I lay down next to her.

"I love this room," Izzy said.

"Why do you like it, sweetie?" Mom asked.

"I don't know. It's just us girls."

Mom laughed. "That it is. Nic, Kayla and Alyssa are probably with Logan."

"I don't like them, either." I crossed my hands behind my head.

Izzy got up and opened her suitcase.

"I thought they were nice to you?" Mom stood next to the bed.

"They're fine."

Izzy extracted her hairbrush and went into the bathroom with it. Already primping. How were we related?

"Things are so complicated for you, aren't they?" Mom asked.

The truth of that statement—and the fact that she'd noticed—really touched me for some reason. I almost teared up, out of nowhere. "Yeah, they are."

"Well, I'm not going to make you spend time with them if you don't want to."

"Thanks."

Her phone dinged across the room. She checked it and said, "Okay, let's go. They're all downstairs. Come on, Izzy."

"Isabella," she called. "Just finishing."

When she emerged, she looked the same to me. She had on jeans with jewels on the pockets and a tucked-in pink t-shirt with flowers on it.

I'd never tucked in a t-shirt in my life.

Everybody had congregated in the lobby downstairs. I saw Logan—coffee in hand—and Caleb talking, over by a large plant, and the rest of the kids were standing nearby, with the adults beyond them.

They were all blocking the sliding front doors, which

wasn't a surprise to me. They were like that. Not thoughtful.

"Hi!" Mom said as we reached them.

Gina and Susan—Alyssa's and Kayla's moms—hugged her in turn while Bridget gave me a quick side shoulder-squeeze and asked how I was. It still weirded me out how much Logan's mom seemed to like me. A couple other moms chatted with Izzy for a second—they loved her because she was cute—before coming over and then all six of them were talking.

The men were similarly bunched up, though Logan's dad, Pete, came over to the women to get everyone moving out. I got stuck walking between the adults and the kids. Kayla and Alyssa came up, and we chatted a little. As we moved into the restaurant, Caleb and Logan brushed past me and Logan muttered "dyke" under his breath.

Nice. "You're such a charmer," I managed to come up with.

"A charmer?" he barked, and he and Caleb cracked up.

I admit, it wasn't clever. Fuck. Why couldn't I be witty? I wanted to be like a girl in a YA novel, not me.

But one of the other boys in the group—Kayla's older brother, who thought he was hot shit because he drove a BMW his parents had given him on his sixteenth birthday—heard us so they all looked back at me and laughed again.

We reached the restaurant and crowded the entryway. We followed the server back and everybody was getting in everyone's way, but then the kids moved off toward another set of tables in the back of the restaurant. I was the last kid left there and Gina and Susan stared at me until I got the message. I headed to the other table.

Izzy was between Alyssa and Kayla because they, too,

thought she was adorable. Don't get me wrong, she was. It irritated me how people were so openly supportive of girls who follow the status quo, even when they're too young for it. Society certainly never encouraged me to be me when I was young.

The only seat left was near the middle, between my brother and the other girl in the group, who I didn't know that well because her parents were part of the outer circle, not the inner. Kayla was next to her and Alyssa across from Kayla, then next to her were the BMW boy and one other boy, another outer circle kid, across from me. Then Logan next to him, and back to Caleb.

All in all, it sucked, though any configuration would suck because it would put me near Logan and the other boys.

"*Hola, señores. ¿Como estás?* How are you?" A short Latino server with a bushy mustache started setting down water glasses.

"Can we get chips?" Logan asked, taking another sip of his coffee he'd brought in.

"They're coming." The server set down the fifth water in front of me and continued along.

A thin woman with a tray arrived and set an order of chips and salsa down on our end of the table and then one on Kayla and Alyssa's. The salsa's tangy smell tempted me, but I didn't want to be the first one to reach for the chips. It would inspire fat jokes.

She disappeared, and the water guy asked, "Drinks for anyone?"

Logan said, "A Coke."

Caleb got one too, and then the server looked at me and said, "For you, *señor?*"

The boys snorted as one, and the server apologized and corrected himself. "*Señorita, lo siento.*"

Through my raging blush I muttered, "A Coke."

The rest of the evening went pretty much as you'd expect. The girls talked about stuff I wasn't remotely interested in, and the boys talked about video games.

I'd hoped things would be different if I left Oklahoma. Though I guess Dallas probably wasn't far enough to be a true test. Maybe if I went really far away, it would be better.

Chapter 58

The next morning, we met as a crowd in the hotel foyer again and then headed out to Six Flags. The plan was to drop the kids off there, and then the adults were going on an art walk. There was an outside one in the art district. Obviously, I wanted to do that rather than hang out with the kids. I mean, spend hours seeing art, or being deeply uncomfortable? No-brainer, that one. Izzy wanted to go to Six Flags so Alyssa and Kayla said they'd take care of her.

We all stood in line at the entrance plaza to buy the tickets to Six Flags Over Texas for the kids, and Izzy and I stood with Mom while the other women talked amongst themselves, as did the men, and the girls and the boys. Everything was so predictable and boring.

Once the tickets were bought, all the parents shooed their kids, and they headed toward the front gate.

"Aren't you going, Nic?" Gina asked, sounding a little alarmed.

I guess Mom hadn't told all her buddies that I was going with them.

"No."

"Are you sure you don't want to?" Susan asked. "You'd rather hang out with a bunch of old fogies?"

"I don't think you're old fogies," I said.

The two of them shared a disapproving look, and the group started heading back to the cars. We left a couple of the cars there and piled into the minivan and two other SUVs. I sat in the front seat, which I think caused some grumbling.

I was excited about the art walk. We were starting at a Henry Moore sculpture.

After struggling to park, we regrouped at the sculpture, which was a giant bronze composed of three pieces. It was called "The Dallas Piece," or "Vertebrae," because it looked like the vertebrae of a giant creature, but we'd be talking monstrous, because each piece was, like, sixteen feet tall.

For some reason, I wondered if Zach would think this was cool. Given his sister's interest in art, and his apparent fondness for her.

"Is this phallic at all, do you think?" Gina whispered to the women as they huddled around one side of it.

"No," Bridget said. "What do you think, Nic? Do you like it?"

I shrugged, still blushing from the phallic comment coming right after my thoughts of Zach. "It's cool, I guess. I'm not really into giant sculptures at this point."

Gina and Susan looked at each other again, like, what's she doing here, then?

Nearby were these two large red spheres that sat in the middle of a large shallow pool. They had cylindrical pieces cut out, which gave them the look of crescents when you looked at them from the right angle, but globes otherwise.

There were several other big pieces, plus a Confederate memorial, which seemed a little tacky and not very artistic, anyway. Pioneer Plaza had a big and involved sculpture representing a cattle drive, with dozens of six-foot-tall bronze steers.

As we were wandering around looking at the different steers, I heard one of the men say, "I thought these things were supposed to be realistic. Where are their nuts?"

One of the other guys said, "They're steers, you dipshit."

The women rolled their eyes.

It was like being with a bunch of teenagers. When I was younger, I had always thought adults were so much better than kids. Kids were mean, and interested in childish things. But then I got a little older and noticed that a lot of adults were no better. Like teachers. They were as swayed by the popular kids as other kids were. It was disgusting. I mean, grow up. Jesus.

After we left Pioneer Plaza, we headed over to check out this giant 2-D neon red Pegasus that sat on top of a small oil derrick in front of a building. Apparently this was a big Dallas icon.

I didn't get it.

As we stood there staring at it, one of the men said, "What do you say we give up on this and head to a bar?"

Gina helpfully pointed out that I was there, and we had the whole day to spend there.

In the end, the men decided to find a sports bar and hang out, and the rest of us continued on. It got good when we ended up at the Dallas Museum of Art. I loved that. There were so many nice pieces, though to be honest, looking at paintings by the masters always made me realize I'd never be that good with paint. Drawing was one thing, but painting was something else. But if I went to art school, I'd have to learn, wouldn't I?

Chapter 59

I was reading on the bed in the hotel room Wednesday morning after breakfast while Mom got ready to go hang out with all the other adults. They'd decided on a day of relaxation and were going to the hotel bar. Caleb was already with all the other kids in the suite Kayla's parents had got for her and her brother.

The blow-dryer roared in the bathroom as Mom got ready.

I set my book on my stomach and closed my eyes. It was good, but what I wanted to do was work on my dragon drawing, but that was at home. I did have my sketch book with me, but it wasn't the same.

"Come on, Nic, I want to go, too," Izzy said. She shook my shoulder lightly.

"I don't really see the point. It will be boring. Why are you so interested, anyway? There's nobody your age there."

"Alyssa and Kayla are nice to me."

"You know they'll be busy flirting, right? Kayla's

brother is there and Alyssa likes him. And if the Campbells are there, then Kayla will be talking to Mark, and Caleb will be scheming with Logan."

"Come on, it will be fun."

Such a social butterfly, this one.

The blow-dryer stopped, and Izzy lay down next to me.

I listened to my breathing, nice and steady. I didn't want to go hang out with the kids. The idea kind of made me queasy. I'd be bored, at best. Tortured, at worst.

I could bring my sketchbook, though who knew what kind of reaction that might get. I had been thinking about some other things I might enter into the art contest. I needed to get going on some projects for it. I was behind. The dragon drawing was obviously the main thing, but I needed more than that.

The dryer started back up. I didn't understand Mom's pressing need to make herself look conventionally perfect just for her friends. She was on vacation, for God's sake.

At the last art club meeting, Ms. Tolliver had asked me if I would consider running for secretary for the next year. The idea was kind of cool. Maybe I'd get to know some of the other kids better. Who knew?

I crossed my hands on my stomach and listened to my breathing some more. I still didn't want to go.

The blow-dryer stopped again, and I opened my eyes and saw Mom standing in the bathroom doorway. "Did you consider going over there? I hate to think of you alone here all day."

I didn't mind too much. I'd brought several books just in case. I could entertain Izzy if she got bored with her tablet.

Izzy was lying on her side facing me, elbow out and with her head propped up on her palm. "Please?"

When I didn't say anything, Mom continued, "Alyssa and Kayla will be there. You can spend time with them, right? They're nice."

They weren't *that* nice and she knew that. "I really don't want to."

"Honey, I think you should. Izzy wants to go. Sometimes you need to do social things even when you don't want to. I'm not going to make you go, but I think you should."

They were both making me feel all guilty. But I knew what she meant. Sometimes it was better to make the effort even though it was uncomfortable. Sam said so, too. "Okay, fine. I'll go." Maybe I could practice conversation with some of the outer circle kids.

"Yay!" Izzy said before hugging me awkwardly.

When Mom was ready, we all headed out. Izzy and I took the elevator up to the sixth floor, and I knocked on room 614.

Logan opened the door and instantly said, "What the fuck are you doing here?"

It felt like someone had slapped me, and I instinctively stepped back. Without meaning to, I looked over his shoulder and could see several of the kids—including Alyssa, Kayla, and even Caleb—watching this. Nobody said anything, and before I could come up with something myself, Logan shut the door.

Why had I thought this was a good idea? Why should I force myself into social situations I didn't want to be in?

"Nic, why did he say that?" Izzy asked in a small voice.

"That was all for me, not you. That's my life, Izzy. Don't be like me."

We went back to our room. Silent all the way.

I knew it was probably an overreaction, but I felt numb

and in shock. I fumbled with the key card in the slot and didn't get the door open until the third try.

Izzy sat on Mom's bed, and I lay back on the other, listening to my ragged breathing while I fought stupid tears.

Why did it bother me so much? I hated Logan and didn't even like the rest of them.

"Nic, why are people so mean to you?" Izzy asked. She was obviously upset, from her wobbly voice.

"It's just how it is. I'm ugly. People don't like me."

"You're not ugly!"

"Yes, I am."

"Why don't you wear makeup? You'd be pretty then."

"Why should I have to wear makeup to be acceptable, Izzy? Don't you think it's so messed up that girls have to change their faces and their bodies just to be considered normal?"

"I don't know." Izzy sniffed.

"And if you don't, you're ugly."

We didn't say anything else but she got into bed with me. We lay there for a bit until I could hear her even breathing.

I shouldn't have brought her into my philosophical quandary. She bought into all the normal crap.

Izzy's mouth was open as she slept and she looked so cute and innocent. I loved her so much it hurt sometimes.

Back to reality.

I got out my sketchbook and drew a sword, imagining beheading Logan with it.

Which was a little violent, I know, but it's not like I was going to do anything.

But then it occurred to me that this was my life. No friends. Even kids who were almost obligated to involve me rejected me or were amused by said rejection. This was how it was going to be forever, because I couldn't imagine how it would change. Obviously, there was something wrong with me. It was more than being ugly. Other people would have been able to come up with something clever to say to Logan, or would have just pushed their way in. Kids would have respected that, and it would have been fine.

Not me. I didn't have even the most basic social skills. And how was I supposed to get them if no kids would let me spend time with them? I mean, I guess they were things you were supposed to pick up when you were younger. Elementary school had only taught me I was a freak.

I didn't know what to do. It was hopeless. Without Sam, I didn't know how I could ever do anything. I couldn't stop the tears this time. Matching floods running down my cheeks.

The crying lasted longer than it should have, and by the end I was exhausted. So I went into the bathroom and splashed cold water on my face before dozing on the bed.

After a couple hours, I woke. Izzy was watching a movie on her tablet, earbuds in. I didn't feel any better. My chest hurt from loneliness, I guessed, but I looked over and saw the sketchbook on the nightstand. Maybe drawing would help.

I put my own earbuds in and listened to some classic metal and turned the page from the sword I'd been working on and started drawing a baby dragon emerging from an egg. I made sure he was covered in egg goo, which did make me feel a tiny bit better because it was gross and funny. And when I thought about Logan, I was getting pissed now.

Then the door opened, and Mom came in.

"Oh, hi, honey." She shut the door. She dropped her phone on the bed. "Did you get bored after all?"

Izzy took her earbuds out and dropped them on the bed. "Mom, Logan was so mean to us!"

"What do you mean?" She looked at me in confusion as Izzy ran into her arms for a hug.

"It was for me, not Izzy."

"Isabella." She said it half-heartedly.

"What?" Mom asked.

"They wouldn't let us in," I said.

"What do you mean?" She still looked confused.

"Yeah, so Logan opened the door and said, 'What the fuck are you doing here?' and nobody else said anything even though they all watched him say it. Nobody missed it. And then he shut the door. Not that I was going to go in at that point, but he wouldn't have let me anyway. So."

Mom's face had gone quite white. "Logan said that to you?"

I nodded.

"He did!" Izzy said. "I hate him. He's such a jerk."

Mom sat on the bed. "Bridget would die if she knew."

"Yeah. But it would make it worse if you talked to her."

She sighed. "I'm so sorry that happened, honey."

"What are you doing back here, anyway?" I asked.

"I came to get my purse. We're going to dinner."

I nodded, dread filling me. God, more time with Satan and his minions.

"I don't think we'll go with them," she finally said. "I can't stand that boy."

"Logan?"

"Yes. Did your brother just sit and watch this, too?"

"Yeah."

She looked off to the side and shook her head. "I'm sorry, honey. I don't know what has happened to him. He used to be such a sweet boy."

"I know. I remember."

She put her fingers against her forehead and closed her eyes. Then she opened them back up and texted someone.

"The four of us will go out alone," she said. "We're having a talk."

Chapter 60

Thursday morning, we met the group at the hotel restaurant for breakfast. Somehow they got us all in one long table. I got stuck at the end with the kids, but Mom was on the other side of me, so they wouldn't say anything, which was a huge relief, if embarrassing.

Everyone acted like nothing had happened. None of the boys said anything disparaging. The talk Mom had with Caleb last night had been anti-climactic. Caleb said my existence was ruining his social life. Mom reminded him of the times when we used to be friends, including the time I'd more or less saved his life. I'd kept him from suffocating in an old leather trunk once when he'd thought it was a good idea to fold up inside one and have his friend shut the top.

In the end, although he said some of the right words and looked maybe a tiny bit guilty, I knew nothing would change.

I didn't talk through the whole breakfast, other than saying hi back to Kayla and Alyssa when both greeted me in a super-friendly way—their moms were right there, after all.

The plan was for everyone, including the adults, to go to Six Flags today. Mom had already told me it was fine for me to spend the day with her, and Izzy could hang with Alyssa and Kayla again. The other adults would be annoyed that Mom wasn't there, but neither of us cared.

After the meal, when the men and Mom were busy settling the bill, Alyssa made a big production of saying, "Nic, we sure hope you'll hang out with us today."

It made my cheeks flame—God knows why—but I knew she didn't mean it. Gina and Susan were watching, and she was only putting on a show.

"No, thanks. I'll probably just stay with my mom."

Then Gina loudly whispered to Susan, "Well, if she doesn't want to try, whose fault is it?"

Something in me snapped. Such subtlety on their part. And I was basically being shamed for other people's bad behavior.

I looked at Mom, whose eyes were wide. She'd heard, too.

Then I glared at Gina and Susan, whose heads were still together, whispering something more quietly this time. I glanced back at Mom, who shook her head a little, but she couldn't stop me as I turned my attention back to the gossiping duo.

"Do you know why I don't want to 'try'?" My voice got louder as I got to the air quotes.

Gina and Susan both looked at me with wide eyes, stunned into silence.

"Because yesterday when I went to Kayla's hotel room, Logan opened the door and said, 'What the fuck are you doing here?'"

Bridget gasped.

I wasn't done. "Then he slammed the door in my face, but not before enough time had passed for somebody in the room to have said something. But they didn't. Not a peep."

"I'm sure they didn't hear," Susan protested.

"They heard. He was loud and your perfect progeny were all watching the whole time, waiting for my reaction." I couldn't keep the sarcasm out of my shaking voice.

"Is that true?" Bridget asked Logan.

"With a mouth like that …" Gina whispered to Susan.

"No," Logan said. The other kids were all staring at their plates.

Bridget looked to me, her face as horrified as I expected. "I don't believe you," she said to Logan.

That's when I glanced around and noticed some other people in the restaurant were looking at us, and I blushed fiercely again.

"Logan, come with me back to the room," Bridget said as she got up.

He sat there like he wasn't going to.

"Logan." Her voice was more commanding than I'd ever heard.

He got up, and I looked back at Gina and Susan, who were still whispering to each other. They didn't give a shit, or they still thought it was my fault.

Which was fine. I already knew they were assholes.

By this point, the men had started paying some attention and knew something had happened. Pete looked down the table. "What?"

Bridget said, "Come on. We're going back to the room."

"Why?"

"Come *on*."

Pete threw some cash on the table and followed them

as they left. The other men were looking around, still confused.

I wanted to get up but I didn't know what would happen now.

After what seemed like an eternity, Mom got up. "Come on, Caleb. You're coming with us."

"What's the plan now?" one of the men asked.

Mom looked at him. "Let's regroup at ten."

We were quiet on the way back to the room, but Izzy held my hand. I was afraid I might get in trouble, and I thought she was afraid of the same thing. I'd thrown a huge wrench into the vacation.

Well, it wasn't exactly my fault, but that was how everybody would see it.

When we got back, Mom told Caleb to sit quietly, so he put his earbuds in and relaxed on her bed.

My nerves were going haywire because I thought for sure I was in trouble. I sat on the bed.

Mom sat next to me. "I can't believe you did that." But instead of anger, there was awe in her voice, which totally surprised me.

"Well, I was mad."

"With good reason. I'm sorry Gina and Susan weren't more sympathetic. At least Bridget was mad, too."

"Yeah, but now it's going to be worse at school. Logan will be an even bigger dick to me."

"Somehow I think you can take it. You've gotten stronger lately."

I didn't think she was right about that, but maybe it would become true. Standing up for myself had felt good. I felt lighter, even proud.

Chapter 61

Mom sent Caleb and Izzy—Alyssa and Kayla promised to watch her—off to Six Flags with the rest of the group that day, and she and I went shopping. Obviously, this retail therapy didn't involve clothes. No, we went to Barnes & Noble first.

As we parked, Mom said, "I can only buy you one book. But we can get a coffee and sit for a while if you want to."

"Sure."

I headed over to the sci-fi section while Mom went to the magazines.

I perused the shelves until I found something that looked good by an author I'd heard about but never read.

Mom was sitting with a steaming cup in front of her, reading *People* or something like that. She smiled when she saw me. "Hi, honey."

"Found a book." I held it out for her.

She dug her credit card out of her purse. "Get a drink, too, and we'll relax for a bit."

I nodded and went up to buy the book and get a chai tea latte.

We sat there for a while until Mom finished the magazine.

"Honey," she said.

Her hesitant tone made my chest tighten. "Yeah?"

"Your dad and I have been looking for another psychiatrist for you."

"Mom," I said, looking around but observing we were alone. "Is that really necessary?"

"I think it is. You aren't very happy."

I shrugged, blushing a little.

"I don't think it's your fault. I think you take after your grandmother."

"Because of her painting?" She was a great watercolor artist. It wasn't my thing, but she was good.

"She was never like all the other women, you know."

"Wasn't she a hippie?"

Mom laughed. "Yeah, but that's not what I'm talking about. She never quite fit in with the ladies. I mean, she tried to, but it didn't come naturally to her. She didn't like cooking, never learned to sew, stuff like that. She wasn't as into church, either. She had an independent and unique streak in her. It was just hard for women to express that in those days. Harder than now. Especially in small-town Arkansas."

"Huh." Was I like her? As hard as it was, was it easier for me, now, since there was a concept of a gender spectrum? Would she be like me if she was a kid now? She'd died of a heart attack about seven years ago.

"And she struggled with a bit of depression, too. It was never terrible, but it was usually there."

I nodded. My phone vibrated right then but I didn't think I should check it. Mom took the lid off her drink and swirled it. The rich scent of the coffee made the moment seem weird.

"Anyway, I think you may have inherited that tendency."

"You think I'm depressed?" My phone vibrated again. The only people who ever texted me were Sam and Mom.

"Sometimes I worry. Would you tell me if you felt really bad?"

"I don't. I just feel sorta bad a lot, never terrible." Well, except for right after Sam and Zach. But there was a reason for that.

She squeezed my hand. "Promise me you'll talk to me about it if you ever feel worse than that?"

"Okay."

Mom finished her drink. "I'll be back." She left with the magazine.

I pulled out my phone and read a text from Sam. She'd convinced her mom to pay to fly me to Glasgow for a visit if my parents would let me go.

I was in utter shock. Her mom must not hate me as much as she used to. Maybe because of Zach. She no longer thought I was corrupting Sam to lesbianism.

Mom came back, and I could barely contain my excitement. "Mom!"

"Hmm?"

"Sam says they will pay for me to go there for a visit."

Mom grimaced. "Honey, I don't think it's a good idea."

"Please?"

She looked at me and my puppy dog face and said, "I'll talk to Dad."

"Thank you!" That was easy. He would say yes for sure.

"When did they say?" she asked.

"Spring break." Three long months away.

Chapter 62

On the Wednesday we went back to school, we got a new assignment in art: a graphic design, our first one ever. We were to design the yearbook cover. Ms. Tolliver explained that this was just a class assignment, and the yearbook committee did the covers, but we should have fun with it.

"Here are some yearbooks from past years," she said as she began passing around maroon and white books.

The couple she handed my table were both maroon and had an embossed mustang on them. I didn't think they were very interesting, and this year wouldn't be any better. Logan had been on the committee since sixth grade, and I knew he'd designed last year's. I guessed he'd get this one, too.

I had some ideas and started sketching them out. My favorite one had an upside-down white equilateral triangle at the top of the maroon cover with the year written out inside it. At the very bottom, "MUSTANGS" would be written in white. Then there would be two embossed right-angle triangles with short horizontal sides on top of the

"MUSTANGS" and long vertical sides intersecting the top triangle.

I started mocking it up in pastels and soon had a good basic design. Then the class was over, and I had to go, but I took it with me because I wanted to work on it at home. For some reason, I was getting into it.

Once I was home, I pushed the dragon drawing away to give myself more room and mocked up another design.

Soon, I had two more designs, though I didn't like either as much as the first.

Then the front door opened, and Caleb and Logan came in along with another couple of guys, which made my stomach twinge. They stopped in the kitchen to get Cokes for everyone but Logan, who had his ever-present coffee. Logan stared at me in a way that was supposed to be disdainful. Unfortunately, it still had an effect on me, making my face heat and my hands shake. He said something quietly, and all of them looked at me and laughed before going upstairs.

Why couldn't I simply let it roll off my back?

Izzy got home a little after that and came in to bug me.

"What are you working on?" she asked.

"A design for the yearbook cover."

"Oh, cool!"

"It's not going to be on it. It's just an assignment."

"Oh."

She ran upstairs and returned with her sketchbook. "I want to do one, too."

I explained what needed to be there, and we worked in silence for a while.

Dad was working late so I fixed us a quick frozen pizza and got back to the design project.

We sat back down to work some more, and soon I heard the guys on the stairs, which got my pulse going again. They got to the kitchen and Caleb reached into the fridge for a Coke while Logan dumped his coffee in the trash. Then he stopped and stared at us.

"Go away!" Izzy said. "You're a jerk."

All four of the guys laughed and then they were gone.

"It worked," Izzy said.

I relaxed and smiled at her. "If only it were always that easy."

Chapter 63

There were still about fifteen minutes to go before the art club meeting started.

"I'm going to contact the yearbook committee," Ms. Tolliver said, in reference to the yearbook design I'd turned in a couple of weeks ago. She had it out on her desk again. "It's just so sharp!"

"Thanks." I couldn't help but smile. At least there was one thing I didn't suck at, even if I couldn't hold a conversation or entice a boy to save my life.

She squeezed my shoulder and then went off somewhere. A couple of girls came up to me and I was excited for a moment. Someone was going to talk to me?

"So Sam's gone?" one of them asked. I couldn't remember her name.

"Yeah, she left last month."

They both nodded. "Too bad," said the other one, whose name I didn't know, either.

"Yeah, I'm bummed about it," I said. This wasn't going well. I really didn't know what else to say.

"Okay, well, talk to you later." They went off to chat

with someone more skilled at the art of conversation, I guessed.

I leaned against one of the tables in the back of the room and crossed my arms, watching the group. Ms. Tolliver was talking to a freshman girl I didn't know. There were almost twenty kids, all mingling successfully. No one else was standing away from everyone, watching. That was me. Why was this so hard for me?

Then I saw Mia come in. I instantly relaxed a tad and smiled and waved at her, both of which she returned. She stopped to say something to a girl who was in our class and had never come to one of the club meetings before.

Then she weaved her way past the tables and said, "What are you doing all the way back here?"

"Hiding."

She laughed. "At least you'll admit it. You should come talk to people, though. Most of these people are nice."

I didn't agree, but said, "I know."

"Are you getting ready for the contest?" she asked.

"Yeah. You?"

"Sure. What are you entering?"

I listed the various things I already knew, which included the yearbook design. "Plus I think I'm going to enter that giant pot."

"That pot is cool. I'm going to start learning the wheel next week," she said.

"Oh, neat. It's supposed to be really hard."

Wow, I was actually carrying on a conversation. This was amazing.

"Yeah, Ms. Tolliver said she has to work with me directly for a while, which is why I've had to wait."

Now that I'd been looking at her for a few minutes, I thought it looked like her left eye was purple, even though she had on a ton of makeup to cover it up. "Do you have a black eye?" I blurted.

She flinched and looked away. "No. Well, yeah, but it was stupid. I seriously hit my head on the top of my boyfriend's car when I was getting in. It was crazy."

"Oh. That sucks." It smelled like a lie. What had really happened? Not that it was my business. Unless it was? Was somebody beating her up?

"I need to go talk to Maddy." And she was gone, too.

Good job, Nic. Run off the one person who would talk to you.

Chapter 64

Saturday, I sat on my bed IMing Sam. I told her all about the art club meeting and my failure to talk to anyone but Mia.

Sam: mia seems nice

Me: she is

Sam: you think shes a potential friend

Me: i dont know. art class friends, sure, but maybe thats it

Sam: yeah, that happens

I thought of Mia's bruised face the other day, and the way she ran off once I brought it up.

Me: i have a question for you

Sam: shoot

Me: mia had a black eye

Sam: really?

Me: you think you could get a single black eye from hitting your head on the side of a car when youre getting in?

Sam: maybe? the human body is weird

That was true. Still, I had such a bad feeling about it. But I had no idea what to do.

Me: but … i dont know. its just, i dont know

Sam: if you think something is wrong, maybe talk to the art teacher

Maybe I should tell Ms. Tolliver. She'd know what to do. But it still felt weird.

Me: anyway, tell me more about glasgow

Sam: its still very rainy. and cold. i mean, its not freezing, but its so wet it gets under your skin

Me: ah

Sam: people seem okay. they like my accent. im at an international school, but there are a lot of local kids, too. the americans are kind of snobby because they found out im from OK

Me: where are they from?

Sam: NY, LA, other "important" places. somebody actually called me an okie. they were joking, but still

Sam: oh, and they're obsessed with the musical *Oklahoma* here. Like, not americans, but other people keep coming up and singing songs from it

That made me half-heartedly smile.

Me: ha! thats funny. have you ever seen it?

Sam: not since elementary school. i dont remember it at all

At least somebody's life wasn't falling apart.

Sam: are you still seeing that crazy shrink?

Me: no. my mom decided last month to stop because he was such an idiot

Sam: thats cool, i guess

What did that mean? I took a sip out of the can of Coke on my nightstand.

Me: you guess?

Sam: you know. cool

Me: ok

Sam: i joined a jazz band here. its after school twice a week

Me: thats good

Sam: so what else is going on

Me: absolutely nothing

It was too true. We'd already gone over what had happened on the Texas trip in depth, so she knew everything that was important in my life at the moment.

I wondered what it would be like to be starting up a new life somewhere so different from here.

This made me think of that school again. Oklahoma City wouldn't be that different from Emerson, but at least it would be new kids. I could start fresh.

Me: actually, im still thinking about OAMS

Sam: i think you should do it

Me: im not sure. getting away would be good, but its probably a lot of work and i might not have as much time for my art

Why was it so hard to make decisions like this?

Sam: I still think you should do it. so … i have news

Me: whats that?

Sam: i have a boyfriend

Oh. Jealousy surged through me. Of course she did.

Me: did you break up with zach?

Sam: oh, yeah

Me: how did he take that?

Sam: i dont know. hard to tell over IM

Me: true

Now I wondered again if he'd want to go out with me.

I realized how idiotic that was. I was still me and still ugly. Not a real person. Nothing had changed.

Sam: hes local. his name is donald

Me: donald?

Sam: i know, it sounds ridiculous, but its not weird here

Me: if you say so

Sam: i do

Me: whats he like?

This conversation hurt. Sam had somehow turned into this desirable girl while I was still nothing.

Sam: tall, black hair, pale skin, skinny

Me: ok …

Sam: hes funny, but he has a real glasgow accent and half the time i have no idea what hes saying

Me: ha!

Sam: its funny. but seriously, nic, you have to leave OK. things are so different when youre not there!

Me: ive got my college fund

Sam: where are you planning to go?

Me: well …

I had never told her this before. I had big dreams. It always seemed weird because Sam was a better artist than me, and she planned to be an engineer. She was smarter, too. That's simply how it was. The Rhode Island School of Design was at the top of my list, with the School of the Art Institute of Chicago a close second.

Me: RISD, or SAIC, or yale …

Sam: awesome!

Me: you think i have a chance?

Sam: definitely. you do need to really work on your portfolio, but you can do it. plus, even if you dont get into a fancy art school, there are plenty of good programs at state schools that arent in OK.

It was nice that she would say that. I wasn't sure it was true, but she probably thought there was at least a chance, or she wouldn't say it. She wasn't a liar.

Sam: you could probably make friends there. people would be more like you

I wondered if she was right. And then I thought about guys at art school. They'd be different from guys in Emerson, wouldn't they? Definitely. Maybe I would have better luck there with romance. Like, have a chance.

Sam: hey, hold up. somethings happening

Me: what?

Silence. What did she mean, something's happening?

I sat there for a while waiting for her to respond, but there was nothing. I pinged her again with a question mark, but she still didn't reply. I was a little worried, but what could it be?

I went over to my desk and tried to work on some of the D&D figurines I hadn't touched in a couple weeks but my hands were shaking because I was wondering what was up with Sam.

There was a knock at my door.

"Yeah?"

"Ready to go, Nic?"

I'd forgotten Dad was taking me out today to learn to drive Mom's car. "Be down in a minute."

I checked the computer again even though I knew she hadn't replied yet. What had happened?

Chapter 65

I was officially worried about Sam by Sunday morning. Something bad must have happened. It was driving me crazy that I couldn't find out.

Finally, *finally*, at about eleven, she wrote me back.

Sam: omg!

Me: what happened?

Sam: there was a fire. we had to go out so fast, there was so much smoke.

Me: youre ok?

Sam: yes, it was not in our actual flat, just two floors up. but were in a hotel because we cant go back to the flat. theyre going to have to make all these repairs, so were going to have to find a new one

That must have been scary. And crazy, since there she was, just IMing me, and suddenly she has to run out of the building.

Sam: but you havent yet realized the biggest thing

Me: what do you mean?

Sam: *everything* is smoke damaged. all our clothes, bedding, that stuff

Me: ok…

She was obviously getting to something.

Sam: all my drawings and paintings

Me: oh!

Sam: theyll forever smell like smoke. And this isnt like some campfire smoke. it smelled horrible

I couldn't imagine. All her art, permanently damaged. I mean, not the figurines, but any paper.

Me: fuck. im so sorry

Sam: i guess it could be worse. it really was scary with all the smoke. so we could have actually died or something. it kind of makes you realize that life is short

Me: yeah

This sounded nothing like her. It was crazy. But I guess almost dying would change your perspective.

Me: im just glad ur ok

Sam: thanks. k, ive got to go. my dad needs the computer back

Wow. I didn't know what to think. I was so glad she was okay. Imagine if she'd died. I'd have nobody at all.

Chapter 66

I had to go to my new shrink a couple weeks later. Her office was different from Dr. Holmes's—even the outside was warmer and less sterile. It was in a small one-story office building not far from the house.

We arrived a few minutes early and faced the door, a heavy wooden one covered in many layers of white paint. Anastasia Goldberg, a name plate read.

"Should we knock or just go in?" Mom asked.

"I don't know, I'm not the adult here."

Mom laughed and tried the doorknob, pushing the door open when it turned. "Guess we'll find out."

We went into a very small waiting area with one of those blue water dispensers next to a small table with a magazine spread, and then another door that led further into the building. That must be where the session would be. My stomach twinged. A tiny, cushy, brown loveseat was on one wall and a wingback chair was squeezed into the last remaining space on the other wall, a tall plant in the corner between them.

I took the chair while Mom perused the magazines,

finding an old *People*. Even though I teased her about it, she liked to read it. But she was too cheap to buy it, even before our financial woes.

I played a game on my phone and after a couple minutes, the other door opened and a man emerged. He looked about forty. I accidentally made eye contact with him, which was awkward and made me blush. He averted his eyes and went through the front door.

Right after that, a middle-aged woman peeked around the door. "Nicole?"

Mom said, "That's right."

She smiled apologetically and said, "I'll be with you shortly." Then she disappeared again and we went back to entertaining ourselves.

It was one minute past the scheduled time. I wondered if Mom had noticed.

The woman came back out. "I'm so sorry. I'm running a little behind. It's not normally like this." She gave me a warm smile and extended her hand. "I'm Dr. Goldberg."

I shook it—her handshake was firmer than Dr. Holmes's had been, which made me feel better—and she turned to Mom and they shook hands and then she invited us back, gesturing toward a small couch.

The waiting room plant was a triplet, because there two more just like it in this room. I briefly wondered if the other one was lonely. Maybe Dr. Goldberg played music for it after hours.

She also had a desk, and like Dr. Holmes, she sat in a chair next to it that faced the couch.

So this part wasn't that different from the first session with Dr. Holmes, except that she didn't have me take a bunch of tests and didn't make me feel self-conscious. Also, she asked me what name I went by early on, which I appreciated. We talked about therapy goals and family history—this time I heard it all, unlike with Dr. Holmes. She explained about doctor-patient confidentiality. Basically, she wasn't going to tell Mom what we talked about except in extenuating circumstances.

Then Mom went back out to the waiting area.

"Enjoy your *People*," I said.

"I don't read it for the celebrities," she said.

"Sure," I said, stretching it out just as she shut the door.

Dr. Goldberg gave me another friendly smile. She was in a long, crinkly navy skirt and wore a loose white shirt. Her hair was black and curly and she looked kind of like a retired hippie. I didn't feel waves of disapproval rolling off her. I liked her.

"So, I have some more questions to ask you now that your mom isn't here."

"Sure."

She flipped to a new sheet on her clipboard and began going through a laundry list of questions. We established that I didn't smoke, drink, do drugs, or have sex. My sleep was okay—sometimes I couldn't fall asleep, but most of the time I did, and once I was asleep, I stayed that way. My hobbies were art, reading, and painting figurines. Nothing revolutionary.

Then she said, "I'd like to talk about your relationships and family. What's it like at home? Who do you live with?"

I told her about my parents and siblings. She asked if any of them had ever made me feel unsafe or had hurt me, so then I figured out this was the abuse screening, which made me nervous because I wondered if the big question would be asked, and if I'd lie.

"Have you ever been hurt or threatened by anyone?" she asked.

"Not really." I fiddled with a loose thread in my jeans.

She nodded and wrote something down before looking up again. "Have you ever been forced to do something sexual that you didn't want to do?"

Okay, there it was. I blinked. My heart started racing, and I stared at the picture of horses in a field she had over her desk. Then I slowly said, "Yeah." I felt like the word was being pulled out of my mouth like a piece of taffy stuck to my back teeth.

"Can you tell me a little about it?"

"I don't really want to. I know what's appropriate and legal and what's not, and it wasn't." My stomach was roiling, and I was starting to sweat.

I could see out of the corner of my eye that she nodded. "How old were you?"

"Nine." I crossed my arms, trying to calm myself.

"Is it someone you have contact with now?"

"No." Thank God.

"And will you potentially have contact with this person again?"

"Unlikely." I pressed my folded arms into my stomach.

"Can you be sure?" she asked.

"It was a friend of my dad's who stayed with us for a little while back then. He's gone, lives in some other state. I think he was going through a divorce or something." The words spilled out with surprising ease.

"Okay, Nic. If that's the case, I don't have to report it to Child Protective Services. But we can if you want."

My eyes widened. Everyone would know. "I don't think so."

She nodded, tapping her pencil on her clipboard. "Do your parents know about the abuse?"

My face flushed, and I put my shaking hands on my cheeks to cool them. My stomach was flipping over. "No. I don't want them to know."

"It might be a good idea to tell them some time, but I won't pressure you."

"Okay." My shoulders relaxed, and I dropped my arms to my sides.

"Nic, let's talk about something else." Her voice was soothing. She asked me things that I imagined seemed mundane to her. We went back to family talk, which led to what a jerk Caleb had become and how I was worried Izzy would turn against me, too. I gave her the basics and soon enough I was out of there.

Chapter 67

When Zach picked me up the next Wednesday for Key Club, I was already feeling crappy. It was Valentine's Day, which of course reminded me of what a loser I was. They had one of those super-cheesy fundraisers where kids would buy a rose for somebody, and other students delivered them in class all day. It was annoying and disruptive and made me crazy jealous.

So I didn't even watch for Zach's rearview mirror looks. I rested my head against the window and absorbed all the bumps along the way. I wondered if he really wanted to drive me to this thing. Maybe I should come by myself.

It was weird having talked to Dr. Goldberg about the abuse. I'd been thinking about it constantly, remembering details I'd thought I'd forgotten. At least the whole world didn't know about it. I was surrounded by people who didn't know. I still couldn't imagine telling my parents. But I was mad at them about it now. Why hadn't they noticed? I was just a little kid—I shouldn't have had to fend off a grown man all on my own.

We parked in the lot and headed into the building.

Mia found me while we were waiting for the meeting to start, and we chatted a bit. The black eye was long gone. There was just a month until the contest deadline so we were both scrambling to finish things up.

Then she said, "You know the sculpture project we're supposed to work on?"

"Yeah." Ms. Tolliver had assigned us a non-ceramic sculpture, which we had until the end of the school year to finish. Most people were working in groups, but I hadn't thought about that.

"Do you want to work as a group? Just the two of us?"

This made me smile. How flattering. I felt honored. "I could do that."

"It's just, I think we could come up with something cool since we have such different styles. You always go big and creative."

"And you always do such amazing detail work. I see what you mean. This could be really cool." It could. "Do you have any ideas?"

"Not yet. But I wondered if you had time this weekend. Maybe we could get together to brainstorm."

She wanted to hang out outside of school? She must not have thought I was that weird. I nodded. "I can do that."

We made arrangements to meet at a Starbucks on Saturday. Then the meeting was called to order so we sat down.

I found Zach and Evan afterward and followed them out while they talked about video games. Even though I was in a better mood than earlier because of the plan with Mia, I figured I should talk to Zach.

When there was a lull, I said, "Zach."

"Hmm?" He turned around.

"I think I can convince my dad to let me borrow the car so I don't need rides from you anymore."

"But that would be breaking our tradition."

He thought of it as a tradition? With me involved? This was unexpected, and it made me feel happier than it should have. I smiled. "Well, we can keep it going, as long as you don't mind."

"I don't mind."

We reached the car, and he unlocked it.

"Cool." It *was* cool that he didn't mind. But I wondered again why he'd looked at me all those times last fall. And the end of my freshman year. Had he been thinking about me and then decided Sam was better and just went for it? Or had I really misread the whole thing? And had Sam, too?

Why stare at somebody?

I'd probably never know.

Chapter 68

When I got to Dr. Goldberg's office the next day, she was ready for me. She came out as soon as we were through the front door.

We went into the back room, and she shut the door as I settled on the couch. I wondered if she'd want to talk more about the abuse, but she didn't, which was a huge relief.

"Let's talk about something we didn't get to last week," she started. "Tell me about a normal day at school."

"Well, it's just classes and that's it."

"What about lunch? Do you eat with anyone?" She smiled and recrossed her legs under another long skirt.

"I usually skip lunch, or get something fast and eat on the way to the library. I don't have any friends."

"Any prospects?"

I shook my head and looked away, missing Sam. "My only friend moved to Scotland two months ago."

"That must have been tough. Were you close?"

"Yeah." She asked me for details, and I told her a little about Sam and about the failed OSIN.

The nice thing about her was that she seemed sympathetic about thingsm, and she didn't repeat everything I said.

"Have you ever had a boyfriend? Or a girlfriend?" she asked, after the Sam topic fizzled out.

I shook my head, blushing as I thought of Zach and Carlos. God, I was such an idiot. "I'm not a lesbian," I finally said.

"Okay. Boyfriend?"

"No."

"Do you want one?"

I shrugged and stared at the horse picture.

With Zach, it was a more abstract desire now, because although I still liked him—more than I should—I also knew there was no chance.

"Is there anyone in particular you're interested in?"

"Ha. No. There's no point. There's no chance anyone would like me back."

"What makes you say that?" she asked.

"The fact that I live in reality. I'm ugly."

"That's harsh, Nic. You're not ugly."

I gave her my spiel on the American standard of beauty and all that and she nodded.

"I understand. But I don't think it's black or white. So what if you couldn't be a model? Neither could I. Most of us couldn't. That doesn't mean you're ugly."

I didn't agree, but already knew there was no point in arguing.

"Do you think you're ugly because you choose to not present yourself as extremely feminine?"

I laughed, because that was the understatement of the year.

Even Dr. Goldberg smiled a little. I guessed she knew why I was laughing.

"I think some people think I'm ugly because of that,

but I also know that, even if I tried to wear femininity, it would come off all wrong on me." I told her about the incident with the makeover and how that made me feel. Just thinking about it had me stressing all over again. "Everyone thinks I'm a lesbian," I said.

"What do you think of that?"

"I hate it for two reasons. One, they say it like it's a terrible thing, and it isn't. It isn't such a big deal. Some people are gay, so what? Two, it's just not true."

She nodded and said, "But also, if people think you are gay, boys won't be interested in you."

I blushed, because as stupid and pointless as it was, I also thought that.

Not that it mattered. That wasn't the reason no one liked me. "You know what, I sort of hate people," I said.

"In what way?"

"They're so shitty to me, all the time. It's like, it doesn't matter what I do. If I try to conform, they mock me for not doing it right—that happened several times in middle school. If I don't, they constantly judge me. Even adults. God, in some ways, they're the worst. There's that whole complete and utter bullshit message of, 'Just be yourself!' that everybody spews. But almost all the adults in my life tell me every chance they get how I'm not living my life right. 'Why don't you draw girly stuff? You should wear makeup. Blah blah.' I hate it."

She nodded. "I can see that. When you say all adults, do you include your parents in there?"

"No. They're nice. They seem to like me even though I'm all wrong." I paused. "Everything about me is wrong."

"Do you really think that, Nic?"

"I don't know what I think. Sometimes I feel like I know I'm worth something. Like I'm better than all these small-minded idiots. Other times I feel like a freakish loser."

"This is something we can work on. Because I think you do know you're a smart, talented person, and you just need to learn to remember that."

It was nice to be told that by an adult other than Mom or Ms. Tolliver. Even if she probably told everyone that.

I looked at the clock on the table beside the couch. We had, like, four minutes left.

"How would that work?" I asked.

"It's part of the cognitive behavioral therapy methodology. We can go over it in more detail next time. But I do want to tell you that one of the presumptions of the therapy approach is that patients often perceive things as worse than they really are. And the therapy addresses that and helps people see things more accurately. However, sometimes particular things really are as bad as they seem —I'm not going to deny that. I know that Oklahoma is not always a forgiving place for people who dare to be different. But there's still work we can do that will help you."

I looked at the clock again and saw it was time, so I got up.

I decided I liked this woman. I guess because she didn't judge me. She sort of got me, even though we'd just met.

Chapter 69

Kayla and Alyssa were in my room, which was weird. It was Friday night, and their parents were over. Izzy was at a slumber party. It'd been about six weeks since I last saw any of them except the kids at school. I wasn't happy about them being there, but whatever. My mom had just asked me to deal with them for a little bit. Alyssa lay across my bed on her back, and Kayla sat at my desk looking at my figurines. I sat on the floor next to the desk.

"Can I touch them?" Kayla asked.

"Yeah, they're dry. It's fine."

"What're those hooks for?" Alyssa asked, pointing at the ceiling.

I laughed. "Don't you remember the canopy bed I used to have?"

"Oh, my God!" Alyssa said. "How could I forget? I was so jealous of that, especially because I knew you hated it."

"It was cool for hiding out. Back before Caleb was a dick, we used to play all sorts of games up in there. We had one called Boat where we'd pretend it was a boat, and the goal was to not fall off, but of course seas were choppy so we had to constantly rescue each other from drowning. Especially Izzy. She loved to be rescued."

Kayla laughed. "That sounds so tedious. My brother and I used to pretend like we were in a piano bar. He'd play, and I'd sing all sultry-like. At seven. It must have been awful."

"I'm jealous," Alyssa said. "I always wanted a brother."

I snorted. "If you had one, you'd wish you didn't. My brother hates me, and the feeling's mutual."

"Your brother's nice, Kayla," Alyssa said.

"He's nice to you because he thinks you're hot."

A rush of jealousy hit me. Of course he did. What would that be like? To have someone think you were hot?

Not that I cared about Kayla's brother specifically. He was a jerk, despite what Alyssa had said.

Alyssa laughed. "He's not my type."

"You mean short?" Kayla said.

"Yeah, I guess."

"How's Jackson?" Kayla asked.

"He's good," Alyssa said.

Jackson was a popular senior with a reputation for being a player. Was Alyssa with him? I could ask, but I didn't really care.

That was kind of bitchy of me. But also true.

They started back and forth, naming and analyzing boys. Every one of them who I knew I also knew was a douche. Some of them had made fun of me at some point, while others were present when it happened.

Alyssa kicked her feet out where they dangled off the side of the bed. "What about you, Nic? You like anybody?"

"No." What was the point?

A text came in on Alyssa's phone.

"That's Nathan," Alyssa said. She sat up. "He's ready."

"Is he coming here?" Kayla asked.

It occurred to me that it was weird that Kayla didn't have a car. Her brother got a BMW on his sixteenth birthday, and she was seventeen.

Though to be realistic, her parents considered her a disappointment. They always had her on diets.

"What's your address, Nic?" Alyssa asked.

I gave it to her, and she texted it over.

"You want to come to the party with us?" Kayla asked, obviously hoping I'd say no, based on the tone of her voice.

"No, thanks."

"You should come," Alyssa said, not meaning it, either.

"I'm good here."

"Okay," Kayla said as she stood up. Alyssa followed her out the door.

I knew I should go down with them, but I had no desire to put up with their parents trying to convince me to go with them. Talking about how it would be "good for me." What a joke.

I worked on a few figurines before I braved the downstairs and went for a Coke.

Pete and Dad were in the kitchen mixing some kind of liquor.

"Hey, Nic. Why didn't you go out with Kayla and Alyssa?" Pete asked.

I didn't even look at him as I reached into the fridge for the can. Why should I? "Because I didn't want to."

Just then, Gina came in and said, "You should have gone. They would have helped you meet people and make friends."

That was bullshit. Everybody thought I should make an effort to be friends with them, but we had nothing in common, and I didn't even like them. Why was everybody so obsessed with the appearance of friendship? I only wanted to have meaningful friendships. And I didn't meet Sam at a stupid party.

I shrugged and slipped past her back up to my room.

I wondered, if they knew about the abuse, if they'd feel bad for me, or if they'd blame me for that, too. They'd be all, if she didn't act like such a victim, he would have left her alone.

It was probably true. Because the guy had left town eventually, but then a couple years later he visited again for a short time. He cornered me in the bathroom and asked, "Do you remember what we used to do?"

I said yes, and he asked if I wanted to do it again. I said no, and that was that. He'd left me alone. That's all it had taken.

Could I have done that any of the first times? Why hadn't I thought of it then? I should have. It would have been so easy.

Chapter 70

I sat down in Dr. Goldberg's office feeling self-conscious, given everything she knew about me. It was weird to have someone I hardly knew know my deepest secrets.

"Hello, Nic. How was your week?"

"Fine." I shrugged. "I had to see these horrible people my parents are friends with, which was awkward."

"Why are they horrible?"

I told her about everything that happened over the Texas trip, including Logan's "What the fuck are you doing here?" comment. She nodded at appropriate intervals.

"Do you think you did the right thing by telling them what Logan said?" she asked.

"Yes, even though it did no good. Well, except he got in trouble with his mom. I guess that was okay. Of course, he's been extra douchey to me at school, but whatever."

"What happened when you saw them recently?"

I explained. "One of the women implied I deserved a crappy social life since I wouldn't go to a party." I paused. "As if hanging out with people I don't even like would be a satisfying social life for me."

Dr. Goldberg nodded again. "Is that all that's happened since Thursday?"

"Oh, I met with this girl from my art class. We're doing a project together for class."

"Tell me about it."

"Well, we have really different styles." I explained about our different approaches to art. "So we came up with the idea of making a large dragon out of papier-mâché, which would primarily be my contribution. Then we're going to paint it with all these different-colored flowers. That will be her main contribution. Though we're both going to help with each other's parts."

"That sounds fun." She smiled at me.

"Yeah. I'm not super-big on the flowers, but it's what she wanted to do. I'm going to get to make a three-foot-tall dragon."

"That big? Wow."

I nodded.

"That sounds exciting. Anything else this past week?"

"No."

"Okay, then. I wanted to talk to you about something."

I immediately felt a sense of foreboding, and the nervous rumblings started in my stomach.

"I wanted to discuss a diagnosis of a mental health condition."

My stomach plummeted. She would tell me what was wrong with me. Make it official.

"How do you feel about that?"

"I guess it depends on what it is."

She nodded again. "Based on your family history and your own history, which I heard about from both you and your mom, I believe you have clinical depression."

Oh, wow. It was official.

Dr. Goldberg continued, "There is a form of depression called persistent depressive disorder, which is a chronic lower-grade depression, something that's always there and keeps you down. I think this is the form you have. Does this ring true to you?"

I didn't say anything. But then I nodded.

She said, "You're white as a sheet. This diagnosis is something that may last your whole life, but we are fortunate to live in a time when there are good therapeutic approaches available. Additionally, there are medications that can alleviate the symptoms, if it comes to that. Many, many people suffer from depression yet still live normal lives.

"How do the medicines work?"

"They bring you up when you're down. However, I would like to focus on therapy first, before considering medication."

I didn't say anything, still trying to take it all in.

"What do you think?"

"I don't know. It's scary to think I'll never get better."

"Depression is manageable. You will simply have to be more cognizant of your emotional state than some people might."

I nodded. I guessed that made sense. Still, it was horrible.

God. Having a shrink was stressful.

My body hated me. And so did my mind.

Chapter 71

The next night I was working on the dragon drawing, but I was restless. I couldn't stop thinking about my discussion with Dr. Goldberg. I needed to get my mind on something else.

Then, for some reason, I thought about the infamous self-portrait. I could enter that in the contest for the self-portrait category, but who knew what trouble that would cause. Maybe I could just do a more normal one.

Well, not totally normal, but not *too* creative.

"Izzy. Isabella." She was sitting across from me at the dining room table.

She smiled, probably glad I'd self-corrected. "Yeah?"

"Can you take a picture of me?"

"*You* want a picture of you?"

I laughed. Not something I'd want under normal circumstances.

"Yes. But I need a specific one. I am going to make a self-portrait. Come here."

I got into position, working on the drawing, and had her take one with me like that.

"The angle's wrong," I said after looking at it. "Take it from a chair."

She took a bunch as I tried several positions and facial expressions, which had us cracking up. She handed me the phone and got down.

We looked at the pictures together.

"That's my favorite," she said, pointing to the one where I'd crossed my eyes and stuck my tongue out.

"That's not the one I'm going to choose. I'm supposed to look like a serious art student."

"Still. Show Mom when she gets home."

"Fine, I'll keep it." I found one that looked kind of cool. My eyes were narrowed as I leaned forward to study the dragons.

"This is the one," I said, holding the phone out for Izzy to see.

"I like that one."

"Me too."

"I want to do a self-portrait, too," Izzy announced.

Of course she did. "Okay, I'll take a picture of you. We can print it off so you can work from it."

"What should I do?"

"Well, you don't have to be doing anything. You could simply smile at the camera."

"Oh, yeah." She put her finger to her lips, thinking. "I know."

Then she disappeared upstairs. I followed her because I needed to get new paper and colored pencils for the self-portrait. On the way back down I passed her room.

I walked in to see a bunch of clothes thrown on the bed. "What are you doing?"

"Trying to pick the right outfit." She emerged from the closet with a couple of skirts.

I laughed. Of course she wanted to look perfect. She

was hopelessly normal. "Well, you don't want that shirt because the lace would be really hard to draw, and you also don't want one with writing on it. Why don't you just wear a simple t-shirt?"

She frowned.

"And you probably should do the portrait from the waist up. Otherwise it might get hard. Fabric is hard to draw, so you don't want too much of it."

"Okay." She put the skirts back, and we dug through the stack on her bed until we found a green t-shirt. We had to compromise because this one had little decorative bling along the sleeves and collar. She figured she could do it.

We went back downstairs and both got to work. I worked like a dog all weekend and through the week—Izzy petered out on hers—and had it finished by the next Sunday night.

It was as cool as I'd hoped. This would be another contender in the contest.

Chapter 72

I went back to Dr. Goldberg the next Thursday.

"How has your week gone?" she asked.

"I don't know. I can't stop thinking about the abuse." And I couldn't. It was driving me crazy. I felt anxious almost all the time.

She nodded sympathetically. "That can happen, Nic. Do you think that means you want to tell your parents?"

It was strange, but I wasn't sure. I was getting increasingly mad at them about it, too. They'd totally failed me. I shifted my legs to get more comfortable. They brought this guy into my life and didn't protect me from him. I was younger then than Izzy was now. It wasn't fair.

"If you tell them, it will be difficult at first. But then over time, it will get easier. Most people who have supportive families find that they're glad that they opened up about it. It often heals old wounds no one knew were there."

I felt myself blink.

"Sometimes it's hard to move forward in therapy when

you have big secrets," Dr. Goldberg continued. "But it is entirely up to you."

Maybe she was right about the wounds. What if I just kept getting madder and madder? It seemed possible, given how things had been going.

"Okay, I'll do it," I finally said, surprised at my decision.

Dr. Goldberg nodded. "Let's talk about how you think the conversation will go."

We talked about it. She said she would start the conversation off and that my mom might be angry at first because she would be so surprised. We agreed she'd feel guilty right away. I didn't know how she'd act then, honestly. Dr. Goldberg said sometimes people lash out, but I didn't think Mom would. She was too conflict-avoidant.

Finally, she went to get Mom, who came in looking confused. "What's going on?"

I looked at the arm of the couch as I felt it shift when she sat down.

Dr. Goldberg said, "Nic revealed something to me that she wants to tell you about."

I wasn't looking at Mom, but I imagined her looking confused. "What?" There was a pause, and I said nothing.

"Something that happened to her when she was young," the psychiatrist prompted.

"What is it, honey?" Mom asked, sounding as confused as I'd imagined her.

I couldn't look at her.

"Are you really ready to talk about this, Nic?" Dr. Goldberg asked gently.

"Okay," I said. I looked at Mom, whose face was tense with worry, and had to turn away again.

"Remember Dad's college friend, Rob?" I asked. I

noticed I was wearing the jeans with the loose thread again.

"Yes," Mom said. "What?" There was another pause, and she shakily said, "No."

"He … did stuff to me." There, I'd said it.

Mom groaned like she was in pain, and I could feel her looking at me, though now I was staring at the horses again. They went blurry as my mind spun.

"What did he do?"

"I don't want to talk about the details," I said tightly to the horses. "But it was illegal, as it should be."

"Oh, God," she said, her voice cracking. She scooted over and hugged me even though I hadn't turned around. She sounded choked up when she asked, "How could I not know?"

She held on to my shoulders and asked, "How could you not tell me?"

I gritted my teeth. How could she blame me? I was fucking nine.

Mom's eyes widened and she gasped and said, "I'm sorry. It's not your fault." Then she hugged me again like she'd never let go.

"Mom, it happened ages ago." I was glad I couldn't see her face since she had me in a death grip. Which felt better than I might have expected.

She petted my head like I was four years old and asked, "Dr. Goldberg, what can we do?"

"Legally, you mean?"

"Yes."

"You can file a complaint with the police. They will have to investigate. But I'll be honest, these cases can be hard to win, and it will require Nic to go through a lot. I'm not advising you either way, but you should think about it."

"Mom, could you let go?" I asked because I thought I might cry from the emotion I felt rolling off her.

I accidentally looked at her face when she moved away and saw it was tear-stained. She left her arm over my back and gripped my shoulder, but she gave me some space.

Then Mom asked Dr. Goldberg a whole bunch more questions, and I didn't listen. As much as I hated him, I didn't think I wanted to relive any of it. I'd have to talk about the exact stuff he did, and made me do, and that was humiliating, even if I logically knew it wasn't my fault. This was just how things were.

Chapter 73

Saturday afternoon, I finally put the finishing touches on the drawing downstairs. It looked awesome. Both dragons looked good, but it was obvious from the way I'd shaded the one in the background that it would be the victor, even though the overconfident one in the foreground thought it was over.

The foreground one was seen from the back, but he was turning away. Arrogant. The background one had obviously just risen from behind the top of the mountain in a fierce position of power. Her wings and talons were extended and she zoomed toward him.

It was a more subtle variant of my original self-portrait. I could claim ignorance of the deeper message. "No, it's only two dragons fighting," I could say.

I stared at it, flushed with pride. I'd really concentrated and had managed to get it done well before the contest deadline. I had fixative spray upstairs.

I went up to my room and grabbed the spray just as my computer pinged with an IM from Sam. I told her about the finished drawing and we chatted for a bit. While we talked, I started thinking about the last couple days. They'd been hard, because both my parents were acting so weird about the big revelation. The abuse one. They'd handled the depression revelation a couple weeks ago fine. Mom kept breaking into tears when she looked at me. Not every time, but it was getting old. Dad was patting me on the shoulder a lot more and kept asking how I was. For once, he'd looked at the dragon drawing and admired it.

The thought that I could tell Sam about it all crossed my mind, but I rejected it as soon as I'd thought it.

We finished chatting, and I tossed my computer on the bed so I could work on this new dragon figurine I'd just gotten. I started the first coat in silver.

The side door of the house, which was right below my window, slammed shut. Caleb must have someone over.

I finished the silver coat and let it start drying. That was my last unpainted figurine so I lay back on my bed, hands behind my head.

I thought about Dr. Goldberg, which made me feel both calm and stressed, which was weird. It was because of her that there was this new strain between me and my parents. But when I was in her office, it always felt like things were getting better. We'd soon be starting the cognitive behavioral therapy she'd told me about.

She'd also told me something I loved, because it was so true and vindicating. Pessimistic people tend to have a more realistic view of the world.

Sometimes they took it too far, but my interpretation of this was that optimistic people were basically delusional.

For some reason, I thought of Gina and Susan and their unreasonable view of me. They tried to apply the same logic to me that applied to other people, and it just didn't work.

Bridget was so different from them, the way she didn't

think of me as weird. I remembered her reaction when I told the table what Logan had said to me in Texas. It made me smile. I would have loved to have been a fly on the wall in the room for his reaming.

Actually, come to think of it, he hadn't been that much of a bigger dick to me since then. A little, but not bad. Small favors, I guess.

I remembered that I had planned to spray the drawing. I got the fixative off my shelf and headed down the hall toward the stairs to grab the drawing.

I heard Caleb and Logan talking downstairs. For a second, I almost paused, but screw it. I wanted to get this thing sprayed.

When I stepped into the kitchen, I saw Logan in the dining room studying my drawing. He looked up and saw me and then got this evil look on his face. Like dead in the eyes. He took the lid off his coffee and held it over the drawing.

I gasped. "Don't." He wouldn't. He was an artist himself.

Then he tilted the cup until a bit spilled onto the drawing, right in the middle.

"No!" I charged him and pushed the cup out of the way. A bunch splashed everywhere, some on his shirt but most on the floor.

Caleb came in from the den looking shocked. "What the fuck, dude? She's been working on that for ages. Not cool."

Logan looked pleased with himself and set the cup down in front of the drawing. He wiped coffee off his arms. "Come on, let's go," he said. Then he was out the front door.

I stared at the drawing in true horror. There was an

almost circular pool of brown about two inches across almost dead center.

Caleb walked by and stopped for a second. He looked at the drawing and said, "Man." But then he was out the door, too.

Why had I left it out? I should have known something like this would happen.

Chapter 74

I got my shit together and ran into the kitchen to get paper towels to blot up the liquid that hadn't soaked in. My mind was spinning, but there had to be a way to fix this. There was still an obvious stain and the paper was buckled. It was right in the middle, so I couldn't crop it out. It overlapped the edge of the mountain into the sky, and covered some of the fire, so I couldn't just dye the whole mountain and pretend like it was on purpose.

I grabbed the picture and took it upstairs, and started googling anything I could do, my hands shaking on the keyboard. Pretty soon a plan emerged, but it was desperately time-sensitive. Antique paper was kind of brownish, right?

I snagged the coffee from downstairs—the large cup was about half full—and then grabbed a couple of black towels from the bathroom. I set these on the floor and put the drawing face up on top of them.

This was the moment of truth. Did I have the guts to pour coffee on my beautiful drawing? I smelled the liquid in the cup. I recoiled—disgusting. How could anyone drink coffee black? I guess if your heart matched it, maybe. Mine didn't.

First, I snapped a picture.

I took a deep breath and poured coffee on the corner of the drawing. It spread in tendril-like fashion. I poured some right on top of the foreground dragon. Then on the left side where there was more of the burning shrubbery.

It had spread to a lot of places, but there was still plenty of white. So I poured more on it, a little bit here, a little bit there. I had to take a paintbrush to spread it out because it was starting to pool in the middle. I used some paper towels to soak the excess up. But the paper was already starting to buckle in other places, and the coffee was pooling in those areas. I left some of that to give it a more natural look.

Once it was covered, I left it to soak for several seconds, my heart beating like crazy because I'd just poured coffee on a drawing I had spent so many hours on. But Logan's work had sat that long while I was frozen in inaction. Then I used paper towels to blot up all the liquid.

The next order of business was to keep the paper from buckling too much. I grabbed another roll of paper towels. I technically needed newspaper for this, but paper towels would have to do. I frantically pushed everything off my desk so the drawing would fit, barely. Then I put some wax paper down, then a layer of paper towels, then the drawing face down. I put several heavy books on top of it.

A knock sounded at my door, which sent my stomach jumping again.

"Yeah?"

"Hi, honey, can I come in?" Mom.

"Okay." God, she probably wanted to talk again.

She opened the door and poked her head in. "Smells like coffee." As she walked on in, she said, "Did you finish your drawing? I noticed it wasn't downstairs. I want to see it."

Shit.

She looked around for the drawing, settling on the desk.

"What are you doing? What happened?" she asked, sounding alarmed.

"Logan happened. He poured coffee on it." God, it hurt even to say it.

"What?!" Her eyes went wide.

"I guess that's what I get for being stupid enough to leave it out." But my heart twisted again as I wished desperately I'd just brought it upstairs after finishing it.

"This is your house!" Her hand went to her forehead. "Of course it should have been safe to leave out!"

I showed her the picture I'd taken before I poured the coffee on. My hands were still shaking.

"He did this?"

"Yep."

"Oh, my God!" She pulled her phone out of her pocket. "I'm calling Bridget."

"No, Mom, don't." I put up my hands. "What's the point? Besides, I think it will end up okay. It's just going to look like antique paper. I'll pretend it's what I always intended to do."

She sat on the bed, face in her hands. "I'm so sorry, Nic. I don't know why there are always such horrible people everywhere. And we have to work around them."

"I think sometimes you have to fight back."

Mom nodded. "Like you did in Dallas."

"Yeah."

"I still can't believe you did that. I was so proud of you." Her voice wobbled a little, and she put her arm around me.

"Did you hear Gina and Susan whispering about the foul mouth on me after I repeated what he'd said?"

"They did?" She rested her head against mine.

I shrugged. "I can't stand your friends."

"I know. I don't blame you." She shook her head and crossed her feet. "I don't always like them, either."

"Why are you friends with them, then?"

"I'm not like you, Nic. I need friends, and I've known these guys a long time."

"Who says I don't need friends?" I scoffed. "I just have high standards."

"Is that what it is?"

"Yeah."

Then Mom looked at me a while, and I looked away because I could tell she was about to cry again, all because of what had happened seven years ago. Mom and Dad's new weird and guilty behavior was driving me crazy.

"Is the iron in your room?" I asked her.

"Yeah," she said in a thick voice.

I got it and dialed it up to medium low and then turned back around to attend to the drawing. I made sure there was no liquid left on it and set it on the floor next to the paper towels. I put down a layer of paper towels on the desk and then lay the drawing face up on top of them and put the towel, folded in half, on top of it.

Mom sniffed behind me. Personally, I had no time for this. I was all cried out.

I started ironing slowly, making sure not to stop. "Mom, I need to work on this."

"Okay, honey." She sniffed again and stood and I heard her leave.

Once I'd gone over the whole drawing several times, I pulled the towel off and replaced the paper towels under the drawing. Then I spread a layer of paper towels covering the top, and I started piling on books. I would have to change the paper towels every two hours until it felt dry, and then I'd have to leave it with the books on top of it for as long as seventy-two hours.

This meant I'd be getting up in the middle of the night tonight and wouldn't be able to use my desk for three days. All because of that prick.

But I would do what I had to do. I needed to win that contest. It would eventually help me get out of here.

Chapter 75

Friday was the day of the art contest, two weeks after I'd fixed my drawing—it had turned out good, better than I expected. We'd turned them in Monday, and teachers had hung everything up in the auditorium and judged the pieces over that week.

In art class, Ms. Tolliver called me into her office. I went in there with hands covered in wet clay, as I'd been working on a pot.

"I didn't tell you before because I didn't expect anything to come of it, but when I showed your yearbook design to the administration, they decided to have a vote between all the designs in the contest."

"Really? Including Logan's?"

She nodded. "Don't say anything to anyone because it's supposed to be a blind vote."

"He'll win, anyway," I said, feeling my lip curl. "Even though he's evil, he's pretty good."

"He is, but I hope yours wins, anyway." Then she lowered her voice and whispered, "I like you better."

This made me laugh. It was so nice to have one teacher on my side.

I went back to my table and continued working on the pot. I was trying coil again but my style was still lacking. I had it on a mold, but the lines were wobbly and I was inconstant with the thickness. I looked over at Mia's finely constructed tall and narrow coil pot.

"Is that going to be a vase?" I asked.

She nodded. "Yeah, so I'm trying to cover the inside enough so that it can hold water."

"Awesome. Are you excited about tonight?"

She smiled. "I am."

I definitely was. I wanted to see the results because I was still sure I'd win first place with my dragon drawing. I *had* to. I hoped I would win in some of the other categories, too. I'd also entered the colored pencil desert landscape I'd done last semester, as well as my giant pot, which was really cool. I entered a charcoal sketch I'd done. It was a boring image of a bowl of fruit, but I'd thought it looked good. I'd gotten the light just right. The last thing was the new self-portrait. I didn't expect it to win anything, but you never knew. Plus of course the yearbook design.

We continued working on our pots until class was over.

The rest of the day dragged on. The auditorium wouldn't open until six for us to see the contest results, then there would be some kind of presentation at seven, so I went to the coffee shop after school and waited for Dad to pick me up. Mom had to work.

He called to say he was running late, so I told him I'd go over there myself. When I went into the auditorium, there were numerous black dividers placed all over the stage and around the back and sides of the seating area, all with art hanging on them. I first found the pencil category and looked for mine. Before I got to it, my heart nearly stopped when I saw a blue ribbon on a drawing of a flower.

Oh, no. It couldn't be on my dragons if it was here. God. I almost tripped over my feet. I was destroyed. All that work for nothing.

But then hope blossomed. What about second place? My drawing was on the other side of the wall.

Not a single ribbon on it. All the air left me like I'd been punched.

How? I looked closely at the other drawings—the second and third place winners were on this side of the wall. One was a picture of a baseball game. It was precise and technically good, but boring. The other was a still life, the same one I'd done in charcoal. My charcoal one was better. It had actual *life* to it.

I didn't know any of the artists. They were probably juniors or seniors.

I needed to sit down because I was so shocked. But somehow I stumbled to the charcoal category. I saw one with a blue ribbon, but it wasn't mine. Next to it was a white ribbon. I walked along the wall until I spotted mine —it had a red ribbon next to it.

This should have made me feel better, but it didn't. The rest of the charcoal drawings weren't very good. Not very many people tried to work in the medium. If my dragons hadn't won me anything, how could I expect anything good?

My landscape won second place, too. Big whoop. I recognized the third place winner's, too—it was Mia's. For a second I felt superior because I beat her at something. Then I felt bad for feeling that way.

I found the self-portrait category and stared in shock at the blue ribbon hanging next to mine. This time, my heart did pinch from something like pride. Because this was a good drawing.

Holy crap. I was flooded with more pride and general happiness than I'd felt in ages. It was so surprising that it was almost overwhelming. I had to brace myself by putting my hand against the wall.

In a daze, I moved on to the ceramics area, tucked away behind the dividers on the stage.

I first saw the red ribbon on Mia's most delicate and impressive pot. It was a big, perfectly round bowl with roses placed all around the rim. She seriously made these thin flower petals and pieced together several roses. It was amazing to watch.

Then I found my pot, ribbonless.

Finally, I found the graphic design category. I recognized Logan's design—blue ribbon, with a white ribbon on mine. Great. Again, he gets to beat me.

Would the dragon drawing have won if he hadn't done what he did?

I felt sick. How could he have done that? I still didn't get it. He was an artist himself.

There were signs over the yearbook designs saying that we were voting on one for this year's yearbook. A table a bit further down had pictures of each and printed ballots with a tiny picture of each of them for people to circle. There was a big box with a slit in the top. I voted.

"Hey, Nic," Dad said.

I looked over. "Hi."

"How'd you do?"

"A first place, two second places and one third." I grinned stupidly.

"That's great."

"I'm bummed that my dragon drawing didn't even place, though." That one still hurt.

He patted me on the shoulder. "You're really too hard on yourself."

I heard something over by the entrance to the auditorium and saw Mia and a white guy with tattoos, gripping her arm. The guy I'd seen in the car picking her up that time. I think what I'd heard was him yelling at her. Then he dropped her arm and stormed off. I realized a bunch of other people were looking too, so I turned back to Dad.

"Show me your stuff," he said.

"Okay." He hadn't seen some of it, because I didn't bring all of it home. I showed him around and he admired it all. He didn't know anything about art, but Mom said I was good, so he figured it was true.

When we got to the ceramics tables, I saw Mia. She was running her finger along the roses of her winning bowl.

"Hey," I said.

She looked up, and I saw her tense face. Then she smiled, and it went away. "Hi."

"Congratulations." I wondered if she was okay, but didn't think I should say anything.

"Thanks. Congratulations on your wins. I only ended up with two ribbons."

Okay, so I had more than her. But at the moment I only felt bad for the little scene she'd had at the door. I changed my mind about asking.

Dad was looking at some of the other pots so I asked Mia, "Who was that guy?"

"My boyfriend," she said with a little blush. "I just said something I shouldn't have."

"Oh." I didn't know what else to say. What would that be like? To be with someone you had to be so careful around? I didn't think it would be worth it to me, as desperate as I was for a boy to like me. Or would it? It was hard to know what I'd put up with.

"It's no big deal. He'll be back later."

"Cool. Do you know what they're doing at seven?"

"No."

It was only another fifteen minutes before they started their little presentation. We all sat down, and they did everything on the edge of the stage. They had a few extra awards to give out. Most innovative. Most true to life. Then they got to what they were calling the Risk/Reward Award.

Ms. Tolliver explained, "This award is for the piece of art that takes the biggest risk but comes out with the biggest reward."

I didn't know what that meant, but then she said. "It goes to Nic Summers for her Dragons over Fire Mountain piece."

What was that about? It was stupid. It was like winning a prize for graduating kindergarten. I'd only done what I had to do.

"Way to go, Nic," Dad whispered as I went up to accept the purple ribbon.

A senior won the grand prize for a really cool abstract ceramics piece. It was made up of a bunch of cubes and was designed to look like it couldn't possibly stay upright, but it did.

On the drive home, I felt weird. It seemed like the strange award was a consolation prize. I wondered if Ms. Tolliver created it just because she knew how much work I'd put into the dragon drawing.

But it was only two days until I went to Scotland. I would simply have to focus on the first place and on Scotland and not think about being condescended to.

Chapter 76

I had to take three separate flights to get to Glasgow. First to Chicago, then to London, and finally to Glasgow. So even though I wouldn't get there until noon Sunday, I had to be at the airport at one on Saturday afternoon. I couldn't believe the day had finally arrived.

Dad drove me to the airport, but Mom came, too. They were quiet, and I was busy trying to imagine what flying would feel like, when Mom turned around and said, "Honey, your dad and I have something to tell you. We were debating telling you earlier, but we just found out for sure yesterday."

Oh, God. What could it be now?

"We have not been able to get out of this financial situation." She paused and looked over my shoulder. "We are going to have to give up all your college funds."

"What?!" Oh, my God! How was I supposed to go to college without any money? How would I ever go anywhere good? My stomach clenched. "What am I supposed to do?"

"I'm sorry." She did sound sorry, but I didn't care right then.

"Where am I supposed to go?" It felt like my throat was constricting.

"You can go in state. I'm sure you can get scholarships."

This was beyond-the-pale horrible. College was supposed to be my way out. I needed to leave. I *had* to. My stomach twisted more, and I found myself holding my shaking hands together.

Dad hadn't said anything the whole time. He was even worse with conflict than Mom was. He simply rubbed his beard, as per usual.

The rest of the drive was silent. We got there early enough that we parked and all walked into the airport.

I waited in line to check in and showed my new passport. I caught a glimpse of the photo and flinched. It was an especially bad picture. I was looking straight ahead so I almost had a double chin. It was hard to deny that I was ugly. My roving zit was on my forehead in the picture. Today it was on my chin.

The clerk glanced at the photo then me and back. What if she didn't let me on? But then she checked my bag and off it went down the conveyor belt, into the bowels of the airport. She gave me my boarding pass, and I went back to my parents, who were standing there looking weird. Like, excited that I was growing up and nervous I was going so far away.

But I was still mad at them.

"This way," I said, and they followed me. When we got to the security line, there weren't that many people ahead of me.

"Okay, honey," Mom said. "I guess it's time for you to go."

She hugged me and Dad followed suit. I wished they'd waited for me to get back to tell me about the college fund. Now I would spend the whole trip thinking about it. I started snaking my way along the roped off rows and my parents waited until I reached the end of the actual line of people.

I didn't look at them because I was getting nervous about going through security. It was supposed to be quite involved. I guessed I'd have to take my shoes off and whatever. All the people going through seemed to know what they were doing—I hoped I didn't make a fool of myself.

Then I showed the guy my passport and boarding pass and he pointed me to one of the lanes. Another guy was repeatedly saying what we were supposed to do. I took off my shoes and jacket and put them in a bin, put my phone in a little bin, and took my laptop out of my backpack, before putting my backpack itself through. Then I had to go through the body scanner thing. It was quite the ordeal, and my pulse was pounding by the time it was over.

As I gathered my stuff, slowly calming, I looked over to check and my parents were still there, waving at me. I waved back, embarrassed. Then I got everything together, sat down to tie my Chucks, and started looking for my gate.

Then it was a long wait—I was glad I'd brought a good book—until we started boarding. I managed to get on in the crush, find my seat, get my book and headphones out, stow my backpack, and get buckled in. I'd requested a window seat so I could look out. I was over the wing, which was annoying because it partially blocked my view.

The guy next to me was this old guy in a suit, which seemed weird on a Saturday. Next to him was a man in a cowboy hat.

I watched the flight attendant go through the emergency spiel and then sat back as the plane drove along the little roads to get to the actual runway. I was a little surprised by the takeoff, which threw me back in my seat and made a lot of noise.

But once we were in the air, I relaxed a bit.

It was about two hours to Chicago. Soon I was passing over a state I'd never been to. I'd be going over quite a few of those on the way. I pulled out my new passport, thinking about how, soon, it would have a stamp in it. Maybe one day it would have lots of them. It would be so cool to be anywhere other than Oklahoma.

Then my gaze fell on my picture, and I closed it, disgusted with myself again.

I tried to think of something that wasn't negative, per Dr. Goldberg's instructions.

The yearbook design thing. That had turned out well, surprisingly. Even though Logan's had won first place and mine only third, the people had spoken—they'd voted for mine, if that could be believed. So my design would be on the yearbook this year. There were three things about that that were excellent. One, it was my design going on the cover; two, it wasn't Logan's design going on the cover; and three, Logan had to work with my design since he was on the yearbook committee. Number three was my favorite.

Thinking about something positive made my mind uncomfortable, so it looked for something bad, zooming in on the college fund.

Oh, God. Everything was ruined.

My eyes burned but I successfully fought the tears back. Who wanted to cry in front of strangers? Or anyone, for that matter?

I couldn't let myself think about the college fund. I had to just focus on getting to Glasgow and Sam.

I pulled out my book and attempted to read, but everything was swirling in my head. The quiet roar of the plane was distracting, as was the excitement of getting ever closer to Glasgow. And of course the college fund problem.

Finding my new gate in Chicago was a bit of a hassle, but I figured it out. Of course, then I had a three-hour layover, which I spent reading. I would finish this book before I even got to Scotland.

Once I was on the London flight, I read some more before falling asleep. When I woke up, they were serving breakfast. I ate some kind of eggs and had OJ, filled out the customs form they gave everyone, and then we were in London. As we taxied to the gate, I turned my phone back on and it said 8:05. Which meant it was 2:05 in the morning in Tulsa.

This was it—I was in a foreign country. A place where cowboys, pickups, and guns weren't part of the norm. I smiled like an idiot.

Soon enough, my Glasgow flight was landing. I looked for Sam before realizing I hadn't left the secured area yet. I followed everyone out toward the baggage claim. I spotted Sam and her mom. At first I tried to decide if Sam's mom looked annoyed, but then Sam saw me and smiled and waved. I was so happy, it was almost hard to act like the normal me. We met each other halfway.

"Hey!" she said.

"Hey," I said, smiling big.

She surprised me with a hug. We'd never hugged before and at first it was weird, but once the initial surprise wore off, it was nice.

"Where's your bag coming in?" she asked.

"I'm not sure." I looked down at the various carousels.

"Let's go find it," Sam said.

"Yeah, okay. Let's."

Chapter 77

"Everything's so different," I said to Sam as we drove to her flat. There were tall buildings and black streetlights and small cars. And little shops like newsagents and grocers.

Sam's mom parallel parked on the street, and we went into a red door and dragged my stuff up two flights to their new flat, where they'd moved after the fire. I saw a couch in what must be the living room, and we put the suitcase in a bedroom that didn't look like Sam's because there was none of her artwork hanging.

Then Sam said, "Do you feel okay? Can you go for a walk? We have to get your transport pass today."

I was wired and bouncing on my feet. "Sure."

We started down the sidewalk, and I was trying to look everywhere at once.

After a block or so, Sam laughed and said, "Your eyes are bugging out."

"Everything's just *so* different," I said. Now that we were walking, it was even more obvious than when we'd been driving. The sidewalk was dark and the curbs were only a couple inches high and made of blocks instead of poured concrete.

"What's up with the gates?" I asked. Short black wrought iron gates lined the inside of the sidewalk.

"Every building has basement apartments."

"Huh. Those must be cozy." All the houses were made of brick or stone, and four or five stories tall. They were row houses, I guessed.

This wasn't like anywhere I'd ever been, although I thought it might be sort of like this in New York. Not that I'd probably ever see New York. I might never get out of Oklahoma for real if I couldn't get out for college. Fuck.

I had to get my head out of that space. "So different."

"Yeah, it is," Sam said. "You get used to it, though."

"I don't know if I'll have time for that." I was a little jealous of Sam, who had already had time for that.

We approached the end of the street and turned onto another street on our right. There were small, colorful shops on the bottom floor of some buildings. A pharmacy, a "fruiterer," a fish market, a deli, an optician. We walked past a smelly black trash can. I felt like a toddler being taken to a park for the first time.

Doors between the shops must have led up to those apartments above them, too. Flats. I wondered if the people working in the shops lived upstairs.

"That deli is really nice," Sam said as we turned onto another street.

"Is that a bus stop?" I asked, pointing to a glass structure with a metal overhang.

"Yeah."

"They're everywhere."

"Yeah, I ride the bus all the time."

"Cool." I never took the bus. It was totally foreign to me. "Are we going to ride it now?"

"No. We'll take the subway later, though."

Oh! "That's so cool." I'd always wanted to take a subway somewhere. And I would be doing it in a foreign country. This was way cooler than New York.

"Glasgow's subway is interesting. It's a big circle, and the trains are painted orange so they call it the Clockwork Orange sometimes."

I nodded as we continued along. We reached a bridge over a flowing river.

"This is the River Kelvin. Then coming up on the right is the Botanic Gardens. We can visit it, but not right now."

I peeked in the gardens, though I couldn't say I was interested in plants.

We reached a traffic circle, and I watched some cars navigate it.

"Driving here would be a total pain in the ass, wouldn't it?" I asked.

"Probably. My mom hates it. Especially the round-abouts. Though my dad says they're safer and easier than regular intersections. She's not convinced."

We walked a bit further before coming up to a large intersection, and waited for the walk sign. Soon we were walking on a street with even more businesses than I'd seen at the end of Sam's street.

"This is Byres Road, where all the university students go. The university is up the hill, a bit down the road. We have to stop into a newsagent to get your bus and subway pass."

I nodded, not wanting to say "cool" again, but I was thinking it.

I saw a sign up ahead with an orange circle around an S. It said "Subway" beneath it. My heart started beating excitedly. I was going to take the subway!

But before we got there, Sam said, "Here we go."

We went into a shop painted blue on the outside, and she talked to the guy at the counter and handed over the extra passport photo I'd brought. Soon I had something called a ZoneCard.

"It's way cheaper this way," Sam said as we left.

We hiked back to the flat, and I listened to everyone around us talking with their Glasgow accents. They sounded different than what you hear on BBC America. A little grittier. I loved it.

Chapter 78

We spent the rest of Saturday in Sam's flat. It was so small, especially compared to their house in Oklahoma. There was a tiny kitchen off the small living room where they had a couch and one chair, plus a TV mounted on the wall—which was good because it would have been even more cramped if they'd had it on a stand of some type. They'd managed to squeeze a tiny four-seat table into the little alcove behind the kitchen. It was even tighter when they put the fifth chair there for me.

Her mom made stir-fry for dinner, and I went to bed about eight because I was beat. Sam let me have her bed and said she would sleep on the couch. It took me a few minutes to fall asleep because I was staring at the really high ceiling and ornate crown molding and feeling buzzed from being here. But then I remembered the college fund issue, and I naturally felt crappy again. I rolled over onto my side and eventually fell asleep.

Sunday morning, I woke up at about 8:30, which was crazy. I'd slept for over twelve hours.

Sam was already up, having cereal at the little table, her long hair wet from a shower, when I went out there. I got a bowl myself and then had a shower in the tiny bathroom—the only one in the flat. It was freezing because there was no heater. And there was no shower curtain—just a glass wall on the side—so you didn't even get the benefit of steam building up inside there.

Then we left.

"It must be driving your mom crazy to be living in such a small place," I said.

"Yeah, she hates it."

We passed the river and garden again and got to the same giant intersection as yesterday.

After the walk sign appeared, Sam started crossing the intersection diagonally, which seemed crazy. But I followed her because other people were doing it, too.

After we were safely across, I said, "Where are we going?" Because she hadn't told me yet.

"The city centre. Then we'll come back and walk around the University of Glasgow. It's awesome. And then there's a really cool little museum there you will like."

"Is that 'centre' spelled 're'?"

Sam laughed. "Yeah."

"Cool." I kept saying it, because everything *was* so cool.

After a bit, I saw the subway sign again and soon we went in.

"Hold your pass against the orange thing," Sam said. "Then we want the outer circle."

I scanned through the gate and we went down the escalator into the underground world. I imagined tracks tracing all under the city. It truly was too cool. I couldn't think of another word.

We stood on a beige tile platform for a few minutes.

My thoughts meandered to the college fund going away, and I started to get stressed again. I should tell Sam about it, even though I really didn't want to talk about it. Then there was a hum and I guessed a train was coming, which was a little exciting, and I focused on that.

The hum turned into a mild rattle and eventually I could see lights in the tunnel and then there was a whooshing sound as the train breezed in. When the doors opened, I followed Sam on and we sat on orange fabric seats. Then the train took off and it was a weird sensation to be pushed back sideways. I bumped into Sam and we both laughed.

We went through several stations before she told me our stop was Buchanan Street. We took some stairs up to the street level, emerging from a glass enclosure.

We started walking around, kind of aimlessly.

I admired all the people who didn't have anywhere to be during the day—or maybe they worked around there. There were a lot of suits, but plenty of people in jeans, too. No cowboy boots in sight. We reached another glass enclosure that led underground, but this one was much bigger and had escalators.

"St. Enoch's station," Sam said. "But do you want to see a Scottish mall?"

"Sure," I said, not sure what she meant. How would it be different?

We walked further and eventually went into a large building with lots of glass on the top. Basically, it wasn't that different from the malls I knew in Tulsa, until she took me upstairs and showed me the bathrooms.

"You have to pay to go in!" she said, cracking up.

"Oh, my God, really?"

We went back down the steps to the food court. It had a KFC, a McDonald's, and a Subway.

"This is too American," I said.

"I know. Outside, everything is all different, then you come in, and it's like American commercialism at its finest. Let's go somewhere so you can get fish and chips. Or a chip roll."

She turned toward the stairs, and I asked, "What's a chip roll?" as I followed her.

"A roll—kind of like a burger bun, but not pre-cut, and with fries in it."

"What?"

"It's surprisingly good. People put ketchup or brown sauce on it. Or salad cream, which is like mayo but thinner. You wouldn't catch me doing that, though."

"Huh." We headed down the stairs and were soon out the front door.

"You know one thing that is different about the mall here?" I asked.

"What's that?"

We headed around the corner.

"The people. Or the women, at least. They aren't all wearing makeup."

"I know—it's great. I love it. It's the same with girls our age. Some do; some don't. But I don't feel like a weirdo here."

We walked back past the last subway station we'd passed and turned onto another street for a few blocks.

"This is one of the two main train stations in Glasgow," Sam said.

The green building extended far left and right, and the restaurant was under a bridge. We went inside to be greeted by the strong smells of oil and fish and stood at the counter to order.

I let Sam order for me because I had no idea what to get.

"We'll just go traditional," she said. "Haddock and chips."

We got our food and sat down.

Okay, so it was super greasy and salty, and the fish was a little bony (we didn't eat a lot of fish in my house, so I didn't know if that was normal), but the chips were fat and good. Sam made me try vinegar on them, which turned out to be awesome.

"Now to see some modern art," Sam said.

We walked back to Buchanan Street and up it a little before turning right. We passed through an arch across the lane. There was a window next to it with a ton of old Singer sewing machines sort of randomly on display.

We walked a little further until Sam grinned and said, "Check it out." She pointed, and I saw a statue of a man on a horse, with a traffic cone on the man's head.

"That's hilarious," I said.

"It's iconic Glasgow. Apparently they've been doing it since the '80s, and the city keeps taking it down."

Of course I took a picture.

Then we went inside our first Glasgow art museum, the Gallery of Modern Art, which was awesome, even though a lot of modern art is too weird even for me. It was funny, though—the building it's in is made of stone, with classical-looking columns. Not modern at all. But they had a huge Andy Warhol exhibit. Sam and I were usually into more classic, realistic work, so neither of us knew most of the other artists.

After that, we took the subway back to the original station and then climbed up this big hill to the University of Glasgow campus. We walked all over it, which was also cool, and through this covered area called the Cloisters. There were fluted columns making up archways all over the space, which connected a couple of the campus's quadrangles—grassy areas surrounded by four-story buildings—and led into a large and striking Gothic building with a tall, pointy, ornate tower.

And then Sam took me over to the Hunterian Art Gallery. This was also awesome—they had a huge collection of Whistler. And I saw both Rubens and Rembrandt —the real things! And then I found out about this Scottish artistic genius named Charles Rennie Mackintosh. He designed furniture, painted watercolors, and was an architect. Some of his stuff was weird, but it was all interesting and proto-art deco.

While we were walking back to her flat, Sam said, "It's so cheap to go to university here—like, three thousand dollars a year."

"Really?" This was exciting. "Because that might solve a big problem for me."

"For Scottish students, I mean. It's expensive for everyone else."

Disappointment coursed through me. "So, my mom told me something horrible yesterday morning."

"What?" She looked at me, clearly concerned.

"My college fund is gone."

"What?!" she exclaimed. Her jaw fell open and stayed that way.

I frowned and nodded, the reality of it punching me again.

"What do they expect you to do?"

"I guess try to get scholarships and pay for it myself." I shrugged to try to convince myself to be blasé.

"Oh, my God. That's awful."

It was. I still felt sick to my stomach thinking about it. "Maybe they'll help me pay when I go. I don't know. We didn't talk about it. They dropped it on me in the car on the way to the airport." I paused. "How the fuck am I supposed to get out now?"

"Well," she said slowly, "we'll just have to come up with a plan. We'll figure something out."

I was glad I'd told her and I hoped she was right. I had to get out or I'd go crazy.

Chapter 79

Once we got back to Sam's flat, we brainstormed for an escape plan for me, both of us coming up empty. I mean, we thought about me getting a job—or I could skip the first year of college and work then. But nothing we thought of would bring in enough money.

The only thing that would work would be to get loads of scholarships. I could study for the PSAT and take it next year to be a National Merit Scholar, which brought in some money, but not a full ride except at Oklahoma colleges. But at least it would be some cash.

It would be hard. Basically, I'd have to pay. Take out loans. It would be horrible. I'd be paying for the rest of my life.

Eventually, we had dinner with her parents and brother, and then she and I left again.

After a bus ride this time—which was novel for me, as well—we arrived at her friend's flat. I told myself it would be fine—Sam said these people were nice. She pressed the bell, and then we heard a buzz and a click, and she pushed the door open.

Despite trying to talk myself out of it, I was nervous, given that almost every other social interaction I'd ever had in my life had been both painful and nonproductive.

"There's a few stairs," she said. "Fifth floor. Or, fourth floor as they say here."

"Why?" We started up.

"What they call the first floor is actually the second floor, because they call the first floor the 'ground floor.'"

"That's stupid," I said as we reached the "first floor."

"I agree."

We continued up. My heart rate was rising, and I couldn't tell if it was from nerves or the stairs.

"So," she said, "You'll meet Donald. I haven't seen him in a few days so I might spend time with him. But I have faith that you will get along with everyone. They're really cool." She was huffing a little from the effort.

"Alright." Her boyfriend. I wondered if he would be anything like Zach.

I wondered what Zach was up to right now.

We reached the top floor and she held her hand up. "Let's catch our breath first."

I laughed, glad because I was breathing even more heavily than she was. She leaned forward and supported herself with her hands on her thighs, and we both breathed a bit more.

"Ready?" she asked.

I nodded, trying not to feel nervous, even though I totally was.

She knocked, and a short girl with freckles and light red hair answered the door. She was wearing dark skinny jeans and a tight t-shirt.

"It was you!" the girl said. "You took so long, I thought I'd buzzed someone else in."

"Hey," Sam said with a grin.

Then the girl looked at me and smiled. She stuck her hand out and said, "Hiya, I'm Fiona. And of course you're Sam's friend. What's your name?"

She seemed remarkably friendly. It was a little odd.

"Nic," I said.

The girl moved out of the way and swung the big door open wide to let us in.

A sweet smell I didn't recognize emanated from around the corner. I followed Sam around it and saw a living room even smaller than Sam's, crammed full with five people, some of whom were sitting on the floor because there was only the couch for seating.

I froze when I saw them but Sam continued across the room as a tall, skinny guy with dark black hair and very pale skin stood up. They kissed.

So that must be Donald. But he looked nothing like Zach.

Fiona came up behind me and said, "Come on. We're nice." She took my arm and sort of half-dragged me into the room.

Sam smiled at me from the other side of the room as she sat down scrunched up next to Donald.

As we stood in front of everyone, Fiona said, "This is Nic. Nic, this is Donald, and you know Sam, and there's Aidan, then Jack with the mohawk, Ellie, and Katie. Just so you all know, Nic's automatically cool because she's American, too."

They all laughed, and I couldn't tell if they were making fun of me or not. But I didn't see any of the snobby, judgmental looks I was used to getting, so maybe she was only teasing.

Aidan and Jack were on the couch, and there was an empty spot between them. Fiona ran over and sat in it, hooking her arm around Aidan's. He had black hair and was wearing black jeans and a red button down shirt, untucked.

I was still standing there like an idiot. Katie patted the floor next to her and said, "Sit here." She looked nice enough, even though she was ridiculously cute in a short white dress and Doc Martens. I would normally be intimidated, but I wasn't. So I sat.

Ellie leaned forward—she was wearing a blue and white striped fleece and jeans, definitely less intimidating—and said, "Did you just get here?"

"Yesterday," I said.

"Are you from Oklahoma, too?" Katie asked.

I nodded.

Then, to my utter surprise, Jack started singing, "Oklahoma, where the wind comes sweeping down the plains!" in this deep voice. I stared at him, having a hard time with the incongruity of this guy with a short blue mohawk singing that, while grinning like a crazy person.

Then everyone cracked up, and I blushed.

Sam said, "I told you! It's the only thing they know about Oklahoma."

Okay, they were only teasing. I should relax.

"Do you play a bunch of instruments, too?" Katie asked.

"Oh, uh, no. I tried to learn the keyboard but I sucked." I'd never pulled it out again after putting it away when Sam had started going out with Zach.

"Good. Sam makes me feel like a loser because all I play is the flute."

"So what's your thing, Nic?" Ellie asked.

I looked over and noticed Jack was talking with Fiona and Aidan. Sam and Donald were busy cuddling.

"My thing?"

"Everybody has a thing," Ellie said. "I'm a book nerd."

"Oh, me too," I said. "But I guess my thing is art."

This was so bizarre. I was simply having a normal conversation with people.

"She's really good," Sam called. I hadn't realized she'd been paying attention. Then she added, "She won several awards at a recent contest."

I blushed, feeling the pain of the dragon drawing loss all over again.

"She got one they called the Risk/Reward Award. Because she figured out a way to fix a ruined drawing."

"What happened to it?" Katie asked.

God, thinking about that drawing still hurt my stomach, so I put my hand there to calm myself. "This friend of my brother's poured coffee on it."

"Oh, my God," Ellie said. "Why?"

"He's just like that."

"A right arsehole, then," Katie surmised.

Arsehole. That made me smile. "Yeah, he's an arsehole." It was fun to say it.

"So what did you do to fix it?" Jack asked, surprising me. I also hadn't noticed he was listening.

"I dyed the whole thing with coffee. It ended up looking kind of like antique paper."

"You have a picture?" he asked.

"Sure," I said.

This was so odd. They were talking to me like I was a person. I pulled out my phone, brought the picture up, and crawled over to hand it to him.

"Shit, that is pure magic."

I guessed from his enthusiastic tone that that was a good thing.

"Lemme see," Ellie said.

Jack kept looking for a second before handing it over. He nodded as she looked at it.

"Wow," she said while holding it out for Katie to see, too. "That's well good."

"Thanks."

I ended up talking to the three of them for the next few hours and understood most of what they said. The two couples kept to themselves, except to pass around the hash cigarettes around that they smoked all night. I didn't partake though I did think about it. But I didn't know how I'd react to it. I figured things were going well, so why throw a wrench into it all?

Chapter 80

Monday morning we got up early because we had a big day planned. We caught a train from a station near the Buchanan Street subway station at about 8:15. We managed to get two rear-facing seats next to each other, on a train full of men and women dressed up for work. Two men sat directly across from us, facing us, with our knees practically touching, which was a little awkward. One had his head back, eyes closed, and the other was reading a newspaper.

I tried to keep to myself how cool I thought it was to be on a real train. In Scotland. I still wasn't used to it all. And all these people did this every day and took it for granted.

"What'd you think of everyone last night?" Sam asked.

"They were all nice. I started off being suspicious. But they weren't faking, were they?"

"No, unless they've been faking since I met them. That would be quite the elaborate hoax."

"I was especially weirded out by the fact that that guy Jack kept talking to me." He had been so cool. Like, effortlessly cool. I wondered what it would be like to be that comfortable with myself. "I mean, I know he's not and never will be *interested* in me, but he didn't seem to find me repulsive."

"Yeah, I like him. I had a thing for him for a while. But he's how I met Donald." Then she added, almost whispering, "And Ellie told me that he's never gone out with anyone, ever."

"Really?"

She leaned closer and said, "They think he's asexual, maybe."

"Huh. I wish I were that. Because liking guys is totally pointless for me."

"Don't be stupid. Some day it will be different. You know, maybe you won't have a boyfriend in high school. A lot of girls don't. High school boys are idiots. Their brains have been hijacked by their dicks." She looked across at the men, but they didn't appear to have heard.

"Uh, thanks, I guess," I said sarcastically.

"What I'm trying to say is that they have to be worthy of you. You shouldn't date someone for the sake of having a boyfriend. There should be a real connection."

I looked at her sideways. "Are you talking about Zach?"

She shrugged. "I'd never even really liked him, and then he asked me out, and I just said yes because I was so excited somebody liked me. It wasn't a good thing to do."

Wow. I could never tell her now that I liked him. She'd feel too bad. "I can see that."

"It was so weird, anyway. Because I was sure he liked you. He looked at you all the time, not only in the car. But you didn't seem to like him at all."

He'd looked at me all the time. It wasn't all in my head. What had happened? My heart hurt thinking about it.

I changed my mind. "Actually, I did like him."

Sam's eyes widened. "You did?"

I nodded. I wasn't sure if telling her was the right thing to do, but there was no going back now.

"But I asked you, and you said you didn't!"

"I know. Once he'd asked you out, I figured I didn't have any claim on him, and you didn't know about it, so I tried to forget about it." I tried to keep my voice upbeat even though I was feeling the pain of the memories.

She leaned into me. "I'm so sorry. Do you still like him?"

"I don't know. We're friends, I guess. He still sometimes gives me rides home, and I go with him and Evan to Key Club."

"He's not a bad guy. I just didn't have that much in common with him. You probably wouldn't either, really." She sat back up, pulling away from me and looking thoughtful.

"You think?" I looked at her again.

"Not that I'm telling you what to do. Maybe he'll ask you out."

"I don't think so. He doesn't sneak looks at me anymore." I felt okay about it. I didn't have that desperate attraction to him anymore. It was just nice to have a friend —to know that a boy could want to be friends with me. Maybe another boy in another place would want to be even better friends with me. It seemed feasible. I didn't think I was being delusional this time.

"Well, I'm still really sorry I went out with him when you liked him. I wouldn't have if I'd known."

"I know."

"Still, you have to go for a real connection."

"There's definitely not been any guy I've felt a connection like that with." Except maybe Zach, but I wouldn't tell her that. No need to make her feel worse.

"Just, don't worry about not having a boyfriend," she

said, bumping my shoulder. "Like I said, plenty of people make it through high school without going out with anyone."

"Okay." I guessed I did see her point. I didn't feel so desperate for one anymore. I mean, I finally had realized that it wouldn't change everything. It wouldn't make me normal. Some people might treat me a little better, sure, but most people would still look at me as a freak.

"But, anyway, I was curious, so I looked it up. Asexuality is a real thing. And I think it's hard for a lot of people, because of all the social expectations and everything."

"Yeah," I said with a laugh. "I know something about that."

Sam smiled and then her face grew serious. "How are things going, really?"

The earnestness of her question surprised me. We didn't ever talk like that. "Um, well. You know, okay."

"Really? What's been going on?"

To be fair, I didn't tell Sam everything, by any means. I had a hard time with that kind of thing. It wasn't that I didn't trust her, it was just that I didn't trust *anyone* that much, I guessed.

"You stopped seeing that one shrink, right?" She said it quietly enough that probably no one could hear over the hum of the train.

I nodded. "Yeah, thank God. He was an asshat." I hadn't told her I'd started seeing someone else, or about everything that had happened since. Or the reason all that stuff happened.

"So, uh," Sam started and faltered. "Are you going to start seeing someone else?"

I looked at her sharply.

She didn't meet my eyes. "Because I worry about you."

What? "You do? Why?"

The train pulled to a stop, wheels squealing a little. The doors swished open and some more people got on and passed us. I looked out the window and saw a sign that said Bishopbriggs. "Whoa, is this where she's from?" I asked, referring to a musician who went by that name.

Sam laughed. "Her parents are from here."

After the train started moving again, Sam continued. "I mean, you don't have any friends back home yet, do you?"

"No." I stared at my lap since she still wasn't facing me.

"Isn't that really hard?" she asked. "I mean, that's how it used to be for me, too, and then I discovered how nice it is to have people."

"I don't know what I'm supposed to do about it."

She sighed and eyed me. "Me neither. But do you ever feel, like, really bad? Like nothing is worth this effort?"

Her asking that was a shock. "Why? Do you?"

"No."

"I guess not really. I think I just feel a little bad all the time."

Oh." She frowned. "I mean, I'm glad you don't feel worse, but that sucks."

"My doctor told me there's a form of low-grade depression that she thinks I have. Like, it's never super-intense, but it's always there. I guess it's why I'm so negative." It was weird telling Sam all this. But it felt sort of freeing, too.

"That bites."

We were quiet for several more stops, and she texted somebody. I guessed Donald.

I thought about coming clean with Sam and telling her about everything that had gone on recently. She'd dived into new friendship territory and maybe I should answer in kind.

I looked over at her. She'd finished texting and sat with her eyes closed.

I wasn't going to tell her all that stuff on the train anyway, where anybody could hear.

She opened her eyes when we stopped in Polmont.

"The next stop is the town we'll visit on the way back," Sam said.

"Okay."

When we pulled into the next station, I read the sign. Linlithgow. Kind of a funny name.

Sam texted Donald again as the train got going, smiling to herself.

Two stations later, we were in Edinburgh. We came out of the station on a bridge lined with homeless people. I always wondered how people ended up like that. You always hear that most homeless people have some kind of mental illness, and now that I knew I had a mental illness, that seemed scary. Not that my parents would ever let me be homeless. But what if you had crappy parents?

I looked to the left of the bridge and saw a large grassy area, cut through with train tracks.

"This way," Sam said, and I followed her.

We passed a road called Market Street, and then we were going up this steep hill.

"How do you say this street's name?" It was Cockburn Street, but I suspected it wasn't said how it was spelled.

"Coburn, like the former senator." One of Oklahoma's.

"Oh, God. Him." He wasn't my favorite politician. He was definitely someone who wouldn't approve of me and my gender nonconformity.

"Hey, at least he acknowledged Trump's crazy."

"True." I noticed a sort of wailing sound in the distance. "What is that?"

"Bagpipes."

"People just play the bagpipes randomly?" I asked, amazed.

"Actually, I'm surprised we didn't hear anyone yesterday. Yes, people randomly play them. And guaranteed, it'll be a guy in a kilt."

"Seriously?"

Through increasingly heavy breaths due to the incline, she said, "Yeah. Men really do wear them here all the time. Especially when they're watching football. I mean, soccer."

I laughed. "You're going native, Sam."

This was quite the hill. And the bagpipes were getting louder.

"It's true. It's easier to use the right word, even if my accent gives me away."

I coughed another laugh.

We reached the top of the hill and were on a new street.

"There's the piper," Sam said.

There he was, in a kilt like she'd said. I took a picture, of course. I mean, he was just out in the street, in a red plaid kilt, playing the bagpipes.

"Okay, now we're on The Royal Mile. Also known as High Street."

"Where's the castle?"

"Up there." She pointed up another, less steep, hill. We started up it.

It was a townhouse-lined cobblestone road, partially limited to pedestrians only. In the distance I could see a black steeple of some type, which I thought might be the castle. This would be a trek.

"So, Sam."

"Yeah?"

"I didn't want to talk about it on the train, but the

doctor I mentioned is the new shrink my parents made me start going to."

"Really?" She looked at me again. "Is he better?"

"She is." I was going to do it. I could tell her about the abuse. "But something happened that I never told you about. Something a long time ago."

She looked at me, obviously ready to listen.

Chapter 81

We were on the train to Linlithgow. She was still in shock
about my revelation. She'd responded okay to it. I mean, it
was a little awkward because she hadn't known what to say.
Who would?

Actually, what she'd said was, "That's really fucked up,
Nic. How could he …?"

I hadn't been looking at her. So I shrugged as we
headed up the giant hill to the castle.

"Do your parents know?" she'd asked.

"Yeah. They're being cool enough, I guess. Not
bringing it up all the time or anything anymore. For a
while it was weird, though."

She was quiet for a while, and I could tell she wanted
to ask more questions, but thought she shouldn't.

I was glad, because I didn't want to answer any questions about it. Telling Dr. Goldberg had been hard enough.

When we got to the overlook in the castle, she finally
asked, "Do you think you'll try to get him in trouble?"

We leaned against the wall and looked at the city.

"Probably not. It just seems not worth it. I mean, I'd

have to talk about it and everything."

"I'm so mad for you."

I'd said, "Thanks," and we'd finished the rest of the tour talking about other stuff, only feeling a little awkward.

But now, on the train, we were both quiet. She had her eyes closed, and I wondered what she was thinking about.

The train started pulling into Linlithgow and she opened her eyes and said, "This place is really, really cool. I know you'll love it."

We jumped up to get off. The doors opened, and we stepped onto the platform. The station was weird because it was small, unlike the Glasgow and Edinburgh ones, which were huge enclosed buildings. This was simply a platform with a covered area.

"The palace is stupid close to the station," Sam said as I followed her down the stairs. "It's seriously, like, a five minute walk."

I laughed. "Everything is super convenient here. You totally don't need a car."

"It's true."

We walked down High Street and then up Kirkgate, another cobblestone street that led to the castle.

"That's St. Michael's Church there," Sam said, pointing to a kind of weird metal steeple.

I looked over to my right as we approached an archway that led into the ruins and saw a plaque that said Mary Queen of Scots had been born here. I'd had no idea, and that was awesome, in the literal sense.

We approached a table where they had someone taking entrance fees. The woman said, "Can I help you, sir?"

Ack, not here too. I deflated.

But she looked again and said, "I'm sorry, not 'sir.' You're just quite tall." Then she smiled.

That was new. And it felt sort of good.

Sam paid her for both of us, and we went inside.

"No one has ever apologized for thinking I was a boy before. Oh, except for a guy at this Mexican restaurant in Dallas."

"I know. You *are* tall, that's probably part of the reason people make the mistake."

I shrugged.

We went through the entrance into the courtyard area. Not too many people seemed to be there, which was nice.

"Nic?"

"Yeah?" We walked over to the fountain in the center of the courtyard. Well, it would be a fountain if there were water in it. But it was super ornate and had unicorns, which I'd found out were Scotland's national animal.

"Do you think you might be bi?"

"What?" I looked at her, surprised. "No!"

"Okay. You just never talked much about boys before. I know you said you liked Zach, but I always wondered."

"Neither did you," I said. "We didn't talk about that stuff."

"True. I used to think maybe you were trans."

We were still standing in front of the fountain, staring at it rather than looking at each other. "Seriously?"

"Yeah." She bumped my shoulder.

"Well, that's kind of funny, because I thought I might be, too. I was trying to figure things out before and did some research. Because the thing is, I don't feel like a girl. But I definitely don't feel like a boy. At all."

"But how does that work? Like, you don't feel feminine?" Her head was cocked.

"No, that's not it. It's hard to explain. I hate everything about being a girl, but the idea of starting to really become a boy, and take hormones or whatever they do, doesn't sound right at all. When I look at boys, I don't feel kinship." I studied one of the unicorns on the fountain. "I guess I just feel desire. Or total disgust, depending on the boy. There aren't that many I like."

She laughed. "Yeah, most are horrible."

"But trust me, I am not into girls and am very into boys," I said. "It's just not a mutual thing."

"It pisses me off for you. But sometimes I think *I* might be bi."

I wasn't expecting that. "Why?"

"I don't know. I guess because femininity is so foreign to me." She was touching a fountain unicorn.

"Okay, look. There's kind of a test for it. When I was doing that research, I came across an article that talked about not being sure if you were a lesbian or not. It said you have to like the idea of giving oral sex."

Sam jerked her head and looked at me.

I grimaced. "Well, I tried thinking about that and it sounds kind of gross to me. I mean, not that other people who do it are gross. Just, you know, not appealing. I don't know. But when I think about guys, it just feels different." I blushed, remembering my evening spent thinking about penises.

She didn't say anything.

"So I guess the thing is, if you can imagine doing that to a girl, then you might be bi. Or who knows, maybe you're a lesbian."

"No, I think you're right. I guess I'm probably straight then, because, no." She looked at me and smiled. "Good to know."

"I know what you mean."

"Let's go walk the corridors here. That's where it gets really cool, and I swear, even though I don't believe in ghosts most of the time, here I do maybe a little."

That didn't sound like her at all.

We went through a doorway and were standing in this large room.

"Great Hall," she said.

"Yep." We stood there, taking it in.

"Donald wants to have sex," she said.

I looked at her tense face. She was full of surprises today. "Really? Are you going to?"

"I think so."

"Wow. I guess you'll find out if you're a lesbian then." I couldn't help teasing her a little. I didn't want to admit it, but I was a little jealous.

"I want to. It's just … you know. A big deal."

I nodded. It was a big deal. "Well." Then I didn't know what else to say. Should I encourage her or caution her or what?

I thought of her in sixth and seventh grade, when she was as much of a social pariah as I was. Skinny, unshaved legs, dorky shorts. She still wasn't really feminine, but she looked like a girl, at least. She was obviously more comfortable with it than I ever could be.

We strolled some more in silence and went up some stairs so we were in an actual corridor.

And then I knew what she'd been talking about. It felt like there was some kind of presence. Not malevolent or anything, but definitely there. Probably just the weight of history.

We walked down the corridor and looked down on the courtyard, then out toward the lake. This place was very cool.

Some rooms later and we still hadn't said anything else, but it didn't feel like we were avoiding talking, only that nothing needed to be said right then.

We turned a corner and Sam said, "Do you think I shouldn't?"

Then I felt terrible. I realized she must have thought I'd disapproved of her plan with Donald. "No. You should do what you want. Just make sure that's what you want. That's all."

"Oh, good." She sounded relieved.

We walked down another magical corridor. Mary Queen of Scots had walked here.

"So you really don't feel like a girl, then?" she asked.

"Not really. I mean, sort of. I think the term for what I am is 'gender nonconforming,' but I hate it. How I feel is not a choice, which is how that sounds."

"I can't imagine what that's like. I've always felt like a girl, but I had to rebel."

I nodded. "I don't feel like I'm rebelling against anything, which, I guess, is why it's different. I'm only being me. There're also people who consider themselves non-binary, but that doesn't feel quite right to me, either. I think I'm okay with being a girl physically, it's just all the other stuff that I can't take."

"I guess."

"But can you imagine trying to get people in Emerson to start using the pronoun 'they' with me?"

"Yeah." She was quiet for a moment before saying, "Life is weird."

"It is." But since I'd brought it up, a new and unpleasant thought had popped into my head. "Can I ask you something?"

"Sure." She started walking down the corridor, and I followed.

"So when I was reading about being gender noncon-forming, it talked about how a lot of people who identify that way had stuff, uh, happen to them. Like me." It was still hard to say it.

"Okay," Sam said.

"Do you think that means that it made me this way?" My stomach twisted waiting for her answer.

"Huh. I don't know. What if it did? Would it matter?"

"It just seems like if that's true, then if it hadn't happened I wouldn't be like this. So it's like I'm not my real self. Like my real self might love pink and have a YouTube makeup channel. Or at least be teaching Izzy how to do it."

"Ha. I don't think that makes sense, Nic. Everyone has life experiences. So what?"

"You don't think I'm really supposed to be a girly-girl?" I stopped and leaned on an old window ledge and looked out on the courtyard.

"You are who you are. I don't think it matters. We're all blank slates when we're born, right? I don't believe in predestination." Sam came back and stood next to me.

"Me neither, I guess. If I did, I'd probably be more comfortable with this, since it would have been predetermined that I'd have all those experiences, anyway."

She rolled her eyes. "I really don't think any version of you would have run a YouTube makeup channel. Did being abused make you like art, or sci-fi, or real music?"

I thought about that. She had a point. "I guess not." Maybe she was right. It was still hard to know and it really mattered to me.

"I think you're perfect the way you are," Sam said in this really cheesy voice.

"Shut up," I said, laughing.

We wandered the rooms and corridors some more without saying much, and then headed back to catch the train to Glasgow.

"What did you think?" Sam asked once we stood on the platform.

"Awesome. I know what you mean—it felt enchanted."

"Definitely."

"If there were portals that took you back in time, I'd bet one would be there."

"Just as long as we didn't step through it by accident. Can you imagine? Being a girl back then?" She shuddered.

"Ugh." I wondered if I would have felt like a girl back then, or would I have been one of those girls who tricked everybody to pass as a boy. Who knew?

The train was approaching. Somehow the rattle on the track made my brain spring into action and generate a thought.

"Sam, I know what I need to do about the college fund."

"What?"

"Go to OAMS. It will make me more competitive for college."

"Oh, my God! You're right." The train doors opened and we got on.

"And it will be a fresh start." It made loads of sense. "I hope I can still apply."

Sam started messing on her phone again, and I assumed she was texting Donald. But then she said, "They're still accepting applications."

"Really?"

"Yep. Due next week, on Friday."

"Oh. That's soon." Even thinking about it made me nervous. I hated rejection, and what if that's what happened? Would it mess with me? Because I'd been starting to think the therapy might be doing something good for me. I seemed to be thinking less about how ugly I was than before.

"We'll start working on it tonight, okay?" Sam said.

It seemed like a logical path. Excitement was bubbling in my heart like a hot spring. "Let's do it."

Chapter 82

The Thursday after I got back from Scotland, I was at Dr. Goldberg's office.

It was weird, getting back to all the mundane stuff. Going to school. Being at home with my parents and my brother and sister. Sleeping in my own bed. Just, weird. Going back to school sucked.

"So, how was Scotland?" Dr. Goldberg asked.

"Amazing."

I couldn't help smiling, thinking about it. The rest of the trip *had* been amazing. After Linlithgow, we went to the Glasgow Cathedral, the Isle of Arran, this more modern castle in Ayr, south of Glasgow, and Loch Ness. I was a little embarrassed by the fact that I'd bought a plush Nessie. But it had to be done.

"What did you do?"

I went through a quick summary, which took longer than I meant, because we did a lot of stuff.

"How was seeing your friend?"

"Really good." I paused, and she didn't say anything,

apparently waiting for me to continue. "We talked about stuff we'd never really talked about before."

"Like what?"

I was getting a little anxious, thinking about telling Dr. Goldberg. I mean, she knew a lot of uncomfortable things about me, but I wasn't used to talking about this kind of stuff with other people.

But I trusted her. So it seemed. I'd given up trying to guess why. It was just a fact.

"Gender, I guess."

"In what way?"

"Well, she asked me if I was a bi, because she thought she might be. She wasn't sure."

She tapped her chin. "And did you help her figure it out?"

"Maybe? I don't know. I told her about what I learned when I was trying to figure out what I am."

"What do you mean, figure out what you are?"

"Well, I'm not normal, obviously. I'm not like other girls."

She smiled. "And do you think that's a bad thing?"

"Not that, not really. But for me, it's more than being a little different." I paused, and she was quiet. The silence stretched between us until I expanded on it. "I don't feel like a girl. Like, emotionally. Physically, I'm fine, I think. Maybe. Probably."

She nodded and asked, "What do you feel like?"

"Just a person. Not a boy, that's for sure."

"I'm curious." She recrossed her legs. "How do you decide whether you feel like a particular gender? What's your criteria?"

I cocked my head, thinking about it. "I think it's a kinship thing. Like, I look at boys, and I don't feel like they're my people. But it's the same with girls. I feel fundamentally different from them."

"Do you ever feel kinship with other people?"

"Not like what I'm talking about. Even over there, where people are so different from here. Sam's friends were genuinely nice to me. They didn't judge me the way everyone does here. But even there, I felt just so different from the girls *and* the boys. Everybody."

Dr. Goldberg nodded.

"If I believed aliens had been here, I'd think that's what I was."

She smiled.

"So, you mentioned that you tried to figure out what you are. Did Scotland help you with that?"

"No. I had found out before then what it's called."

"What's that?"

"Gender nonconformity." Saying it to her for the first time felt weird. Scary, but nice, too. "Though I hate the term because it makes it sound like a choice."

"And how you feel deep down isn't something you choose, is it?"

I shook my head. "It's like being gay. I mean, I think I would be better off being a lesbian, honestly. If I could choose that, I would. But I can't. I've only ever liked boys."

"Was this what you told Sam to help her decide if she was bisexual or not?"

"No." I laughed, uncomfortable again. I shifted on the couch. "That was something else." I wasn't sure if I could say it out loud to an adult.

"Yes?"

"I found an article that talked about what you're willing to do … uh … to the other girl … below the belt." I blushed.

Dr. Goldberg laughed. "I see. And does she think she's willing?"

"No, probably not."

She smiled again. "It is a good mental test, I think. However, it's not foolproof. There are women who consider themselves lesbians but who won't do that."

"Really?" I was taken aback. My test was undermined.

She nodded. "Yes. Everyone has their own way of thinking about their sexuality. And sex can be complicated. You have to look inside yourself to find the truth."

"It's so hard." Had I just not met a girl I was attracted to yet? I mean, I knew I liked boys. That felt too real to be a subconscious front. But was I bi? I was starting to freak out a little, my pulse starting up.

"It is."

Then everything slowed down as I realized it didn't matter. Truly, as much as I'd thought about it, who cared? I didn't need to know what I was right now. And it was nobody else's business. Fuck them. If I turned out to be bi, great. If not, great.

Then I thought about the other stuff Sam and I had talked about—whether or not I'd been destined to be gender nonconforming or was turned that way by a few bad experiences. I told Dr. Goldberg about it.

In that moment I made a decision. "I think Sam was right. You can't separate life experiences from a person. Some people are abused and stay cisgendered, and some gender nonconforming people never were abused. It's not a simple yes or no question. It doesn't matter."

Dr. Goldberg was studying me. "I think you are on to something. A bad thing happened to you when you were young. But if you can look at it that way, you can more easily heal. Some people let it define them and everything in their lives goes through the lens of abuse. It doesn't have to define you."

"Yeah." That whole line of thought didn't matter anymore. I knew the answer. I'd be whoever I was supposed to be, no matter what, because I was always true to myself. It didn't matter what other people thought. Then I remembered something that did matter. "I almost forgot. I decided to apply to OAMS."

"The STEM school in Oklahoma City?"

"Yeah."

"What's the application process?"

"I turned in the application Friday. I'll find out soon if I get an interview. Sam and I talked about it and decided that it would be the best thing for me to do, because my parents are losing my college fund."

Saying that stressed me out a little again, and I started wondering what would happen if I didn't get in. I'd be stuck at Emerson for two more, horrible years. My stomach clenched.

"Oh, that's unfortunate."

"Yep." Understatement.

"And OAMS is what you want to do?"

"I guess so. I mean, it will make me much more competitive for college."

"Yes, I can see that."

And with that, I seemed to have run out of things to say. We looked at each other for a moment, until Dr. Goldberg said, "I'd like to hear more about Sam's friends. How did they treat you?"

Thinking about it made me smile as I remembered the feeling of being there. "Like a person."

Chapter 83

Weeks went by after submitting my application to OAMS, and I became more and more convinced that I wouldn't get in. That I wouldn't even get an interview. I mean, what would they want with an artist? It was a science and math school.

So I was surprised when I got a call the last week of April inviting me to an interview two Saturdays later. Now Mom and I were on the interstate to OKC, on our way to it. It was supposed to last a few hours.

And, of course, she had advice for me.

"Honey, I don't want you to build this up. It's a good opportunity, but it's not the only thing in the world. Don't pin all your hopes on this one thing."

"I know, Mom." I looked out the window in irritation, even though I knew she was right.

"You do that sometimes. And I hate to see you so disappointed."

I looked over at her and sarcastically said, "You sound sure I'm not going to get in."

"Nic, they'd be stupid to turn you down. But you know

as well as I do that other people don't always make the right decisions."

That was certainly true.

But in my defense, the therapy seemed to be helping some. I didn't obsess over everything as much anymore. I wasn't constantly thinking about how I was a loser or whatever. Sometimes I even felt okay.

The school was at the Oklahoma Institute of Technology, a college in Burnside, northwest of OKC. And it took us a while to find it, but Mom had made us leave early so we wouldn't be late.

The OIT campus was all white brick buildings. We finally found the one we needed. There were three buildings facing a grassy yard. Mom parked and we followed posted signs that led us to the one facing the lot.

We went inside the building, which smelled like some kind of cleaner, and found an Indian woman sitting in a chair inside the front door. She got up. "Nicole Summers?"

"Yeah," I said.

She stuck her hand out. "I'm Dr. Kaur." Then she shook Mom's hand, too, and Mom introduced herself.

"If you want to wait here, I'll come get you when we're ready."

I knew from the information they'd given me that first there was an interview, and then I had to take an IQ test.

Another one. These things were a breeze.

"Follow me," Dr. Kaur said.

We went into a room.

There was a man and also an older woman wearing glasses on a chain.

The man was Dr. Smith and the woman Mrs. Callender. He taught chemistry, she was the librarian, and Dr. Kaur taught English.

"Have a seat, Nicole," Dr. Smith said.

I cleared my throat. "I usually go by Nic."

Dr. Kaur smiled and said, "Nic it is, then."

That relaxed me a bit. They were being nice.

"How was the drive here?" Mrs. Callender asked.

"Fine," I said, knowing I needed to say something else, too. "Um, my mom tried to distract me with pep talks."

They laughed.

"So why don't you tell us a little about why you want to come to OAMS," Dr. Smith said.

Okay, I wasn't really expecting that. I'd really had no idea at all what to expect in the interview. Which was dumb—this was an obvious question. "Well," I said, stalling.

Think, think. My heart raced, and I hoped they couldn't hear it. "I want to go to a good college, and I know this is a good school that will make me more competitive than Emerson would."

They nodded.

Dr. Kaur asked, "What do you know about OAMS?"

I had done some research, but I still wasn't sure what they expected. My stomach twisted, again and I eventually said, "Well, it's an academically challenging boarding school offering advanced courses in math and science."

"All true," Dr. Kaur said. "Do you know anyone here?"

I shook my head. "No."

"It's truly challenging," Dr. Smith said. "You will be expected to work harder than you've ever worked before here."

"Okay," I said, not sure where they were going.

"Do you think you will be able to make the necessary sacrifices?" Dr. Kaur asked.

Oh, man. They were scaring me a little. "Sure."

Dr. Smith cleared his throat. Something about it made me nervous. "Your social life will suffer," he said.

"I don't have a social life, really," I said.

I shouldn't have said that. They'd think I was antisocial and didn't get along with others and they wouldn't want somebody like that there.

But Mrs. Callender laughed. "A lot of our kids spend more time on their studies than their social lives. But we do encourage and have opportunities for social events."

Oh, thank God. They didn't think I was horrible.

"So, Nic, what three adjectives best describe you?" Dr. Kaur asked.

What? "Um, creative." That was one. I wracked my brain for more. I spent a lot of time drawing. "Dedicated." One more, one more, one more. The old habit returned. Crazy, depressed, negative, friendless. Tall. Fat.

Ugly.

Oh, God. Rabbit hole. Think, think, think. Why was this so hard? Surely I could come up with something else good. I wasn't used to thinking about myself like this. "I guess also humble."

The two women smiled. Mrs. Callender asked, "How are you creative?"

"Well, I'm an artist. I'm very dedicated to it, and I draw a lot."

Dr. Smith nodded. "What do you like to draw?"

Should I say flowers? Fashion? "Dragons. And knights. Stuff like that."

"Are you a reader?" Dr. Smith asked, clearing his throat again. Did he disapprove?

I nodded. "More sci-fi than fantasy, though."

"What's your favorite book?" Mrs. Callender asked.

My brain froze, and I couldn't think of a single book I'd read. Ever. "The impossible question," I managed.

They all laughed, which felt sort of amazing because it was with me, not at me.

I started mentally scrambling to come up with something. "I mean, it depends on my mood." Think. They stared at me.

Ah, finally. "If I want to laugh, I like *Cinder* by Marissa Meyer. If I want something deeper, I might read something by William Gibson or Neal Stephenson."

Recognition dawned on all their faces.

I tried not to grimace, not sure if I'd messed up or not.

"So, tell me about your favorite artwork that you've created," Dr. Kaur said.

That surprised me. "Well, I made this beautiful scene of two dragons battling at the top of a mountain. Big." I motioned with my hands to indicate how large. "Then when I was done, someone poured coffee on it."

"On purpose?!" Mrs. Callender said.

"Yeah. So I took the whole thing and dyed it with coffee. It ended up looking like antique paper. It was kind of cool." I paused. "Though I still liked it better when it was just regular white paper."

"That's a shame," Dr. Kaur said.

"Yeah. It's still my favorite, though."

Dr. Smith cleared his throat yet again. "It's impressive that you figured out a way to fix the damage. But besides drawing and reading, what extracurricular activities do you participate in?"

What was with his throat?

"I belong to Key Club," I said.

"What kind of activities do you like to do with them?" Dr. Kaur asked.

"I always do the food drives, stuff like that."

I guessed it was going okay. It continued on like that for several more minutes. Afterward, Dr. Kaur took me to another room and, after taking my phone, had me take an IQ test.

By the time I left, I had no idea how I'd done, but it seemed unlikely I'd wowed them enough to get in. It just didn't fit my life story.

Chapter 84

Sunday, Mia came over so we could try to finish the dragon, which my dad had dubbed Opus for no apparent reason. We'd ended up having to bring it to my house for the weekend because we were behind. I wondered if we'd end up friends. It would be different from how it was with Sam.

Opus had ended up being a little under three feet tall. Mia had helped me shape the face and wings, and it looked really realistic. I'd given Opus a base coat paint color of sky blue. Friday at school, I'd gotten all the flower bases painted—basically a circle in one of a few colors—and Mia had already started following behind me to paint the petals in her detailed way. It was so easy to work with her, the way we complemented each other perfectly.

She was sitting cross-legged on the garage floor painting a yellow flower on his back foot.

I stepped back and looked at Opus. He was in a crouched position with his wings partially up—not fully extended, but enough that you could see they were real wings. He looked weird, for sure. But working on him was a lot of fun.

Mia scooted over to work on his tail, which was curled so that he wouldn't be too long. "Did you see the mess Brian and Diego made?"

"No." They were a couple of jerks in our class. Boys who took it as an easy elective, not because they cared about art in any way.

"They actually made a toilet."

"No way."

She nodded as her brush moved delicately over the top of the tail.

"Do you think I should paint his eyes and teeth realistically?" I asked.

Mia looked up, her black hair falling across her shoulder. "Like how?"

"Well, I guess the eyes should be black. But maybe I could put a bit of white on there to represent a glint."

"That sounds cool. And you could do his teeth in white." She checked her phone and sent a text.

I nodded. I started working on that.

"So guess what was in the toilet?"

"Oh, my God. Seriously?" I started on the bottom row of teeth.

"Yes."

"What did they use?" I asked.

"Papier-mâché."

Most people had done that. The classroom had been a mess for weeks.

"What is it with guys and potty humor?" I asked

"I don't know. It's so juvenile. Trevor's not like that, thank goodness."

That was her BMW-driving asshole of a boyfriend. I was even less of a fan now that I'd gotten rides home with him a few times when Mia and I had stayed late at school to work on Opus.

After that, we continued working in comfortable silence except for her text messages until I had painted all the eyes, teeth, and toenails, and she had the tail done.

She got another text. "Oh, Trevor's on his way."

"Okay." She was at his beck and call. When he said jump, she did. "Are you sure you can't stay a little longer? You could finish the right foot, too."

"Trevor wants to go somewhere."

"Do you always have to do what he wants?" I asked.

"It's not like that." She avoided looking at me when she said this, so I didn't say anything else.

She painted a few more flowers before he got there. Then Trevor's black car rolled up, bass thumping, and she was gone.

Chapter 85

During the third-to-last period the Friday after the interview, there was a required assembly. It was some end-of-the-year thing where they awarded student government superstar, teacher of the year, that sort of thing.

I hated assemblies because I had no one to sit with, and it was awkward. Not that awkwardness was new to me, but still. At least in classes you established your seats at the start of the year.

I filed into the auditorium with the rest of the sopho-more class.

My heart twisted. The last time I'd been in here had been for the art contest.

When I'd gotten that stupid Risk/Reward Award.

I sat at the end of a row because I didn't like being in the middle. I watched more kids come in and get settled. Then to my unhappiness, Carlos and Kyle came in and sat two rows in front of me, also on the end. As he was sitting, Kyle saw me and waggled his eyebrows.

I mean, seriously. What an ass.

Carlos was okay, but how could I have ever thought he'd been flirting with me? Jesus. I mean, duh.

The principal got up there and started blathering on about what a great year it was and what a fine bunch of students we were, blah blah blah. Then they got to the awards. Some teacher I didn't know won teacher of the year. That sort of thing was so dumb. How could you really judge people who were teaching different subjects and different students? It wasn't possible to be objective. You couldn't make direct comparisons. Then there were some awards for volunteer service, environmental efforts, and some other stuff. Honestly, I wasn't paying that much attention.

I was staring at the back of Kyle's head, trying to bore a hole into it with my mind.

I heard, "And now for sophomore artist of the year," and thought, that'll be Mia.

Then they said, "Nicole Summers."

What? Holy shit.

I was frozen for a few seconds.

"Is she here?" the principal said.

So I finally got up, my feet weighing a ton, and started making my way to the stage. As I climbed the stairs, I really wished I wasn't so fucking big because there were a hundred and fifty pairs of eyes on me now.

I smiled and took the award, then fled back toward my chair. When I got close to Carlos and Kyle, I saw Mia sitting across the aisle from them. She smiled and said, "Congrats, Nic."

This caught me off guard, but then I managed to string together the words, "Thanks, I was surprised."

A teacher sitting nearby shushed me and said, "No talking," as I quietly settled back into my seat, the award heavy in my lap.

Seriously, most adults here hated me. I was so sick of it. I hadn't heard from OAMS yet, but I knew there was no way I'd gotten in, so I was stuck here for the next two years, which was depressing.

I studied the trophy. It had a rectangular marble base with a medallion-shaped gold plastic piece screwed into it vertically. The medallion said, Winner. The plate across the base had my name and Sophomore Artist of the Year 2018 written on it.

It made me feel weird. Like, I knew I should be happy and honored, but instead I felt suspicious. Mia was a better artist than me—why didn't she get it?

I hardly listened to anything for the rest of the assembly. Afterward, I dumped the trophy in my locker and finished up the rest of my classes.

After school, I stuffed the award into my backpack and headed down the hall toward the buses.

"Hey, Nic," I heard. I looked over and Zach had just turned a corner and was walking with me. I said hi back. It had been a few weeks—we usually only saw each other at Key Club meetings—and I was glad to see him. We were still at least sort-of friends, which was nice.

"So I heard you won Sophomore Artist of the Year. That's awesome."

I blushed at the praise. "Thanks."

He pushed the door open. "I'd offer you a ride home, but I have to meet someone downtown in, like, ten minutes."

"No problem. The bus is fine."

"Later." And he was gone, heading toward the parking lot.

Despite what Zach said, on the bus ride home, I couldn't stop thinking about the award and how I shouldn't have gotten it.

I eventually came to the realization that they'd given it to me because of the whole self-portrait fiasco. They were worried about me and wanted to make me feel better about myself.

It had the complete opposite effect.

By the time I got home, I was feeling crappy. I went straight upstairs, set the award on the desk, and lay on my bed. But I kept looking at the trophy there, taunting me, until I went over and unscrewed the medallion from the base. I left both on the desk, but faced the base away so I couldn't read it.

I was still lying on my bed, wallowing in the fact that I hadn't done that well in the art contest and probably hadn't gotten into OAMS, when there was a knock on the door.

"Come in."

Mom poked her head in. "How are you, honey? I was surprised not to see you downstairs working on your drawing."

I had started a new big one, which I left covered with a trash bag consistently now so nobody could easily destroy it. Still, I didn't think Logan would do that bullshit again.

This one was cool. It was a leopard sitting up and looking off to the side, but instead of regular spots, I was putting in celestial shapes—stars, moons, etc.

"I wasn't in the mood." Truth.

"What's wrong?" She stepped further in.

I guess that the therapy had helped enough that going back to my natural state caught Mom's attention.

"Nothing."

She glanced at the desk. "What's that?"

"Nothing. Just this stupid thing."

She picked it up. "You won Artist of the Year?"

"I didn't win it—they just gave it to me because they felt sorry for me."

"Nic," she said, sounding a little exasperated. She sat in my desk chair. "Honey, they wouldn't have given it to you if they didn't think you deserved it."

"But Mia's a better artist."

Mom sat at the end of the bed. "You've shown me her work, and I agree she's very talented." She took the screwdriver and began screwing the medallion back onto the base. "But I've always thought your work was more interesting—more creative—than hers. Her technical skill is very high, but she's kind of predictable, don't you think?"

I was stunned. I'd never thought about it that way.

"Maybe they think so, too," she continued.

"I don't think so. I think it's because of the self-portrait and all that."

"Even if that's it, honey, they like you enough to do something like that for you. That's nice. I know that even a lot of adults in your life are just overgrown bullies, but your art teacher genuinely likes you."

"But if that's true, that still means I didn't earn it," I said in a small voice.

"Nic, let me tell you something about life. Things are never one hundred percent fair. You know this, and it's not cynical to acknowledge it. But it's true for awards, too, which are hardly ever given based only on merit, unless they're judged truly blind. It's always a little about popularity or politics." She looked to the side. "Everything in life is political, despite how much everyone claims to hate it."

"Is your work rant over?"

Mom smiled. "Sorry. Bernadette got Server of the Month again despite being a table-thieving hussy."

I snorted despite myself. "Did you just call her a *hussy*?"

She laughed. "I did. And I'm not saying you're a thieving hussy of any type. I think you did earn it, despite what you think. Just try to go with it and see how it feels."

"Okay, fine."

"I'm going to go make dinner." She got up. "Come down in an hour to set the table."

"Okay."

Once she was gone, I looked again at the trophy sitting on my desk, staring right at me. Maybe I could at least try to think I deserved it.

Chapter 86

The day after getting the award, I was at this sandwich shop for lunch, working in my sketchbook. I had about an hour before I needed to be home to meet Mia to work on Opus.

I finished my sandwich and crumpled the wrapper off to the side of the table. I was sitting in a booth just next to the Coke machine, working on some detailed shading, when the door opened. I kind of glanced up and saw it was a couple of kids I'd seen before at school. They glanced at me, and one of them whispered something to the other. Probably juniors. I got back to work.

One of them said, "What do you think it is?" pretty loud. It was clearly for show, which meant it was directed at me since I was the only one in the restaurant except for the sandwich maker.

The other guy said, "I don't know, it's so hard to tell." He snorted. "Could go either way."

"Whichever, sure is ugly," the first said.

Ah, they were talking about me. Nice. It was a testament to the therapy that I didn't want to die.

I was pissed instead.

Here I was, totally minding my own business, and they had to go after me. Why? What was wrong with them?

Why was it everyone always acted like I was the one in the wrong?

"What do you think," the second asked. "Boy or girl?"

He must have been asking the sandwich maker, because she muttered something I couldn't quite hear. My back was toward them. I stared at the door, considering leaving.

But by this point, my blood was boiling, and I decided not to leave. Why should I let a couple of douchebags dictate what I did?

They continued to work their way along the counter, going back and forth with a few more snipes at me. "We need to see what's on top."

Then one said, "I'll find out."

I heard him come closer. He took his tray to the table facing mine. The whole restaurant was empty and they were going to sit next to me. He put his tray down facing me, and I could feel him looking. Then he returned to the Coke machine and filled his drink up. He moved away until he was right next to me. Then, after he'd stopped, he made a big show of spilling some of his drink, the liquid splashing on the floor.

"Crap," he said in this exaggerated voice. It was so obvious that he was trying to get me to look up so he could see what was "on top."

Something in me snapped, and I put everything back in my pencil case, closed my sketchbook, took the lid off my drink. Then I stood up and threw my entire Coke into his face, in one fluid motion as if I'd practiced it.

"Did you figure it out, you stupid fuck?" I snarled.

I didn't even have time to be stunned by the fact that

I'd done this, because I knew I had to get the hell out of there. I grabbed my sketchbook and pencil case and literally ran for the door. His Coke hit me in the back and then the sandwich maker yelled, "Hey!" and I was out the door.

I walked quickly to the minivan, got in, and took the fastest route home.

I'd just assaulted somebody.

And I'd never felt happier.

Chapter 87

I was still feeling good—but also a little weird—about the sandwich shop incident when I came out into the garage and opened the door. It rose up, squeaking a little in the tracks, and Opus came to life in the light. He lacked a few flowers, and his teeth were too white.

Mia was coming over so we could finish him up. We were so behind, but Ms. Tolliver was letting us turn it in late.

I was expecting Trevor's black BMW, but instead a silver Lexus pulled up in front of the house and stopped. Mia got out, looking beat-down, and then a short older man got out of the driver's side. Her father? What did he want?

They walked up the driveway. He was wearing a polo shirt and slacks but Mia was obviously ready for another potentially messy work day, with her jean shorts covered in paint stains and an old t-shirt.

Once they reached me, Mia said, "Dad, this is Nic."

"Hi," I said awkwardly, not sure if I was supposed to shake his hand or what.

He nodded. "You can call me Mr. Tran."

"Nice to meet you, Mr. Tran."

He looked around the garage, which I was now aware was kind of messy. My mom's car was in there, but then there was an old fridge, a table with a bunch of tools and who knew what else all over it, and some shelves, all bowed so the boxes on them had slid toward the middle. Opus took up most of the front left corner, with newspapers covering the floor.

Mr. Tran took this all in with an intent look on his face. Mia stared at the ground.

"What is this project you are working on?" he asked.

I wasn't sure if he was talking to me or her, so there was this pause, and then Mia said, "It's this, here." She pointed to Opus. "It's a dragon."

He made a disapproving click sound, and then looked at me and said, "Are your parents home, Nic?"

"Yeah, my mom is."

"I'd like to meet her."

"Okay." I glanced at Mia and she was staring at the ground again, hands clasped in front of her. "I'll go get her."

Mom was in the den reading. "Can you come out? Mia's dad wants to meet you."

She looked surprised but got up and followed me out.

I went to stand over by Mia and Opus while our parents greeted each other, and Mom invited him inside, which seemed unnecessary.

"Sorry," Mia whispered.

"It's fine. How come your dad brought you? I figured Trevor would be dropping you off."

She blanched. "Don't mention him in front of my dad, please."

Weird, but I nodded and suggested we get started.

She crouched down to work on painting the petals, and I worked on Opus's teeth. I'd done them in white but decided to give them a more realistic look, so I was adding a thin yellowish coat over them.

We worked in silence—Mia obviously didn't feel like talking—for quite a while before Mom and Mr. Tran came back out. Mom was smiling, but it looked forced.

"Mia, I'm picking you up at five," he announced. Then he said something in Vietnamese and she nodded and responded in the same language.

He turned to go, and Mom called, "It was nice meeting you!"

Once the Lexus was gone, I watched Mia paint a pink petal in silence. I worked on the teeth.

"So, Trevor was arrested last night," she eventually said.

"Oh my God!" I said. "What for?"

"Selling drugs." She continued painting and didn't look at me. "And my parents didn't know about him before. They were a lot more lenient with me than they were with my older sisters, but now Dad's going to be so strict. I'll never see Trevor again."

"But he's a drug dealer." How could she want to stay with him?

"You don't know him. He's not a bad guy."

That statement could definitely be challenged. "He's not very good to you, though. He's so controlling. How come you put up with that?"

She pursed her lips and kept painting, but didn't say anything right away.

I blushed as I realized I'd overstepped. "Sorry, it's none of my business." I couldn't help but think of Izzy and her crush and how she had enough self-confidence to demand to be treated well, at least after a little guidance from me.

She looked at me. "Maybe. It's just so hard—when I'm around him, it's the only place I want to be. But when I'm not, sometimes I wonder. He's under a lot of pressure from his parents."

"I think it can sometimes be hard to think straight around guys."

"It doesn't matter. I'll never see him again because my dad's going to watch me like a crazy person." She put a hand to her forehead and looked off to the side.

"That will suck." I thought that might be a good thing, actually. If she was away from Trevor long enough, she'd surely get over whatever spell he had on her.

"Oh, I forgot!" she suddenly said. "That's really cool about your award."

That was quite the subject change. Then I felt the same suspicions I'd felt yesterday, but tried to channel my mom. "Thanks. I was so surprised. I think you should have gotten it."

"Maybe next year. But you deserved it this year."

I didn't know what else to say so I stayed quiet. She finished her last flower, and I finished touching up around Opus's face. Her dad was due in about fifteen minutes, so we just chatted about art, and I told her about OAMS and how, if I was lucky, I wouldn't even be at Emerson next year.

By the time she left, I felt like we were still friends. So I had someone else to be friendly with if I didn't get into OAMS. Zach and Mia. It was something.

Chapter 88

I sat on Dr. Goldberg's couch again the next Thursday. I'd just told her about the sandwich shop incident, and while she had not reacted much, the corners of her mouth both went up a wee bit.

This made me even happier.

"How do you feel about doing that?" she asked.

"Proud. Happy." I smiled, reliving the look on the prick's face.

"Why do you think that is?"

"I mean, I know it was 'wrong'"—I made air quotes—"but I don't regret it. Because it's like, for once, I actually did something about it instead of just taking what they were dishing." Just thinking about it had my pulse going again.

She nodded. "Do you think it's something you'll do again?"

I thought about that. It probably wasn't worth it. "I doubt it. I mean, I don't want to end up a juvenile delinquent. What if things escalated?"

"That is undoubtedly true. The police wouldn't care

what he'd said to you, or what everyone else has said to you over the years."

"Yeah." My stomach dropped as I thought about what could have happened if a cop had been around or something.

"What else has gone on in the last week?"

"I sort of won Sophomore Artist of the Year." I still had very mixed feelings about this.

"That's really nice." Her voice grew excited. "How do you feel about that?"

"I think I just got it because they were worried about me." I thought of what Mom said.

She raised an eyebrow. "It sounds like you have something else to say about it."

She read me pretty well, which was surprisingly comforting. So I told her about Mom's theories.

"I think she's right," Dr. Goldberg said. "I agree with her about the way awards are given. Some companies have done away with such things as Employee of the Year because they engender jealousy and resentment in many people while only making one person happy. So the net effect is negative. But my bet is that they thought you deserved the award. I doubt it was a pity gift."

"You don't know for sure, though. Nobody does." I shifted on the couch.

She nodded again. "That's true, but sometimes it's good to have a little faith. Give people the benefit of the doubt."

I shrugged.

"Have you heard anything from OAMS yet?"

"No. I'm sure I didn't get in." I couldn't keep the frown off my face. This would be horrible. "But still, I'd like to hear for sure. I want to know before school's out."

She looked at me over her glasses. "I don't think

anything's decided yet. So you definitely want in?"

"Yeah."

"What happens if you aren't accepted?"

"I don't know." I wished this didn't matter so much to me. My stomach churned. "I guess everything stays the same. I'll be the secretary of the art club at school, if it works out that way."

"That should be fun. I'm impressed you'd volunteer." She smiled, looking impressed. "Is this you trying to take life by the horns again?"

"I guess. I don't know what I have to do. I forgot to ask."

She chuckled. "What if it's something you don't want to do?"

This made me smile, too. "I'm sure it will be fine."

"What about if you do get in?" She tapped her pencil on her clipboard. "Have you really thought about what that will mean?"

"How?"

"Leaving your family. Having to follow somebody else's rules. I bet they're strict."

"Yeah, I don't think we're allowed to leave campus."

She nodded. "You won't miss being able to get away and go to a coffee shop or restaurant for a bit?"

"I don't know, maybe. But hopefully it's worth it. If it's not, I can always quit, right, and go back to Emerson?"

"You could."

"But I don't think it will be a problem. I'm not overly attached to my parents. Or my brother. I'd miss Izzy, though."

I stared at my Vans. Nothing was about to change dramatically, unless it was. There was no way to know until I got some stupid piece of paper in the mail telling me my fate.

Chapter 89

I spent most of Saturday finishing painting the last of my figurines. But I started thinking about it. Was it worth doing anymore? It was something that Sam and I had done together, and now there was no one to share the hobby with. It sucked.

What was I supposed to do with all of them now? I had them displayed on one of my shelves, but I was coming close to running out of room. At least where I'd be able to see them. I could scrunch a bunch of them all close together, but what was the point of that?

For that matter, what was I supposed to do with Opus? We'd finished him, and he looked awesome. I'd covered him in glossy clear paint so he was super-shiny. But Ms. Tolliver didn't have room for him at the school, even though she loved him as much as we did. Mia lived in an apartment, so there was no room there. He was currently in the garage.

I waved a dismissive hand and went downstairs to work on the new drawing. I'd made good progress on the leopard and done all the basic shading. I'd put some of the celestial spots on, but it was tricky to do because when you looked closely, real spots were two colors. Kind of a ring of black around a slightly darker orangish brown than the rest of the leopard's coat. So I was doing something similar. Trying to make it look natural, despite the weird shapes. Sort of like how I'd like to be. Me—weird—but still seeming normal enough from a distance.

My goal was that people would look at the picture at first and just see a leopard and only then notice that the spots were weird. Like a drawing Easter egg.

But also, I couldn't help but think about how leopard spots are like people. Everybody's a little different, but most of them look more or less the same, with only a few truly standing out.

I did five more spots—two quarter moons, two stars, and one sun—just a circle. To achieve the Easter egg effect, the shapes weren't perfect stars or moons or circles. They were slightly distorted and also shaped to correspond with the curves of the real animal.

I was in love with this drawing, and it wasn't even done yet.

The neighbor's dog started barking, a sign that someone was in the front yard. I looked out the window and spotted the mail truck.

I was still waiting for the letter. They'd told me I should have an answer within three weeks, and it had been two now. So I hurried out to the mailbox, trying to tamp down my nerves, which were threatening to go haywire like they had been every time I saw the mail.

To my surprise—and terror—a letter from OAMS was on top of the stack in the box.

With shaking hands, I studied it for a moment, realizing that it held my future. I tore it open, my heart doing all sorts of acrobatics, and tried to get to the good part. It was short, which had me concerned. But when I was able to focus, I saw the words, "We have decided favorably on your application. Welcome to the newest class of The Oklahoma Academy for Mathematics and Science."

My heart nearly stopped in shock.

I *was* going to get out. I would have a real life. I would leave Oklahoma in one piece. Unbroken.

Acknowledgments

This book benefitted from my critique partners and beta readers, who helped me improve the story and the writing. Thank you to my oldest writing group: Shari Duffin, Stacia Leigh, and Karrie Zylstra Myton; to my other critique partners and beta readers: Anne Shaw, MC Austin, Debra W., and Gwen Sharp; and finally of course to my ever-supportive mom, Kathy Vincent.

Thank You and More

Thanks for reading *Ugly*! I hope you enjoyed reading about a gender nonconforming girl figuring out how to navigate her world. If you are willing to leave an honest review, I'd really appreciate it. Reviews help authors out a lot.

You might enjoy my other recent YA novel, *Always the New Girl*, about a girl destined for mediocrity who manages to rise above everything. It also has a prequel called *Binding Off*.

And if you're interested in what Kirkus Reviews called "an offbeat spin on the YA suspense genre" in a starred review, check out my first YA book, *Finding Frances*.

To find out more about me and all my books, check out my website at kellyvincent.net.